CHECKMATE

This is *Reckless*

USA TODAY BESTSELLING AUTHOR

KENNEDY FOX

Checkmate

/ˈCHekˌmāt/

Noun
(Chess)

1. A position in which a player's king is in check and the player has no legal move (i.e. cannot move out of or escape the check). A player whose king is checkmated loses the game.

2. Utter defeat

PROLOGUE

COURTNEY

ONE DAY AFTER THE WEDDING

Once upon a time, in a faraway land, lived a queen who ruled her own kingdom. She didn't need a king beside her because she was confident, strong, and smart without one. She knew men only brought heartache, and there was no time for that, but if there ever was a man who could stand beside her, he'd be the strongest, smartest, most protective guy she could ever ask for. He'd be her best friend and The One.

…Excuse me while I drown in my own tears.

There is absolutely, positively no way a guy and a girl who live together as roommates could ever become anything more. I hoped it would, but after several clear-as-day hints, I've come to terms that *just friends* is all we'll ever be. He doesn't see me the way I see him.

And *he* was Drew Fisher. My best friend's older brother. *Cliché, I know.*

I remembered the day I first met him. I'd nearly broken my face when I walked into a beam because my mind had

1

stripped him of his cop uniform. He's built like a rock, his chest and back are covered in ink, and his long strands of dark hair are just asking to be pulled. You can see his chiseled jaw under his nicely-trimmed beard, which gives my girl parts all kinds of weird tingly feelings—and don't even get me started on the handcuffs in his duty belt. Every time I see them, I want to handcuff myself to him.

Okay, that might sound a bit over-the-top and maybe even obsessive, but I swear I'm not. Drew's been my roommate for over a year; his sister, Viola, is my best friend, and just married his best friend, Travis. Not to mention, Travis is also my boss at King Marketing, where Drew stops by to bring me lunch every Friday. So, we're linked together in more ways than one, and it'd be way too complicated anyway. I know this. I've reminded myself of this several *dozen* times.

But that doesn't mean my heart has gotten the memo. I can't help the way I feel for him, and I've tried dating other guys to get over the pathetic crush I have, but so far it hasn't worked. Nothing has, so I just suffer in silence as I watch him give his heart to a girl who absolutely, positively *does not* deserve him in any way.

Mia *Fucking* Montgomery.

She's the classic tall, skinny, dark-haired goddess who thinks she rules the world and everyone in it. I don't get what Drew sees in her—okay, maybe I can—but too bad her attitude is as ugly as her botched boob job. He doesn't see her for who she really is—conniving, manipulating, cheating, lying whore. I don't typically shame other women for being outspoken and confident, but Mia is the exception, and I don't even feel bad for hating her slimy guts.

All right, that might sound like jealousy and all

considering I just admitted to having the biggest crush on one of my best friends, but those aren't feelings of jealousy. Those are feelings of disdain. Take one look at Mia Montgomery, and you'd feel the same way.

Too bad Drew Fisher is blind as a fucking bat.

All feelings aside, I hate that she's hurt him more times than I can count and that he's taken her back every single time. He's the sweetest guy I've ever met and gives more second chances than she deserves.

I can't help but feel like maybe, just maybe, one day he'll open his eyes and see what's been in front of him the entire time. I hate that he sees me as his sister's best friend or the Southern redneck girl who prefers cowgirl boots over high heels or the loudmouthed one who yells at the TV during football season. I'm just *one of the guys* to him, and even though I'd rather be his friend than nothing at all, I can't help that feeling of *what if*.

Coming to terms with the way things are between us comes to a complete halt the moment I wake up Sunday morning. Blurred flashbacks of the night before surface and I can't tell if they were all a dream or if...

I peel my eyes open as the sun glares through the window. I hate that damn sun. And fuck that window, too. Jesus, I feel like I ran a 10k marathon last night. My feet are more than likely swollen from wearing those damn shoes Viola made the bridesmaids wear, and I can feel the pins jabbing into my skull from having my hair done. Being Viola's maid of honor was a blast, but between the over-drinking and the too-tight shoes, I'll be paying for it for at least a week.

It takes me a minute to clear my eyes and realize I'm not

even in my own room. I'm in Drew's room, which could only mean one thing.

Last night wasn't a dream.

My body stiffens because I'm too nervous to look and see if Drew is lying next to me. My heart is pounding, and my head is aching from the excessive alcohol I drank last night. I don't normally binge drink like that, but it was my best friend's wedding reception with an open bar, so it's not really my fault.

Okay, yes, it is.

I shuffle around as quietly as possible, gripping the sheet in my fist as I turn slightly to check if I'm alone or not. Before I can look, I feel the cool fabric rub against my bare nipple. Glancing down, I see I'm completely naked and groan inwardly to myself. Searching the floor, I don't see any of my clothes. *Fuck me.*

My heart is racing so hard; I'm sure if Drew is next to me, he can feel the vibrations against the bed. If last night wasn't a dream, and I'm naked in his bed, and he's next to me…*stop panicking*, I tell myself. Maybe it's not even Drew. Maybe I brought another guy home, and I was too drunk to realize we went into the wrong room. That *has* to be it. Drew's probably asleep on the couch right now waiting to curse me out for all the damage I've done.

Feeling a bit calmer, I decide it's now or never. I need to take a good look at the strange guy next to me and kick him out before he thinks we're a couple now or something. I don't typically do one-night stands; hell, I've barely done relationships since my ex-boyfriend, Toby, broke up with me over two years ago. The last thing I'm looking for is someone to have casual sex with, well *unless*…

No. I can't go there.

Pulling the sheet up over my chest, I turn over as slowly as possible to avoid any movement on the bed and prepare for what I'm about to see.

Or rather, *who* I'm about to see.

Blinking, needing to clear my vision once again just to make sure I'm seeing him correctly, I nearly gasp aloud. There's no fucking way. This has to be one of those dreams within a dream type things because *holy fuck*!

I'm in Drew Fisher's bed *with* Drew Fisher.

How the hell did that happen?

CHAPTER ONE

DREW

SIX MONTHS BEFORE THE WEDDING

DON'T ASK me how I got here. Most days I wonder the same thing, but if there's one thing I know for sure, I wouldn't change my decision to become a police officer for anything — even when a prostitute is currently sleeping off the alcohol in the back of my patrol car, drooling all over herself and the seat.

"Another day, another pro," my partner, Logan Knight, mutters from the passenger seat. He shakes his head as the girl slurs something in her sleep. Working on the Sacramento PD the last several years has its ups and downs. I wouldn't necessarily consider this situation a pleasant one, but there've been worse ones.

"At least this one hasn't tried making out with your ear," I say, laughing as I think about the last time we brought one in.

"The night's still young," he mutters, annoyed.

Logan is a bit uptight. He's former military and holds a no bullshit stance ninety-nine percent of the time. It makes for an awesome partner, though. I know he has my back no matter what, which helps ease the tension when things get intense.

"So, what's your plan for the long weekend?" I ask. Our rotation ends tonight, and then we're off for three days.

"Driving up to see Skylar and probably staying up there so we can go do some stuff together." His expression doesn't change, and I can't tell whether he's excited to go there or not. I know things with his ex aren't the best, so I assume he has mixed emotions.

"How is Skylar, by the way?"

"Great. We FaceTimed last night, actually."

The conversation is over before we drive into the parking lot of the station. The girl is still passed out in the backseat, and once we park, we team up and carry her out.

"Hey, Mr. Grabby Hands!" she yells. "This isn't a free ride, ya know?"

We each hold an arm as she stumbles to walk. "Send my bill to the district attorney," Logan tells her, and I hold in a laugh.

"I'm serious," she says. "Touching is extra."

"Extra what? STDs?" Logan spits back, having zero tolerance.

"Oh, honey…" she purrs.

"All right, that's enough chitchat." I tighten my grip as we walk through the doors. "Save it for the judge."

Once my shift is over, I pat Logan on the back and tell him to have a good time this weekend. He's a good guy to have around, but he's very jaded. He's been through shit I couldn't even fathom.

Once I'm packed up, I wave to a few other guys and head out to my truck. I check my voicemail and see Mia has left me three messages already. She lives a couple of hours away, so the only chance to see each other is on my days off.

"Finally," she says, answering my call. "I was getting worried."

I check the time on my dashboard. "My shift ended six minutes ago."

She lets out an impatient sigh. "I know, but when your boyfriend is a cop, and you don't hear from him, one tends to get worried." She reminds me of this regularly, which makes it hard to get mad at her when she gets like this.

"All right, I'm sorry. I'm fine. Everything's fine."

"Good. So, when are you heading up here?" Her tone changes, and I smile.

"Probably in an hour or so. I have to head home first, shower and pack; then I'll be on my way."

"You haven't packed yet?" she scolds. "Why didn't you pack before work? You knew you were coming after your shift," she whines, sounding panicked.

"Mia, relax. It'll take me two minutes."

"Well, I just really miss you," she says, her voice softening. "I want to spend as much time with you as possible."

"Don't worry, baby. I'll be there before you know it."

We hang up as soon as I pull into the driveway, and I notice my roommate's Jeep is parked in my spot. *Dammit, Courtney.*

As soon as I walk in the door, I smell her blueberry muffins baking in the kitchen. It's something I've become accustomed to since she moved into the house a year ago, and although I don't eat muffins, she pushes me to try them every single time. She knows my routine with working out before or after work and my daily protein shakes, but she doesn't give up trying. She's persistent; I'll give her that.

The oven begins beeping as I walk into the kitchen, the smell getting stronger. Courtney isn't around, and the constant beep noise is making me panic.

"Court!" I shout, looking around for an oven mitt. "I think your muffins are burning! I'm going to feed them to the dog if you don't come and —"

"We don't have a dog!" she yells from the living room. "Just turn off the timer and quit being a baby."

"Not wanting the house to burn down doesn't make me a baby. Now, which one is the timer button?"

"Oh, for goodness sakes," she spat, marching into the kitchen in only a sports bra and short spandex shorts, and finally presses the damn button. She turns around and flashes me a look. "And you call yourself a police officer?" She grabs the oven mitt, pulls them out and places them on top of the stove.

"Sorry, I don't get a lot of baking hazard calls." I open the freezer door and grab a bag of frozen fruit.

She rolls her eyes, adjusting her straps over her shoulders. Her face is flushed, and her hair is pulled back with sweat.

"Wouldn't you rather have a delicious, warm, homemade blueberry muffin instead of your smoothie that tastes like wood?" She waves her hand over the pan, pushing the scent closer to my nose.

"Muffins don't create abs," I tease, pulling my shirt up and flashing her my stomach. She blushes immediately, and I laugh.

"I might not have an eight pack, but the girls have gotten their fair share of free drinks." She waves a finger over her chest, arches her brow, and now I'm the one blushing.

I clear my throat, looking away. "Why are you in workout clothes anyway?" I grab the ingredients for my fruit protein smoothie and turn away to the other side of the counter. Her walking around like that wasn't something I had anticipated when my little sister, Viola, suggested this arrangement. They've been best friends since college, and when Viola and my childhood best friend, Travis, shacked up, I was left with an empty room, and Courtney's lease had just ended.

"I'm trying yoga," she explains, and I snort. "It's harder than it looks."

"Aren't you supposed to do yoga in a class or something?" I pour all the ingredients I need into my blender and hit the button.

"I watched a tutorial on YouTube!" she shouts over the noise. "I think I'm finally starting to get it!"

I switch the blender off and lift the lid. Grabbing a spoon from the drawer, Courtney comes and stands right next to me, wrinkling her nose. "That looks like something the garbage disposal ate."

I ignore her comment, as I usually do when it comes to anything I make, and stir it up before pouring it into my glass.

"Should you be sweating that much?" I ask as she dabs her forehead with a towel.

"Huh?"

"Isn't yoga supposed to be relaxing and calming? Why are you so sweaty?"

She narrows her eyes at me and glares. "I broke a mental sweat."

I chuckle and shake my head as I start chugging my smoothie.

"The guy on the video said—"

"I can't believe you YouTube everything," I interrupt, shaking the cup in my hand to mix the protein powder better. "Just go to a class, and they'll teach you properly."

"I have learned a lot from YouTube, thank you very much. How do you think I learned to repurpose old furniture and properly fold a mattress sheet?"

I chug the rest of my drink down and set the glass in the kitchen sink.

"Figured one of your brothers would've taught you some of those skills?" I tease.

"They've taught me plenty, but I couldn't really transfer my skills in changing a tractor tire or gutting a fish into the city life," she says matter-of-factly as she begins cleaning up the kitchen and storing her muffins in Ziploc bags. Courtney is an obsessive baker and hoards them like an apocalypse is coming.

"Except in Texas, men happily try a woman's blueberry muffins when offered." She flashes me a look, and I roll my eyes at her pathetic attempt.

"Well, we aren't in Texas anymore, Dorothy."

"Ha. Ha. It's called having a little Southern hospitality. You should never refuse a woman's cookin', drink sweet tea like water, and say, ma'am, a lot." She gives me a wink, pops a piece of muffin into her mouth and releases an exaggerated moan. Her eyes flutter closed, and she tilts her head back like that muffin just gave her the most amazing orgasm of her life. "Now I need to take a shower...and get this stench off me." I walk out of the kitchen with her following behind.

"The only stench I smell is your girlfriend's expired hair products." *Ugh, not this again.* "Seriously, I don't know how she hasn't choked to death on the amount she uses."

"Court," I say in warning. "Stop."

"I'm not starting anything, but as the roommate, I think I have some say on who gets to stay here." I turn around, and she's standing with her arms crossed. I'm not in the mood to have this conversation again.

"You only get a partial say, and unless she's stinking up your room, you don't get to say who's in mine."

"Fine, have it your way." She marches off, and I know this is far from over.

COURTNEY

THREE MONTHS BEFORE THE WEDDING

"Drew!" I scream, stumbling over my feet as I rush out of my bedroom. Booking it to his room, I smack my palm over and over on his door. "Drew! Get up! She's having the baby!"

I don't wait for his response because I need to get dressed. I fell asleep looking up baking tutorials on my phone and forgot to change out of my running clothes. Well, my sweats. I hadn't actually gone running.

"What the hell, Court?" Drew finally comes stumbling down the hallway. "It's three in the goddamn morning."

"Well, tell that to your nephew. Apparently, he's ready to

make his debut." I shuffle around my room for something to wear.

"*Now*?" It finally hits him.

"Yes, now!" I turn around and see him in only a pair of boxer shorts, and by the looks of it, Drew Jr. is also awake. I blush so hard and turn back around before he takes notice. "Get dressed so we can go to the hospital."

"Okay, can I at least take a shower first?"

My brain momentarily freezes as I hold onto the image of him in the shower with Drew Jr. and what it'd be like to be in that shower with him. *His hard body, my hands gliding over his tattoos, my fingers combing through his wet locks.*

"Courtney," he says, pulling my attention back.

"Uh, no. No shower. There's no time. We gotta go." I can't look at him right now, so I pretend to search for a hairbrush. Seeing him half naked never gets old, regardless of how long we've lived together.

I hear him groan before he walks back to his room. Thank God. I couldn't chance looking at him again and him noticing the way I was staring at his groin.

This is what happens when you crush on one of your best friends who's also your roommate. It's not a new crush by any means, but that doesn't mean it gets any easier to be around him either. He's obliviously in love with a girl who thinks Skittles really are at the end of a rainbow, and I'm in love with a guy who sees me as only a friend. Like *one of the guys*. I don't pretend to know how a guy's brain works, but I'm pretty sure Drew's is broken and in need of a major repair. He doesn't see Mia for what she is—a train wreck.

We carpool to the hospital, and once we arrive, we nearly sprint up to the Labor and Delivery floor. Drew called Travis on the way over, and he let us know the baby would arrive any minute. Not wanting to miss it, we rush as fast as we can.

"We're looking for Viola Fisher," Drew tells the lady at the nurse's station as soon as we push through the doors. "She's having the baby, and we can't miss it."

"Are you family?" She looks at the both of us expressionless.

"Well, he is," I say, interrupting. "He's her brother. I'm her best friend. So, basically family. Please, where is she?"

"Just a moment, please." She picks up her phone and dials.

Ugh, we don't have time for this.

Drew brushes a hand through his hair—frustration and annoyance evident on his face. I glance at the nurse who's not paying attention to us and down the empty hallway. Drew notices and furrows his brows at me, curious as to what I'm up to.

Deciding I can't wait any longer, I grab Drew's hand and pull him down the hall with me.

"What are you doing?" he whispers as we shuffle down the hall before the nurse can stop us. "You're going to get us in trouble."

"By who?" I ask. "The cops?" At least if I did get arrested, there'd be handcuffs involved.

Grinning, he rolls his eyes at me and the both of us go searching for Viola. We round the hall and both start speed walking as soon as we see Travis. He has a plastic cup of ice in one hand and his cell in the other.

"Finally," he groans, shoving his phone back into his pocket. "Viola's been asking about you guys."

"Don't look at me," I say, suddenly realizing Drew and I are still holding hands. I release his hand and miss his warmth immediately. "Nurse Stuck-up gave us a hard time."

Forty-two minutes later, Viola delivers a baby boy. James Travis King. Chunky thighs, dimpled cheeks, and dark hair. This kid is already stealing hearts, especially mine.

Travis and Viola have a long history together—since before middle school. I've heard the story over and over since Viola and I first became friends back in freshman year of college, but it's one of those stories romance novels are made from.

Ginny is their feisty one-year-old and the coolest kid I've ever met. Her name was inspired by Viola's obsession with Harry Potter, as is the name James, but I'm going to make sure they grow up knowing more than just spells and Hogwarts. As their auntie, I'll make sure they're corrupt in all the right ways.

"He's so cute, Lola," I gush, using the nickname I've called her since we first met. "I think he looks a lot like Travis."

"Nah, he's got some good Fisher features," Drew says, hovering over me as I hold James in my arms.

Viola smiles and nods.

"When is your mother-in-law bringing Ginny up here?"

"Probably not until after her morning nap. We called her in the middle of the night, so his mom probably needs the nap more than Ginny does."

"Well, you should get some rest, too," I tell her.

"I will." She smiles sincerely, and I can tell she's just over the moon in love with her new baby. "Three months 'til the wedding," she reminds me.

"Don't worry, Lola. You're going to be the most gorgeous bride ever."

She frowns. "Well, just in case, start looking around for the best Spanx on the market. Three months to lose this baby weight will probably be the death of me."

"Spanx to flatten the stomach and a corset to lift and separate the girls. I'm on it."

CHAPTER TWO

DREW

TWO WEEKS BEFORE THE WEDDING

Mia Montgomery is the only woman I've ever truly loved.

I know our relationship hasn't been perfect over the last few years, but working for it makes the good times that much sweeter. Today is one of those days I look forward to.

Travis swears I'm whipped. He even has a bet on the table that if I sleep with someone else, I'll realize that Mia's pussy isn't made of gold. Although he knows I have no desire to be with anyone else, he's still holding out hope. The only person I want is on her way over, and I plan to make every minute we have together count.

Sitting on the couch, mindlessly flipping through the channels, I hear the low growl of Courtney's Jeep pull in the driveway. I let out a deep breath, rubbing my sweaty palms against my jeans. If only she would've stayed away a little longer. It's her house too, but she and Mia have never gotten along since the drama she caused with Viola and Travis a couple of years ago. She's Viola's best friend, and though we've become close over the last few years, there's nothing between us other than our friendship and being roommates. I've got her back, and she's got mine. I know she's there for me no matter what.

Mia admitted to being intimidated by her looks, and while Courtney is obviously pretty, I have to constantly remind Mia that Court is one of the guys. She chugs beer like it's going out of style, calls football plays before the referee, punches like a guy, and has no filter. Also, she can appreciate a nice ass and isn't afraid to say so. She's basically replaced Travis since he's no longer living the bachelor life. Regardless, Mia doesn't see it that way and is too stubborn to let it go. The fact that I won't and don't have anything negative to say about Courtney pisses her off, but I refuse to play into her games and ego strokes.

Right on cue, Courtney stalks in, drops a large bag on the floor and plops down on the couch next to me.

"Do you have any idea how exhausting your sister can be?" she asks, reaching over and grabbing the beer out of my hand.

I give her a smile and a firm head nod. "Actually, I do." I reach for the bottle in her hand, but she pulls away before I can grab it. Her fingers feel cool, and it's hard not to notice the way she lingers them against mine. I look over and study her, recognizing her hair is a windblown mess. She looks like she just walked off the beach in her short shorts and cropped t-shirt that hangs off her shoulder.

"I need vodka, muffins, and a nap, and it's barely noon. Helping Lola fit into her wedding gown and playing with Ginny made me break out into a sweat," Courtney says, grabbing the remote from the coffee table and changing the channel back to one of her reality reruns. She leans her back against the sofa with her legs crossed. There's no use mentioning I don't want to watch this shit because she keeps score and will probably bring up some other time I made her watch something she had no interest in. Either way, I don't want to get into it now because I need her to leave. If Mia arrives and Courtney is here—sitting right next to me—it'll be a battle of wits, and I don't want to deal with it right now.

"So, what does Vizilla have planned for you the rest of the day?" I can't even hold back the smile on my face. Whether they want to admit it or not, Viola has turned into a bridezilla, which is how I came up with her most recent nickname. I *almost* feel sorry for Travis, but I know he'll take care of my little sister.

"Please tell me you didn't forget, Drew. We have a lunch date with her, your mom and dad, and Travis in about an hour. I know it was last minute, but it's important you're there. She group texted us earlier. Didn't you get it?"

Shit! I try to hold back my reaction. "Yeah, of course." *I didn't read it.*

"I hope so because if you miss this, she will speed over here, use your handcuffs against you, then proceed to cut off your balls and feed them to you."

"Jesus. A little graphic, Court," I say with wide eyes, knowing she'd probably just stand by and watch the whole thing go down while acting as Viola's backup.

Courtney faces me and arches a brow. "She's a nervous wreck and wants everything perfect, so don't mess this up. Got it?"

"I've dealt with Viola for all of her life, Court. Even the crazy parts of her."

She rolls her eyes, not taking the bait.

"I need a shower. I smell like baby shit." She lifts part of her shirt up to her nose and sniffs. "Probably because I'm wearing a little of it." As she stands, she lifts both arms over her head and stretches. I catch a glimpse of her flat stomach and boney hips. Not sure how that girl is so slim considering she eats carbs and chocolate like it's going out of style. She takes notice and playfully rolls her eyes before walking away, knowing I'll call her out for her horrible diet even though it doesn't show.

I grab the remote she dropped on the couch and turn my show back on. Moments later, I hear the water running in the bathroom, and all I can think about is having to go to that fucking luncheon and Mia arriving in the next thirty minutes. I mute the sound and stare past the TV. Skipping isn't an option, and neither is ditching Mia. *Fuck it. She'll just come as my date then.*

This would be a lot easier on me if everyone could see Mia the way I see her. She's beautiful, sweet, and goes out of her way to check up on me when I'm on duty. She has her bad days, but we all do.

My show finishes up just in time as Courtney walks back into the living room, dressed up in new clothes. Her long blonde hair is damp and pulled back into one of those messy buns, but her face looks freshly put on and clean.

"Do you want to ride together? I'll drive since I want to actually be on time," she offers with a chuckle, bending over and picking up her purse. She unlocks her phone and glances at the time. "Come on, Drew. We really need to get going if we want to miss the traffic."

I tense up, not having the nerve to tell her why I can't go with her. "Nah, I'll meet you there. I'll be right behind you."

"You better, Fisher." She points one of her fingers at me

as if I'm in trouble. "If you set Lola off, I'm smothering you with a pillow in your sleep."

I give her an evil grin. "You wouldn't dare."

She licks her lips and shakes her head before walking out the door. I hear the Jeep travel down the road and breathe a little lighter. Moments later, knocks ring out on the front door. I open it and pull Mia into my arms.

"Baby!" she says. "I've missed you."

"Me too." It's only been two weeks since we were last together but it's felt like an eternity. I lean in and give her a kiss. She smells so good, like spring water and fresh air, and I just want to lead her to my room and make love to her. But she's made it very clear that we can't rush things this time around and that we need to take our relationship more seriously. I'm hoping this time is different. *Fifth time's a charm, right?*

"So, what are we doing today?" she asks, looking around. I'm sure she's wondering if Courtney's here because the smell of her raspberry soap still lingers throughout the house.

"I thought we'd have lunch with my family," I say, nonchalantly grabbing my keys from the counter in the kitchen, knowing we have to leave now or we'll be late.

She takes a few steps forward and looks at me as if I've grown a third head.

"I'm not up to anything, I swear. Viola is having a prewedding meeting, and I want you to be there since you'll be my date and all."

"Oh, baby," she gushes, running toward me. She throws her arms around my neck and kisses me. "You really want me to be your date?"

"Of course, I do. I can't imagine going with anyone else. And you'll be the prettiest girl there…and mine."

"I'd love to join you. I love weddings," she adds, running her finger down my chest. "Honestly, I'm still kind of upset Viola didn't ask me to be a part of the wedding party since we've been together for years."

I was hoping she wouldn't bring this up again. We've already talked about this several times before, and Viola would die before ever allowing Mia to be a part of one of the biggest days of her life. She's very open about how she feels about Mia and hasn't yet forgiven her for the drama she caused years ago. We're all adults and have significantly grown up since then, but Viola refuses to forget. She's like a damn elephant; she remembers everything and jokes it's one of her mom superpowers.

"You know she didn't want a big wedding party. It's not personal, babe."

She pouts. "I know. But we would've looked so great together walking down the aisle."

I pull her closer and whisper in her ear, "We'll walk down the aisle together one day."

She tenses then relaxes by my touch. I may have pushed the limit that time, but I'm not giving up on us.

"Are you ready? We have to get going, so we're not too late."

"Yeah. I can't wait to see your parents again. It's been too long," Mia says.

"I agree. That's all about to change."

As we walk out the door, I text Travis and let him know I'm running a little late. He doesn't reply.

COURTNEY

Mia *Fucking* Montgomery.

What the fuck is she doing here, is my only thought as I watch Drew and her walk toward the table where we're all sitting. They've been broken up for months, but they've had this weird on-again, off-again relationship that drives me and everyone else insane. Viola and Travis loathe her as much as I do, but since their wedding is only two weeks away, Viola's playing nice to accommodate everyone. If it were my prewedding lunch, I'd be escorting her dirty skank ass out of the building. *And the country.*

"Hey, you finally made it," Travis says as he stands up and greets them, unfazed by Mia dangling on Drew's arm. "We were just about to order."

Noticing the way Viola tenses, I mutter, "I thought this was a *family* restaurant. When the hell did they start letting dogs in?"

She jabs her elbow into my ribs, shushing me before anyone else can take notice, but I can tell she's holding back a small, pleased smile from my words. Viola and Drew's mom and stepdad are having lunch with us, making this situation even more awkward than ever. Drew knows better, and when we're alone, he's going to get a mouthful.

As soon as Mia locks eyes with their mother, she puts on the widest, fakest smile ever, showing off her perfectly straight and white teeth. She's a trust-fund baby, so I know she's probably bought most of her *assets*. She's fake inside *and* outside. The difference between Mia and me is while my parents have helped support me, I actually know what it's like to work, to get my hands dirty, and take care of myself. I'm pretty sure the most work she's ever done involves walking from point A to B in six-inch designer heels.

"Mia, it's so great to see you again," their mother says, placing a cloth napkin over her lap.

Drew slides a chair out for Mia and she sits down right next to her. Drew sits between Mia and Travis. Smart. He knows there needs to be some kind of buffer between her and well, *everyone.*

"It's wonderful to see you, too, Mrs. Hennessy. And of course, Mr. Hennessy." She nods over to him, but his eyes haven't moved off her chest since the moment she walked in. "And of course, you too, Mr. Fisher."

"Oh, please. Call me Carla."

"Drew," Viola grabs his attention from across the table. "We're doing *family* wedding stuff. You should've told me you were bringing a friend with you."

I want to die with laughter at the way she just called him out. We never know what they are, relationship-wise, and I'm pretty sure they don't either. They're never together long enough during one stretch to be anything aside from a week-long booty call.

"What's it matter? Mia and I already had plans when you called this *little get-together.* And plus, Courtney isn't family."

I gasp, and I swear Viola is ready to punch him in the face. "Yes, she is," she says between gritted teeth.

"Oh, don't worry," Mia interrupts in a sickly-sweet tone, and I can tell by the way Viola's clenching her fists that she's ready to jump over the table and claw her eyes out. "I won't get in the way. I have a hair appointment tomorrow, so I'll have to drive back home at some point anyway." She turns to gaze into Drew's eyes, and I have to swallow down the vomit before the words come out of my mouth. Hair appointment? She acts like she's going to work or something.

"What a shame," I blurt out, grabbing my napkin and

25

aggressively shaking it out before I fold it on my lap. Viola turns and looks at me just as Drew does. *Shit*. I guess I said that too loud or maybe it was the pop of my napkin that caught their attention. Either way, Drew's eyes are burning holes into me.

"It's going to be so fun," I quickly add with a smile that says I'd rather eat dirt than be anywhere near Mia. I grab the glass of water on the table and take small sips to stop the words from flowing freely.

"Oh, no worries!" she exclaims as she turns toward Drew and gazes into his eyes, overly exaggerating her movements and silently marking her invisible territory so I know he's taken. "I'll be back to visit my *Drewberry Muffin* every weekend starting now."

The way she says his name in a nasally baby voice has me spewing water out of my nose and mouth faster than I can cover my lips. It flies across the table and nearly reaches her face before she squeals and backs away. I cannot handle her being at my house every weekend until the end of time. I will fucking die.

I hear Travis chuckling at my expense, but Drew is giving me those eyes. Those same eyes I dream about at night and fantasize to in the shower. Except this time, they aren't bedroom eyes I'm seeing; instead, they're shooting daggers at me. He clears his throat, making it known that he doesn't appreciate the way I'm acting, but my heart is beating so hard in my chest, it might break through and punch Mia between her eyebrows that are on point.

I wish I were sitting in front of Viola so then at least we could exchange eye rolls, but I'm stuck in hell, sitting in front of Drew and the devil incarnate. He sneaks glances at her, and I can see her hand on his lap. As she giggles, I can't help but roll my eyes. What makes this situation even sweeter is Mia hates me as much as I hate her. She's always been weird around me, probably because she's intimidated, which she should be. I'll snatch her man so fast, the Gucci bag she has hanging off the back of her chair will be out of style before she can order lunch.

During one of their many breakups, Drew agreed to have me as his roommate. After graduation, I refused to return to Texas, which didn't make my Dad happy, so he refused to renew my lease. Considering my circumstances, I had to find a more affordable living arrangement and Drew conveniently had an extra bedroom. He worked weird hours, so for half the week, I'd be home alone which was perfect considering I lived alone for years. Viola loved the idea but only because she secretly wished we were sharing the same bed. But that hasn't *ever* happened, and by the looks of it, I don't believe it'll be happening anytime soon.

When they got back together—once again—Mia wasn't happy to see that a girl moved in with him. Countless times, before I accepted his offer, Drew begged her to move in with him, but each time she rejected him. When she felt threatened by me, she'd bring up moving in, but the next week they'd be broken up again. It's a psychotic cycle. Though it's been over a year since we've been roommates, and she's had plenty of time to accept it, she blatantly refuses.

Just like Viola, Drew had house rules, but even now I continue to push his boundaries on a weekly basis. I've never been controllable, and I think it's hilarious Drew thinks he can tell me what to do when I'm paying half the bills.

Mia's annoying laughter brings me back to reality, and I

realize how pathetic I am. I have a crush on a man who's given his kind heart to the devil herself.

Our food arrives, and surprisingly enough, I'm not hungry. Seeing them together makes me sick to my stomach, and I twirl spaghetti around my fork and move it on my plate while Viola reads her itinerary aloud. I almost feel like I'm back in college because she gave us handouts with a schedule of times for each day leading up the wedding. I can't help but laugh, but she doesn't think it's funny. Viola's all business, and if anyone ruins her perfectly planned-out day, God help them.

When Drew places his arm around Mia, and she leans into him, she makes sure to look at me with an evil-ass grin on her face. I set my fork down on my plate and can't stop my nostrils from flaring. I thought I could handle being around her with Drew, but in reality, I can't. It's killing me inside. I've successfully avoided them together until their next breakup, but right now, there's no escaping them. It's absolute torture.

At that moment, a silent conversation is exchanged between Mia and me.

She kisses his neck then glances back at me as if she's hoping to get some sort of reaction, like she does each time she's around me.

Instead of making a scene, I give her a smile just as sarcastic as her own and hope she understands who she just started shit with. If she wants a war, I'm ready to fight. I'm not passive. I'm not Viola. I don't play games. Maybe Mia *Fucking* Montgomery has finally met her match. I want my best friend happy, and I'll die helping make that happen.

Game on, bitch!

CHAPTER THREE

DREW

THE WAITER COMES to the table and picks up empty plates, and I take the opportunity to go to the bathroom. I open the door, and before I can close it, Courtney pushes her way in. She stands there with her hands on her hips like she's about to rip off my head.

"What the hell?" I scold.

"What the fuck?" she fires right back.

"I have to piss. Do you mind?"

She crosses her arms. "Go for it, *Drewberry Muffin*."

I shake my head at her and walk to the urinal. "Why are you being like this?"

"I should ask you the same question. You know exactly how Viola and Travis feel about Mia. You know how I feel about her, too. The only neutral people out there are your mother, your stepdad who loves her tits, and your father. Everyone else, even the children, despise her. She's a witch, Drew."

I zip up my pants. "Mia's my girlfriend. You, Viola, and

Travis will have to accept it just as I accepted their relationship."

She sighs. "So, you're *officially* back together again?"

I nod my head, knowing it's not the answer she wants to hear.

"I know you can't see past the bullshit. You can't see how she affects everyone, even you. She's poison," Courtney says.

A knock rings on the door, and it slightly annoys me.

"One minute," I shout and can hear a man's voice mumble something.

"Are we done here?" I glare at her as I turn the faucet on and wash my hands.

She takes two steps forward until she's inches from my face then pokes her finger hard into my chest. "You deserve better than her." She lowers her eyes and then murmurs, "God, I wish you could see that."

I open my mouth but then close it just as another knock pounds against the door.

Courtney shakes her head at me then opens the door and walks out. As soon as I open the door, Travis is standing in the hall, confused.

"That was unexpected," Travis says.

"I'll tell you later," I walk back to the table. The rest of the time Courtney doesn't look at me and pretends Mia doesn't exist. No one really notices the cold shoulder, but it's painfully obvious to me because I know her. I may know her better than Viola at this point, especially after living with her for almost two years, but I don't remember a time when she's completely ignored me.

Mia leans over and whispers in my ear. "Are you ready to go?"

Courtney picks up James and holds him in her arms. She whispers something to Viola who cracks up laughing.

"Yeah," I whisper back. "Let's get out of here."

"Whoa, where are you two headed?" Mom asks when we both stand.

I glance over at Mia and wrap my arm around her. "We've got some things to do."

Viola looks pissed that we're leaving but doesn't say a word. Travis gives us a head nod, and we turn and walk out hand in hand. I don't dare look at Courtney. Once we're to the truck, Mia climbs in and scoots close to me then places her hand on my thigh. It's the closest we've been in weeks—hell, in months.

"I was ready to go as soon as we arrived. Boring! And your sister with that itinerary...pfft, *please*." She laughs as I start the truck and head home.

I glance over at her, ready to say something, but she leans her head against my shoulder, and I forget about it.

"I want to snuggle."

"Yeah?" I can't help but smile.

"That's not code for anything," she adds.

We make small talk on the way home, and as we pull into the driveway, I turn and look at her. This 'no sex' rule she came up with is ridiculous considering how long we've been together, but I'll go along with it for as long as I have to. I lean over and give her a kiss, and she places the palm of her hand on my cheek.

"Let's watch a movie," I suggest.

"Here?" She scrunches her nose, and I tap it with my finger.

"Come on. I'll let you choose."

After we walk inside, I rummage through Courtney's

DVDs and name them off until Mia agrees to one. She chooses *Mean Girls*, which I'm not really pleased with, but I don't argue about it. I turn off the lights, turn on the surround sound, and grab a blanket. Once we're comfortable, Mia leans into my arms, and I hold her as we watch this stupid-ass movie. It takes everything I have not to fall asleep because I'm so comfortable.

Before the movie ends, I hear the Jeep pull into the driveway, and my eyes bolt open. The best thing I can do is keep Courtney and Mia away from each other.

"Babe," I say. "Let's go to my room."

"But the movie isn't over yet," she whines.

I let out a calm breath as soon as the door bolts open. Courtney turns on all the lights and pretends we're invisible. Going straight to the kitchen, she makes all sorts of noise opening plastic wrappers, opening and closing the fridge, and cabinets.

Mia looks up at me and groans. I kiss her on the forehead before getting up and going into the kitchen.

"We're trying to watch a movie." I stand in the doorway as Courtney mixes a preworkout drink together. Yeah, she's pissed. Pissed enough to go for a run.

"*Mean Girls*? Ironic since you're sitting next to the real-life Regina George," she whispers, pointing to the living room where Mia is waiting.

I take a few steps toward her, keeping my voice low. "Are you going to tell me what's crawled in your ass and died?"

We're inches apart. I can feel her breath brush against my face as anger radiates from her. She hasn't been this mad in a long time.

"You're my problem, Drew." She looks like she's about to

punch me in the face or push me away from her. I'm not sure which one it is yet.

"What are you two doing?" Mia asks, noticing how close Courtney and I are. Courtney wraps her arms around me and gives me a big, tight, angry hug, and I instinctively hug her back.

"Just telling my best friend how much I've missed him." Courtney flashes a wide grin.

Mia narrows her eyes, groans, and then storms out.

I release my hold on Courtney and glare at her.

"What?"

"Real nice, Court." I turn away and follow Mia to my bedroom.

"What the hell, Drew? I need to know the truth. I need to know if you secretly have a thing for her."

I actually laugh. "Not at all. The only person I have a *thing* for is you."

"I see the way you look at her."

"Really? Please enlighten me, Mia." I hate arguing with her. I especially hate arguing with her over Courtney because Mia always wants me to choose sides, although she's the only one that has my heart and has for years. This is exactly what I wanted to avoid today, but I suppose it was inevitable. It's just the kind of relationship we have.

"You look at her like she's a piece of cake or something." Mia is furious.

"And you know I don't like cake, so there you go. I'm not going to explain this to you again, Mia. We're just friends. We'll always be just friends. There's nothing romantic between us at all. I don't know how I can be more clear about this."

"You promise? I'm the only woman for you?"

I move toward her and pull her into my arms. "Yes, I promise. You're the only woman I want." I pull her close, and before my lips touch hers, I tell her how much she means to me.

COURTNEY

Mia doesn't want Drew unless someone else does. If she feels slightly threatened, she'll do whatever she can to make sure he doesn't move on. It's happened so many times over the last few years it's almost sickening. At one point, Drew considered going on a date with someone who worked dispatch, but as soon as Mia found out, she freaked out and immediately wanted him back. And what did he do? He took her back, so they could work it out—again. *And again. And again.*

I walk into my room, and I can hear them arguing through the thin walls as if I'm standing right beside them. I roll my eyes and change into some workout clothes. I need to go for a run before my brain explodes. Before leaving, I hear her say my name like it's poison. Once she sees me in nothing but a sports bra and the smallest shorts I have, she'll really lose her shit. *Perfect.*

I'm sure she wouldn't care if Drew lived with some slob. She wouldn't care if I were ugly or had a third head. But since I'm not any of those things, she's intimidated and always has been. I think it's hilarious because our relationship is so platonic and harmless. Since we've become roommates and besties, I've tried to be nice to her, include her in on things, and each time it's a disaster. The girl doesn't have a nice bone in her body.

I grab my headphones and cell phone before heading out the door. After running three miles, I decide to turn around and run back. Before I walk back in, all sweaty and out of breath, I hope whatever argument they were having is over. It's a nonstop rollercoaster that I'm not waiting in line for.

Hardly able to catch my breath as I walk toward my room, I realize how much better I feel. All my frustration with Drew and wedding stress has almost vanished. Once I turn the corner, I see Mia exiting the bathroom, and she looks me up and down then gives me a death glare. She's totally not amused with me or my choice of clothes.

"Bitch," she whispers under her breath as she passes me and then she hits me hard with her shoulder. I'm actually shocked she brought it to that level.

"Oh, I'm so sorry," she says sarcastically, covering a hand over her mouth when I slightly stumble before I gain my footing.

My jaw is clenched as tight as my fists. Being the polite little Southern girl I am, I'll never throw the first punch regardless if provoked, but that doesn't stop my mouth from running. Taking a few steps forward, I'm getting ready to tell her exactly what I think of her skank ass and before I can spew out a single cuss word, Drew walks down the hallway toward Mia. He places his hands around her waist, but she ignores his touch as usual.

"Everything okay, babe?"

"Yeah, *fine*." She glares back at me as I rub the shoulder she hit pretty hard.

Without a doubt, she wanted me to act out, and it's eating her alive right now that I didn't. He glares at me, and I put on a big smile because this time I'm actually innocent. Somehow, I hold back what I really want to say and wait. I won't let her see me lose my shit in front of him because it's childish, and I won't let her win.

She groans before walking past him with an attitude. He glances back at her then looks me up and down before narrowing his eyes at me.

"Are you being rude again?"

"No. Not this time." I turn away from him, not waiting for a response and walk to my room. Honestly, I pity her for being so jealous of the relationship that Drew and I have because she has him in ways I only dream about. It's sad that he's traveling down a dirty road with her that leads straight to Heartacheville. If only I could help him see he's brainwashed by her fake tits, hair extensions, and spray tan, but I'm pretty sure it's hopeless because he's too committed. When I hear her voice raised again, I realize I need to find my escape for the night, so I text Viola.

Courtney: I need a distraction. Can you break away for an hour?

Viola: I'm exhausted. Get your cheesecake to go and come over.

Courtney: You've already got your pajamas on, don't you?

Viola: You know me too well. I'm sure Kayla is free and it will only be carby temptation for me. Text her!

Courtney: Fine! I will. :) Get some rest!

I take a shower, put on my red lipstick and smoky eyes, and dress in overly-scandalous clothes before I text Kayla to hang out tonight. We've become good friends since being in Viola's wedding party together. We're two single ladies who have no outside life, so it makes it easy to drop random things on her, plus she loves it as much as I do.

Courtney: Get dressed woman, we're having a girls night!

Kayla: How much time do I have?

Courtney: Thirty minutes?

Kayla: Perfect. Come get me!

I can't stay here and listen to them argue all night, so hanging with Kayla is a perfect escape. Mia needs to go and I have a feeling she's staying. Them together again is already making me crazy, and I need to have fun and ignore it. Viola usually makes sure I don't get into too much trouble, so no telling what kind of shenanigans I'll get in without her.

CHAPTER FOUR

DREW

"I WANT HER GONE," Mia demands as she plops on the couch with her arms crossed.

I stare at her confused. "Who?"

"Courtney. I don't want you living with her anymore," she explains, her voice firm.

I shake my head at her. "That's not your decision to make."

She stands, cocking her hip out. "As your *girlfriend*, it is."

"Where is this coming from? Courtney isn't the issue in our relationship, Mia."

"She spews hate and jealousy, which obviously isn't good for us. So, you can choose—me or her."

"That's not true. Courtney isn't the reason we fight."

"No? Well, we're fighting right now and look who just happens to be here." She waves her hand up in the air, and I follow it behind me. Courtney is standing by the table, digging in her purse. I can tell she heard everything by the somber look on her face. Her blonde hair curled and down, makeup that makes her look like a supermodel, and a tight little skirt and low-cut shirt. She's almost eye to eye with me in those high heels. When she's dressed like that, it's hard to remember she's one of the guys, which really doesn't help my plea with Mia about it. *Fucking fantastic.*

"Mia," I hiss, my jaw locked as I look back at her. I can't believe Mia's doing this right now.

"You'll make your choice and you'll make it *right now*." Her voice is full of venom, and her eyes are narrowed and threatening.

"You're being ridiculous."

She grits her teeth together and speaks between them. "If you don't, it's over. So, let me know when you make up your mind, okay?" Mia's shaking in anger as she grabs her purse from the couch.

I place my hand on her shoulder, turning her back around. "Please, don't do this."

"I don't like you and her being around each other. And it needs to stop." She tilts her head around me, and I turn to see what she's looking at.

Courtney's no longer there, but that doesn't mean she can't hear us.

"Perhaps if we had some privacy once in a fucking while, we could talk about this like adults."

"Fine, if it'll make you calm down, I'll talk to her about it. Can we drop this for now, please?" I plead with my eyes, grabbing her hand in mine.

"Really?" She smiles, stepping closer.

I nod, eating my words. "Yes. I don't want us to fight anymore."

She nods in agreement, but then pulls away and throws her bag over her shoulder.

"Wait. Where are you going?" I ask, confused.

"I'm going home." She walks toward the door. "When you make your decision, call me."

I follow behind and grab her hand. "Stay with me."

She shakes her head. "It'll just lead to sex. And I have an appointment in the morning. This is for the best." Mia stands on her tiptoes and gives me a quick kiss on the cheek before she walks out the door and gets in her Mercedes then drives away.

Once she's gone, I can't contain the anger I feel. "Fuck!"

I hear rattling in the kitchen and glance in to see Courtney messing around in the fridge. Shit, I didn't realize she was in here.

She slams it shut and jumps a little when she sees me in the doorway.

"I didn't mean to eavesdrop. I was just grabbing a few things before heading out."

"It's not your fault."

The air between us is thick, and I know she's probably thinking the worst. "Listen, Court—"

"You want me to move out," she interrupts. The words sound worse aloud that I anticipated. I can't imagine Courtney leaving. Nor do I want to.

"I really don't," I begin, hoping she can see how awful I feel about this. "Mia will get over it."

"And if she doesn't?" she asks, raising her brows. She knows Mia as well as I do it would seem.

I shrug because I don't know the answer to that.

She steps toward me and places her hand on my arm. "You deserve better, Drew Fisher. I'll leave if it's what you want, but when you come to your senses, it might be too late."

Her words hit me like a ton of bricks. She walks away

before I can respond, which is probably best because I have no response to that. I can't imagine not having Courtney in my life, but I also need to give my relationship with Mia a real chance.

My heart pounds in my chest, thinking about everything, and what each decision would mean. Courtney and I are good as roommates. I know I can count on her to help keep the house and yard clean, pay her half of the bills on time, or be the first one to tell me when our towels need to be washed. It's simple, and between work and Mia, I need *something* in my life to be simple.

I lay on the couch and think about Mia. We've been together over three years, and we've had so many ups and downs, even I get confused on where the ups begin and where the downs end. But I love her, and I want to make this work. I have this weekend off, and I had hoped she'd stay so we could spend some real quality time together before the wedding.

Closing my eyes, I drift off, thinking of Mia and Courtney and how I'm going to figure this one out. When I finally close them for good, it's not Mia face I see or her voice I hear.

"*Drew*," Courtney says, sauntering into the living room with nothing on but a red thong and matching bra. I'm confused by her boldness and wonder what the hell she's thinking. She's never walked around the house like this, and somehow, I'm not complaining.

"What are you doing?" I give her a pointed look.

She walks toward me and sits on my lap, straddling me. Her perky breasts press against my bare chest and my heartbeat pounds harder. I take short breaths as I try to understand what she's doing.

"Court—"

"Shhh," she shushes me, placing a finger over my lips and offers a sultry smirk.

"But," I challenge, but it's no use.

"*Shut up*," she demands with a sly smile. She leans in closer and drags her pouty lips against my neck and plants kisses up my neck to my ear. "I'm tired of waiting for Mr. Right, so I'm finally taking what I want."

I should be pushing her away, but her lips on me feel right. She begins grinding her hips against me hard, and it feels so fucking good that I can't stop the moan that releases from my throat.

Instinctively, I run my fingers through her wavy hair and forcefully kiss her, taking control of the situation. It's hard for me to hold back when she's giving herself to me. All my inhibitions are gone and not once does it cross my mind that she's my best friend. Right now, all my dick knows is that she makes it hard and now I fucking want her.

She moans against my lips, which is the sexiest thing I've ever heard. She then slides her body down mine until her knees reach the floor. Hooking her fingers in the waistband of my bottoms, she pulls them down to my ankles and runs her hands up my thighs. Smiling, she takes charge and wraps her lips around the tip of my dick. My head falls back, gripping my fingers in the sofa cushion under me. Her mouth on me feels fucking amazing.

Courtney licks from the bottom to the top, paying extra attention to the head until I'm throbbing for more. Her fingers dig into my thighs as she opens her mouth and places every inch inside, deep throating me until she's gagging. Before she finishes, she stands and removes her bra and panties until her beautiful naked body is on full display. She stands there, staring at me with a sexy little smile on her face and all I can do is admire her. I pinch one of her taunt nipples then slide two fingers deep inside her as I thumb her clit. She moans and sinks lower. I kiss my way up her naked body until I'm standing eye to eye with her as I slide my fingers in and out of her wetness. Nothing is holding me back, and the urge to want to do everything overcomes me.

"I want you, Drew. Fuck me," she says in her cute country accent. Her pussy is so wet that I don't know how much more I can take before I slam my dick deep inside her. I place my fingers in my mouth, hoping to taste her sweetness before grabbing her hips and forcing her against the couch. Slapping her round ass, I want to hear her scream my name as I fuck her dry.

"Fuck me hard, Deputy," she pleads. Wrapping her long blonde hair around my fist, I force her head back so I can look into her blue eyes and demand she beg for it like a good girl, and she does. I'm not sure what's come over me, but there's no stopping now, not while she's looking back at me with hungry, greedy eyes.

I don't go easy.

I give her every inch of me until she's screaming obscenities.

"Yes. Harder. *Much* harder," she demands, and I gladly do what I'm told. She screams out my name as her pussy tightens and she comes, and I continue pounding every inch of my cock until I feel warmth cover me.

"Drew... Please, Drew..." Her moans fade away, and soon her voice is completely gone.

Confused, I blink my eyes a few times until I'm fully awake. I start to realize what the fuck just happened, but I can't comprehend it. I close my eyes tight, knowing I need to clean myself up and calm down. My dick is so damn hard that it hurts. I've not had a wet dream since I was a teenager and what's even more awkward is who it was about.

What the fuck is wrong with me?

Not once have I thought of Courtney that way. It's weird, and I'm not sure what to make of it. It felt real and natural and already the images of her body against mine are haunting me. Since the day we met, I've seen her as one of the guys, my best friend and roommate, and nothing else. My subconscious has played a cruel fucking joke on me, one that I don't think I'll be able to forget any time soon.

Once I decide to get up and change clothes, I hear the front door swing open and click shut. Realizing I've got a mess in my pants because of Courtney, I sit back down and try to pretend she's not here. I can't bring myself to look her in the eye, and honestly, it might take me a while.

COURTNEY

You know you're having a bad day when even cheesecake can't make it better. After my run in with Drew and Mia, I wasn't in the mood to go dancing even though I was all dressed and ready to go. Kayla and I decided to go on a dessert date instead, and she's been catching me up on all the juicy gossip on her horny neighbors. The whole time, I've been distracted thinking about Drew and haven't really been listening to what she's said.

"What's going on?" Kayla asks, taking a huge bite of her strawberry cheesecake. Nothing gets past her.

"Life," I say with a smile.

"Drew?" She winks at me.

"How'd you know?" I laugh.

"Because we're basically twinsies, and it's obvious how much you care about him."

I sigh. "So how 'bout those Cowboys?"

"Don't change the subject." She notices my deflection, a tactic I can never use against her.

"Drew's girlfriend wants me to move out *again*, but it's different this time. I don't want Drew to choose me if she is really going to be what makes him happy, but I don't think she is. It just hurts my heart. The sick thing is I would move if he wanted me to."

Kayla's mouth drops open. "Court, I've got a spare room or a couch if you need a place. And I don't like this Mia chick. Everything I've heard about her over the years is just…ick."

I laugh. "She's a special kind of bitch."

After a few hours of chatting with Kayla, we leave with hugs, and I drive home in silence, which is odd for me. Usually, I'm blaring pop music with the top down, allowing the wind to blow through my hair. Though the weather is perfect, I need time to think before I walk in and see Drew. There will be a day when we won't be roommates because one of us will get married or in a serious relationship, but I didn't think that day would be so soon. I never imagined Mia would give him an ultimatum. It's low, lower than I thought she could go. Though it's not the first time she's demanded us apart, seeing the look on her face when she said it made it all too real.

As I pull into the driveway, I notice the Mercedes isn't in my parking spot. I exhale, recompose myself, then walk in. Drew's sitting on the couch but doesn't acknowledge me when I enter, which amplifies the negative thoughts that rush through me. Maybe he's trying to find the words to tell me to leave? I can't imagine him doing that, but I know how women can affect men. Instead of allowing their brains to take charge, they sometimes allow their dicks to make important decisions.

Everyone knows Mia has him by the balls—which makes me even more uneasy about the situation. I'm hoping Drew is stronger than that and he doesn't ask me to move; but if he does, I'll go. The thought makes me so fucking sad. It'll tear my heart from my chest because he's one of my best friends, and I care so much about him. I love being his roommate. It's the first place that's really felt like home since I moved here from Texas. I know my best friend, and I know he's not happy, whether he'll admit it or not. Sometimes he's too proud to talk about how he feels, especially when it comes to her.

I hear rustling around in the living room as I pour a glass of wine, trying to forget about the day. As I lean against the doorway, Drew walks past me like I have a disease.

"Well, hello to you, too," I say before kicking off my heels and walking to the couch with my wine. It's still warm from where he was sitting. The shower comes on, and I finish the glass then put it in the sink. The material of the skirt is itchy, so I walk to my room and change into something more comfortable. Grabbing a tank top and pajama pants, I change and wait until I hear the water stop and the bathroom door open so I can wash my face. Nonchalantly I walk to the bathroom and pass Drew in the hallway. He swallows hard and keeps walking to his room without a word exchanged. Seriously? I really hope he's not mad at me.

After I put my hair in a messy ponytail on top of my

head, I turn on the water and bend over the sink to scrub the makeup from my face then head back to my room. Before I walk in, I stand in the hallway for a second, contemplating knocking on Drew's door. We need to talk about this before it gnaws at my sanity. Sucking in a deep breath, I take a few more steps forward and stand outside his door. Right when I go to knock, he opens the door and is standing there staring at me like I'm a ghost.

"Why are you being so weird?" I ask.

He looks into my eyes then looks away. "I'm not."

"Yes, you are. Listen, I'm sorry about today. Whatever you want in life, I support that. You can always talk to me about anything. Okay?"

Drew nods. "Thanks." He walks past me, and I stand there confused by his shortness.

"So, are you still mad at me?" I yell down the hall when he's out of sight.

It's completely silent for a few seconds, and my heart begins to race. Maybe I shouldn't have blurted that out? Maybe there was a better way to ask him?

As soon as I let out a sigh, Drew yells back, "No."

A big smile crosses my face, and I'm genuinely happy.

"Good," I whisper with a smile. I head back to my room and climb into bed.

CHAPTER FIVE

DREW

ONE WEEK BEFORE THE WEDDING

BETWEEN THE ARGUMENT with Mia and that hot sex dream of my best friend, I've successfully avoided Courtney like the plague for a week. I can't look at her without feeling guilty. Every time I even think about her, all I envision is her perfect, luscious body pressed against mine and it's freaking me the fuck out.

I've never thought of Courtney like that before. Sure, she's pretty, funny, and smart, but she's always just been one of the guys I hang with, minus the being a guy part. Once Viola and she became friends, she just started being one of mine. There was never anything more to us, and I'm not sure how or why Mia thinks otherwise. Now, for whatever reason, Courtney is haunting my dreams. Every night this week before going to bed, I've tried thinking of something else—*anything else*—but nothing's worked. Courtney naked on top of me. Courtney naked under me. Courtney naked in the shower.

Fuck.

However, last night I woke up to a text message from Mia that solidified our relationship. I hadn't told her what she wanted to hear, so she made the decision for us.

Randomly throughout the day, I've opened my phone and read it.

Mia: I can't do this, Drew. When Courtney's gone, we can start over again.

Being given an ultimatum really pisses me off and I think it's the most upset I've been with Mia in years. I let her get away with so much, but this has crossed the line. I don't want Courtney to move out. For Christ's sake, she's one of my best friends who also happens to pay her rent early and doesn't annoy me much. She's a better roommate than Travis because she's OCD about the same things, like our cabinets and refrigerator.

Instead of Mia giving me the chance to figure this shit storm out, she breaks up with me as if she didn't trust me. I've been nothing but faithful to her regardless of how much mud she's dragged me through over the years. Honestly, I'm tired of the back and forth. I love her. I really do, but little by little she's chipping away at my patience.

I haven't told Viola about our breakup.

I actually haven't told anyone but Travis.

Though I don't want to ask, I'm sure she's not going to accompany me to the wedding, which hurts. It isn't the worst thing in the world to happen, but I imagined this week would play out differently and by the weekend we'd be back to the norm again—well what's normal for us.

The day is halfway over, and it's been uneventful.

Sometimes work is like that, though. But the saying *no news is good news* stands when you're an officer.

Logan and I sit in the patrol car on the corner of Broadway and Freeport listening to dispatch. Once we're hungry, we grab food then drive around the city. After a few traffic stops and an arrest for domestic violence, we head back to the station. My mind has been in a different place all day, and Logan is the type of partner who doesn't pry. He listens and offers advice when asked. He's the older brother I never had.

"I'm thinking of applying to become a detective, too," I tell Logan, and he turns his head and looks at me as I turn off the squad car. He's been on the force for a few years longer than I have, and while I have no intentions of leaving my partner, Logan has voiced wanting to train for a detective promotion. Maybe we'd still be paired together if I pursued it as well.

"The training will kick your ass, Fisher. But if that's what you want to do, I'll support it. You'll be on standby for critical situations. It's a fuckload of long hours—working during holidays and weekends. Investigating scenes that will make your stomach turn. Sure your woman will like all that?"

I give him that look that tells him we aren't together anymore—again.

"Damn. Sorry, man. How many times is this now? Five? Six?"

"You sound like Travis," I groan. "I've lost count."

"You should move on. There are millions of fish in the sea. I was going to make some joke about seaman but lost it. Anyway, there are plenty of women that'd make you a happy man, just have to give them a chance."

"This time is going to be different," I say with a small smile.

"Oh yeah?" Logan lifts an eyebrow at me.

"For once, I'm not going to run after Mia like a little, lost puppy with his dick tucked between his legs."

"Well if you need a partner for drinks, let me know." Logan opens the door, and I follow him inside. I grab my gym bag from my office and drive to *24-Hour Fit* to work out before heading home for the night. I have a lot of pent up frustration inside me, and if I'm serious about applying for a promotion in the future, I'll need to make sure I stay in great shape.

I put my earbuds in, crank my music, and start running on the treadmill, barely breaking a sweat when I get a text from Courtney.

Courtney: I'm baking chicken and asparagus with a side of cookies if you're hungry.

I can't help but smile. I have to eventually stop avoiding her, I guess.

Drew: Perfect. I'll be home soon.

It's hard to not think about her since that dream, but I try and force myself to run harder. By the time I'm finished, an hour has passed, and I'm soaked with sweat, but instead of showering at the gym, I drive home. As soon as I walk in, I smell sugar. The music is cranked loud, and I can hear cabinets opening and closing followed by the oven.

I walk past the kitchen and glance over and see Courtney in a sports bra and yoga pants. *Oh, fucking hell.*

When she turns around, she's eating raw cookie dough from a spoon and smiles. I swallow hard because I've avoided her for a week, and this is the first time I've made an effort.

"I'm making fat-free, sugar-free low calorie chocolate chip cookies." She's basically screaming over the music and then laughs as she finishes off the raw dough. She places the spoon in the sink once she's finished. Her blonde hair is wild on top of her head as she sets the timer then begins dancing around the kitchen.

"You're not supposed to eat raw cookie dough; you know that, right?" I say.

She smirks. "I've been doing it since I was five. I think I'll live."

"I hope you're right."

Her blue eyes search my face, and there's a slightly awkward moment.

"Honestly, the statistics of eating raw cookie dough goes down whenever you use pasteurized eggs. See?" She opens the fridge, shows the liquid eggs, then closes it. "I'm well aware of my chances, and I understand that one out of twenty-thousand eggs will be contaminated. And don't get me started on the statistics of consuming raw flour."

"Are *you* sure you're not the one that's really related to Viola?" I laugh.

"Oh, God. Did I just transform into optimus nerd?"

I nod. "And you tried to make a transformer joke. Cute, Court."

She playfully rolls her eyes at me, and I take that as my cue to take a shower.

I have a feeling it's going to be a long one.

. . .

COURTNEY

My mama always said my mouth could talk itself out of a hostage situation or into a fight, not that it's necessarily a bad thing. There are times when Viola's personality leaks out of me. I like to think it's because we're both too smart for our own good.

I hear the water come on in the shower, and I lean my back against the kitchen counter and take a deep breath before I make our plates. The sound of the oven timer beeping brings me back to reality. It's obvious he's been avoiding me and tonight when we first saw each other, I felt a strange electricity stream between us, but then again, I always feel that when he looks at me. That nervousness I had before I officially moved in is back in full force, and I can't help but laugh thinking about the day we first met.

Viola didn't give me an option and demanded we visit her brother's house so she could grab a few books she had left earlier in the week. We've been friends since freshman orientation, which was only a few months ago. When she pulled out notecards and made a joke about forgetting her pocket protector, I knew we'd be best friends for life.

Viola stormed into the house trying to grab everything before Travis came home since they hated each other. I followed behind her, but as soon as I turned my head, her brother Drew, who I had only heard stories of at that point, walked out of the kitchen wearing his cop uniform. It fit him in all the right places, and I swallowed hard as I nearly ran smack into a support beam in the living room.

"Are you all right?" he asked, concerned. His voice sounded like velvet, and I couldn't believe he was Viola's brother. He practically

stole my voice, and I couldn't find words as I blinked at him, completely stunned by his biceps and the tattoos peeking under his sleeves. He stepped toward me with a small smile on his face, and I hurried and spoke before he got any closer. Men didn't usually make me nervous, but being around him, my palms instantly began to sweat, and my cheeks flushed. And it didn't help one bit that I was imagining him naked.

"Fine," *I finally said.* "Just wasn't looking where I was going."

…because I was too busy looking at you, but I wasn't about to admit that.

He nodded and flashed a big grin at me, showing all his perfectly straight, white teeth. He ran his hands through his dark shaggy hair, and I couldn't help but notice the color of his eyes—hazel. When we made eye contact, a strange bolt of electricity soared through me. No one had ever made my heart drop after a few words and a smile.

How in the hell was this Viola's brother? She had never mentioned he was hot as hell or that he was a cop. She didn't mention he'd be home when we arrived either. I felt like I should've been given some sort of warning or something.

Viola returned with a few books tucked into her arms and Drew gave me another smile then walked away. As soon as he was out of listening distance, I let out a sigh, and she glared at me. "Stop looking at my brother like you want to rip off his clothes!" *she said with a groan.*

I couldn't find the strength to take my eyes off him as he walked down the hall to his bedroom. "I want to do a lot more than that…" *I smile.* "And those handcuffs—"

"All right, I get it," *she said, cutting me off as fast as she could.* "You want to go all Fifty Shades on his ass."

Just thinking about him and all the dirty things I'd do, I laughed. "Hot cop fantasy."

Viola gave me another pointed look, and I shrugged

54

unapologetically. The rest of the day, I couldn't help but think about him. It was strange. We'd only exchanged a few words, but there was some sort of unspoken connection that I couldn't explain.

He clears his throat as he stands in the doorway and I swallow hard as water drips from the tips of his long hair. A small part of me is grateful he's avoided me for a week. It's allowed me time to get my mind straight and accept his choices. It's easier that way. Regardless if he's dating someone who's hateful, I have to respect that. I cannot allow my opinions to change our relationship.

I give him a smile and pile asparagus and chicken on two plates.

"This looks awesome," he says as I hand a plateful of food to him. All I can do is smile.

I pull the cookies out of the oven and place them on the stovetop as they cool, then turn down the music and join him at the table. We eat in silence for awhile before I try to find the words to say to him, but I don't want to push him. I make small talk instead about the wedding and weather. He doesn't look at me, and it's starting to bother me.

"Are you going to stop acting weird around me or what?"

Finally, he makes eye contact and gives me a small smile. "Sorry. There's been a lot on my mind lately."

"I get it. But you're avoiding me. I don't like that."

"I'm not," he says, taking a bite of chicken.

"You're a terrible liar. I know you as well as I know your sister," I remind him.

"Mia and I broke up. That's all it is."

My face falls, and I reach my hand over to his and

squeeze. He tenses at first, but then relaxes and grips my hand in return.

"Oh, I'm so sorry. If you want to talk about it…" My words are sincere, and I mean it with my full heart. I can't help but think that this has something to do with me, which would explain why he's being strange.

"I don't. Thanks, Court."

He's being short, but I understand. Every time they break up he's standoffish. It's a part of the cycle.

I suck in a deep breath, and all I can smell is sugar and chocolate chips.

"You should have a cookie. Even if it's just one."

"I might."

"They will make you feel better," I add.

A smile creeps up on his lips, and that makes me happy to know my best friend is still in there, even though he's hurting. Once we're done eating, I pick up our plates and put them in the sink. Drew follows me into the kitchen with his wet hair slicked back, shirtless, with only basketball shorts on and when I glance over I think I stop breathing. The tattoos that cover his body are so damn sexy that I have to push those thoughts I've worked so hard to bury away. I see he has a napkin in his hand with three cookies piled high. Before he starts chewing, I warn him.

"They're actually really bad for you and full of sugar and butter."

"You little shit," he teases. "I should've known there was no such thing."

He puts them down, breaks a corner off one and moans as he swallows the little bitty piece down.

My eyes widen, and I tuck my lips into my mouth.

He narrows his eyes at me. "What? You have a look on your face."

I try not to burst out laughing and shake my head until I completely lose it. "It's better than sex, huh?"

Drew swallows down what's in his mouth then glares at me and turns his head quickly. Just like clockwork, it gets all awkward again. Before I say something incriminating, I wash the dishes in the sink and decide to go to bed. It's even a believable excuse because I've been yawning like a grandma for the past twenty minutes.

"Bedtime already?" Drew asks as I turn off the dining room light.

"I'm going to eat five cookies in bed with a big glass of milk and watch *Big Brother* reruns," I say walking back into the kitchen.

"You're kidding, right?"

I turn and look back at him.

"You're not kidding." He shakes his head.

"Not one bit," I say between bites as I'm piling them high on my plate. I pour a big glass of milk and walk to my room and turn on the TV. As I'm lying in bed eating, I text Viola to fill her in before it gets too late.

Courtney: Mia and Drew broke up.

Viola: I kind of figured they would before the wedding. I just had a feeling.

Courtney: I feel really bad for him. He seems pretty upset this time.

Viola: Only one way to make him feel better.

Courtney: Best friend & roommate status ruined all that.

Viola: I'm still holding out hope.

I place the empty plate on my nightstand and pull the blanket up to my waist. Silently I hope he's going to be okay this time and he doesn't push the world and me away like usual.

CHAPTER SIX

DREW

TWO DAYS BEFORE THE WEDDING

THIS WEEK HAS FLOWN BY, and soon my sister will be a married woman to my best friend.

I arrive at the rehearsal dinner on time because there is no way I'm going to be the one to set Viola off. She's already in her bridezilla mode, and I got the warning text from Travis super early this morning after my shift. Over the years, I've seen Viola stressed to her max with school projects and finals, and while she goes into hyper speed mode, she gets emotional. It's best just to go with the flow.

Our mother is giving everyone instructions while the orchestra warms up. Travis walks up behind me and pats me on the back. He reaches inside his blazer and hands me a wedding ring box. My eyes go wide.

"Don't lose it. The ring is really in there," Travis says. Mom is busy breaking the wedding party into couples. Andy, Travis's cousin, is standing right behind me cracking jokes with Ashley. I'm really happy Travis asked him to be in the wedding party. He's been a jokester for as long as I can remember. Courtney walks over to me with a big smile on her face, and I must force back all the thoughts that are streaming through my mind.

"At least pretend like you like each other," Mom says and pushes Courtney and me closer to each other. I glance over and smile at Court, and she smiles back.

"Now you'll loop your arms together and walk down the aisle when I say go. It's very simple but needs to be timed just right. Everyone understand?" Mom has taken on the role of wedding planner, which is fine for everyone—even Viola.

I turn and look at Viola who's behind us with our father. I give her a wink, and she smiles back at me. Travis is standing at the front of the church with the minister, waiting with the most genuine, happiest smile I've ever seen him with. To say I'm happy for them is an understatement. I'm fucking ecstatic.

I stand next to Travis and watch as the girls walk down the aisle. Courtney's the last to walk down before Viola and when I make eye contact with Travis, and he gives me a head nod then reverts his eyes back to my sister. I know this isn't the real thing yet, but the way they look at each other is intoxicating. They have that all-encompassing raw love that I'll find one day.

The minister runs through the verbiage, then I hand over the ring, and they kiss. The violins explode into the wedding march and Viola and Travis exit, then Courtney and me, followed by everyone else.

As we make it to the back of the chapel, I can see Courtney's been crying though she's smiling the whole time.

"Need a tissue?" I ask.

"Nah." She sniffles. "But weddings get me every time."

"You're cute," I say, and I swear her grip tightens just a little. Once we're in the foyer and so is everyone else, Viola makes an announcement.

"So, I'll see everyone bright and early Saturday?" She's smiling so big as Travis has his arm tightly wrapped around her.

The group bursts out into laughter when Courtney makes a joke. Travis glances down at her still attached to my arm and gives me a look, and it feels so natural I didn't even notice. I'm feeling too comfortable with her.

Courtney eventually lets go. She walks to Viola, and they exchange big hugs. They're standing there hugging and crying in front of everyone, mascara running down their cheeks. Travis comes to me and gives me a hug, making a joke out of it, and we pretend to cry on each other's shoulders. They both turn around, and Viola flips me off.

"In church? I'm telling the minister," I quip.

She gasps. "I cannot believe I just did that in the house of God."

"Drew deserved it," Courtney adds, smiling at me.

I shake my head at her. "I will tickle the shit out of you."

She gives me a mean face before she and Viola walk off.

Travis stands close to me and watches them walk away.

"So…" Travis lingers.

"Yeah?" I'm confused at his tone.

"You and Courtney finally do the dirty deed?"

I scrunch my nose and step back. "Dude, no. You know it's not like that."

He grins, rubbing the stubble along his jawline as he looks intently at me. "If you say so. Although, you'd be more convincing if you weren't smiling like a fool."

"Don't make me give you a black eye before your wedding, King." He knows I'm giving him shit, but he glares at me anyway.

"Viola would mount your head on the cross of Jesus herself."

"Yeah, she's good at getting her revenge." I laugh, knowing he'll get the reference. Viola and he nearly killed each other before they finally admitted their feelings and hooked up.

"Yeah, she's good at getting what she wants." He looks at me and smiles. "Must be a Fisher thing." He chuckles, amused.

"Well, she's soon to be a King," I say. "She's your responsibility."

"She's soon to be my queen," Travis says, staring at Viola across the room.

"You two are disgusting."

He bursts out laughing. "I know. And I love it. You have no idea how dirty your sister can be."

Gross. "And I don't ever, ever, *ever* want to know."

COURTNEY

ONE DAY BEFORE THE WEDDING

At work, I've become a professional daydreamer. Travis has demanded I get to work so many times over the past week that it's now an inside joke. Even when I'm working, he demands I get to work. I've used the excuse that it's wedding week for three weeks now and so far, it's worked, so I keep riding that wave while I can. But in an hour, the bachelorette party begins, and I've got so much fun stuff planned for the girls. Thankfully, Travis agreed to let me have a paid half-day. If he didn't, Viola would've withheld sex for a week. I totally made that up, but he believed me enough not to test it.

The other girls in the wedding party were Viola's dorm roommates from college. Ashley and Kayla are sweethearts, and over the last few months, we've all become great friends. The bonus is we all like the same things, so planning was easy, except the fact they all requested Drew to be the stripper for the night. I had to remind them it was Viola's *brother* and how weird it would be the night before her wedding to see his hot little ass. While it might scar Viola for life, it'd be something I'd never forget. But it was a big n-o.

Travis rented out a day spa for the afternoon and had a limo waiting to pick up Viola and swing by and get all the girls. It'll be mimosas, manis and pedis, then we're going to a karaoke bar downtown. I've got a cute little sash and tiara for Viola and sashes for the rest of the girls. Mine says Maid of Honor across the front, and the others say Bridesmaid, and we plan to be those stereotypical wedding party girls tonight. We'll be the sexiest, smartest, women in all of Sacramento, and I can't wait to go out and let loose.

Right on time, the limo picks me up at the house, and I make sure to bring the goodie bags and my purse with a change of clothes. I'm so freaking excited I can hardly contain myself. I climb inside and see a disco ball spinning around, reflecting shards of different colored lights throughout the back of the limo. The music is cranked, and the drinks are already flowing.

"The party has already started? Without me?" I ask, and they raise their glasses and give me high-pitched *wooos* in return. My happiness can no longer be contained as I sit next to my bestest friend in the entire world. I give her a big hug, and she hands me a drink.

"Oh stop, Court. If I start crying now, my fake eyelashes will fall off," Viola says.

"I love you so much, and I'm just so excited for you. Totally being an emotional whore." I fan my face. "Weddings always do that to me, but yours will be the most special one I've ever been to."

"Aww, my little sensitive Southerner." She chuckles. "It's not like I'm moving away."

"I would never allow it again. You basically had me confessing my undying love to you the last time you did that." I smile thinking about everything that's happened over the past year. She left for Boston a couple of years ago, and it was the worse six months of my life. And of course, Travis' too.

However, each step has brought us to this exact moment in time, and through the thick and thin, Viola will be marrying the love of her life tomorrow. It makes me realize that one may have to put up with the bullshit to get to the unicorns and rainbows. She hasn't had a perfect story, but it's been a beautiful one, and I'm so honored to be a part of it.

Kayla is laughing at us as she pours more champagne to the brim of my glass. "Thanks, babycakes." I really like her, and I'm so happy we became better friends over the last few months.

"You're welcome, sugar pants!" she replies back, getting me.

The limo pulls up to the Elite Spa, and the driver opens the door. We all climb out, looking like supermodels with our perfect hair, long legs, and tight clothes. As we change into our robes for our massages, the woman brings mimosas for us along with a bouquet of flowers with a card attached to it for Viola.

Viola opens it, and I look over her shoulder and read it.

I love you, my Queen.

She gives me a big smile, closes it, and holds it against her heart then sighs.

"Oh my God. You two," I say with a smile. "Team Traviola for the win."

"You'll be Team Drewtney in no time," she says, the alcohol obviously taking over her mind.

"Don't get your hopes up." I snort.

We're escorted into the massage room where four tables are set up. The only male therapist chooses me, and for some reason, I feel like I've won *The Bachelor* when his strong hands rub the kinks out of my neck.

"You're so tight," he says, and all I want to say is *'that's what he said'* but I decide against it. He digs his thumbs deeper into my muscles, and I'm putty in his strong hands. For once I wish there were happy endings with these things.

After our massages, I thank him stupidly and look around the room. Every single one of us has on our orgasm faces as we walk to the manicure room. I'm giddy, and my body is so relaxed; I feel weird.

"He was so hitting on you," Viola says as we sit down next to each other. Kayla is on the other side of me.

"I wish I would've been lucky enough to get him. Damn girl," she says, and I smile, happy that I was the chosen one.

"I wish I could get his number," I say, *almost* joking as our tubs are filled with hot water.

We're all completely relaxed and are given leg massages, warm wax and towels, along with our pedicures. Every time the woman runs the foot scrubber along my foot, I start giggling, which causes everyone else to start laughing.

"I can't help that I'm ticklish as fu— Well, you know," I stop myself as I hold the arms of the chair tight, trying not to flinch as I laugh. It happens every time.

Viola is sitting in the chair with her eyes closed relaxing. I know that if I even dare do that, I'll be out in five seconds if my feet aren't being touched.

"What color would you like?" the lady doing my feet ask.

"Whore red," I blurt out. Kayla and Ashley burst into a chuckle.

"I want whore red, too," Viola says, and we all get the same color.

Once the pedis are done, we get our manicures and allow them to dry before we head to the backroom to get our clothes.

"Miss," a woman behind the counter says to Viola with a box and a big red bow tied around it. "I was told to give this to you once you all were finished." She opens the box, and it's the tightest, black dress I've ever seen. Her eyes go wide.

"Is he serious?" she asks me.

"I think he is," Kayla says as I hold it against my body.

"Put it on! I wanna see," Ashley says, and we all wait as Viola changes. When she enters, my mouth falls open.

"That ass!" I can't help it. "Hot!"

She smiles. "Yeah?"

Everyone nods and agrees.

"Travis knows what he has and apparently knows your best *assets*," Kayla says.

Viola is so damn happy that it's contagious.

Once we're all dressed and makeup is freshened up, I

look at my phone. It's close to six. Next up is dinner and then we're going to rock the fuck out of some karaoke.

As I'm walking out of the spa, Mr. Hottie Hot Hands Massage Therapist meets me in the foyer and hands me his number. Of course, I take it and give him a wink before I walk out the door. Not looking back, all I can think about is if he knows Kama Sutra. What a perfect distraction that'd be.

CHAPTER SEVEN

DREW

THE NIGHT BEFORE THE WEDDING

I VOTED FOR A STRIP CLUB, but of course, Travis shot it down. Apparently, strange titties weren't on the list the night before one of the biggest days of his life. Instead, he planned a night at his friend's cabin and had the house stocked with premium cigars and whiskey for all of us. I can't complain too much, but I know he was tempted to text Viola the moment he packed his suitcase.

"Do you want me to check in on them?" I ask.

His eyebrows lift, and I already know the answer.

"I just want to cancel it all and meet them at that stupid karaoke bar," Travis says as he cranks the Range Rover. Since we graduated college, he's driven a black Challenger but after the second baby was born he traded it in for a utility vehicle. But I'm happy he did. I couldn't listen to Viola bitch about putting car seats in a two-door car anymore. Since he rented them a limo, we took the Rover to the cabin.

I pull out my phone to text Viola then decide against it

because she'll know I'm checking up on her. Instead, I pull up Courtney's number and send over a text.

Drew: Just expect nightly check-ins. Travis is going crazy without her.

Courtney: Considering what he dressed her in, I imagine he is.

Courtney snaps a picture of the girls and Viola's wearing the tightest black dress I've ever seen her in.

Drew: That explains a lot. Please watch her.

Courtney: Duh. But you might have to come arrest me.

I'm not sure what to say in response until a picture comes in of her flexing.

Courtney: Because I've brought the guns tonight. Also, Viola has already given us a curfew, too. We can't stay out past eleven. *eye roll*

I instantly start laughing, hard.

"She's crazy. Actually, they both are," I say out loud.

Travis speeds down the highway. "But that's why we love them."

That's why he loves Viola, of course. He loves everything about her—the good, the bad, and the nerdy.

"They're eating dinner then going to karaoke. But they are leaving at eleven."

Travis smiles. "That's my girl."

Drew: Be safe. Have fun. Give me updates.

Courtney: You too. Wear protection. Stripper titties can sometimes be gross.

Drew: You must know from experience.

Courtney: A proper southern lady never tells.

Somehow Courtney and I have transported back to how we were before Mia and I got back together, and I had that crazy dream. I'm happy that it feels normal again. I didn't want it to feel strange with her. Pretending it all never happened is the best thing for us both.

Actually, I'm a bit shocked because it's the first time I've thought about Mia all day, which is an odd feeling. She still hasn't texted me, and I haven't made an effort either. Usually, when we break up over something, it's obviously stupid, and I don't push the issue, but this time is different. I always allowed her to get her way. More times than not, I'm tripping over myself to prove I love her, that I'm the man for her, but now, I feel done with it all. When a person steps away from the manipulation they've been smothered in for so long, the real issues become obvious. At least that's been my experience since we've broken up. It feels like I've finally seen the light—again.

Over the years, Viola has complained about Mia's control over me, and by taking a step back, I can see it all too clear. The bottom line is if Mia wants us to be together, she's going to have to prove herself to *me*. That's just how it's going to be this go-around. And if not, I'm man enough to get over it and move on. It'll take time, but if I have to, I will.

We pull up to the cabin, and I can hear the whooshing of the lake water against the shore. Once I'm out of the car, I follow behind Logan and Travis as Andy sucks in fresh air.

"Whiskey and cigars. You know the way to a man's heart, King," Logan says. Over the years, Travis and Logan have become close. They're cut from the same cloth and have been my right and left-hand men when I needed a shoulder to lean on. Without hesitation, I'd die for them both.

Andy, one of Travis' groomsmen, opens the fridge and pulls out the rock glasses and begins filling them with ice. Travis walks over and pours whiskey halfway and hands us each one.

"I'd like to make a toast," I say before everyone takes their first sip.

"To Travis. You've always been a brother to me, and now it'll be official. I couldn't be happier for you, man."

"Hell yeah," Logan says, and we all crash our glasses together and drink.

"Finally, making it official," Andy adds. "Happy for you, Travis."

I can't help but think about Mia. I don't want her to ruin this, not now, not while I'm celebrating with my best friend. Over the years, she's placed the spotlight on herself, and now she's seeping into my thoughts. Tomorrow she won't be my date at the wedding, and we haven't spoken since the big blowout and she texted me letting me know my choices. I refuse to allow her to ruin it or my mood. I'm half tempted to text her, but instead, I lock my phone and place it back in my pocket. I have nothing to say to her anymore.

After another drink, all of us walk outside, down to the

patio area. The fire pit is full of wood and Travis bends over and lights a piece of paper on fire and nestles it into the presoaked wood. Once it's lit, we all bend over and use the flames to light our celebratory cigars. We shoot the shit as the California breeze surrounds us. The sun finally sets, and the crickets greet the stars as the wood crackles in the flames. Along the shoreline of the lake, I can hear the waves pressing against the sand.

Logan turns around with his cigar between his teeth, and a smile overtakes his face. Puffs of smoke leave his lips as he speaks. "So, what's new?"

I know this question, he's not pushy or anything, but when he asks it, he's getting ready to dig deeper into my thoughts. I know I've been quiet tonight, but I have a lot on my mind.

Andy stands and stretches and looks out to the lake. "I'm going to the water. I'll be back."

Travis is unfazed, caught up in his own thoughts, and when I look over at him, he shrugs.

"What's on your mind?" Travis asks, taking a sip of whiskey as the fire cracks loudly.

"Nothing," I say.

Logan laughs. "Bullshit."

"Are you both ganging up on me now?"

They laugh, and I crack a smile. "Anyone need another drink?"

Each of them says yes, even Andy yells out as he gets closer to the water.

I walk up the stairs leading to the house and close the sliding door behind me. It whips open, and Travis is staring at me with a shit-eating grin.

"Mia's jealous of Courtney," he tells me.

72

"Thanks, Captain Obvious," I mumble as I pour whiskey to the top.

Travis chuckles. "And you give no fucks about it."

I turn and look at him. "I don't. I'm not going to choose one of my best friends because of it. It's petty."

He narrows his eyes at me. "Wait. Wait a damn second." He's staring at me. "Holy shit, you have a thing for Courtney."

"Don't start this matchmaker bullshit again, King. It's not like that."

"I'm willing to bet it is." He smiles slyly.

As if she was cued, Courtney sends me a text.

Courtney: Viola is already yawning. It's barely ten. We're probably going to head out of here soon. Well they will. I might stay behind and meet up with someone.

Drew: Ha! Who are you meeting?

Courtney: This hot massage therapist that worked on me at the spa. His hands are strong enough to break bricks.

It takes me a minute to process the thoughts that are speeding through my head. Courtney's made it very clear that she's not looking for a relationship with anyone so what's the point of her doing this? And why do I give a shit about it?

"What's wrong?" Travis asks. "Are they okay?"

I smile, realizing he never stopped watching me. Between

him and Viola, I have no secrets. They both know me way too well.

"Yeah, everything's fine. Apparently, Viola is getting tired and they, well everyone is going to leave except Court. She's going to stay behind."

"Tell her I said absolutely not. If something happens and she isn't there for the wedding, it could be really bad."

"You can't control her," I remind him.

"Oh, yes I can. I want Viola stress free tomorrow," he says, grabbing my phone. He reads the texts above, and a wide smile crosses his face. "And you're clearly jealous."

I shake my head. "Am not."

He types something then hands my phone back to me with a smirk before grabbing the whiskey bottle and heading back outside. "It's taken care of. She'll leave with everyone else."

I look down at my phone and read what he sent her.

Drew: I'll make it worth your while if you leave with Viola.

Not even a second later, my phone vibrates with her response.

Courtney: Deal.

COURTNEY

I don't even know what the hell that text means but I'll take it. Just as I predicted, Viola rounds us up like cattle and tells us she's tired. But in her defense, she's been running around like a mad woman for the past two weeks, while being a mom, fiancée, and best friend. Honestly, she might sleep for a month after the wedding, especially after all the sex they'll be having during the honeymoon.

Travis still hasn't told her where he's taking her, which is totally romantic, but I demanded to know so I could help pack her suitcase. After the wedding, they're flying to London for a week. It's been one of her dream vacations for years but not because it's freaking London, but because of the Harry Potter shit they have there. If I had to hear one more thing about Platform 9 ¾ and a muggle tour, I swore to myself I'd buy a plane ticket and ship her off, but thankfully she's mentioned it to Travis enough he got the hint.

As soon as I found out, I kicked her out of their bedroom and packed her wand, cloak, and Gryffindor scarf in the bottom of her suitcase. I wish I were exaggerating, but I'm so not. I know, without a doubt, as soon as she gets on that plane and realizes where they're heading, she's going to ask Travis about her Hogwarts uniform or whatever the hell it's called. Viola is a nerdy ass, but I love her. And I can't wait to see the pictures.

The limo drops off Ashley and Kayla, and before they get out, we give each other hugs. We're stupid drunk and tired. On the way back to Viola's, she's smiling like a crazy person.

"Tomorrow I'll officially be Mrs. King. Do you think that's weird?"

I can't help but laugh. "Yup. But totally awesome too. Maybe one day, I'll be Mrs. Fisher."

Viola leans over and gives me a big hug. My jokes about her brother don't even faze her anymore. "I hope so."

Though she begs me to stay, I decide to go home to sleep in my own bed, plus it would be easier in the morning to get ready. The limo pulls up to my house, and I pull out a one-hundred-dollar bill and hand it to the driver for being awesome. At first, he refuses to accept it, but I use a little bit of my Southern charm and talk him into it. I like him; he reminds me of my Uncle Jack with his big curly mustache.

As soon as my heels hit the pavement, it's impossible to ignore the big truck sitting in the driveway. I love a man with a truck who's confident and not trying to overcompensate for something. Just give him a baseball cap, tattoos, and a pair of handcuffs, and I'm putty in his hand. My heart pounds hard just thinking about Drew and that damn text he sent. He's made it very clear over the last few years that he's not interested, but a girl can wish.

I swallow hard, pull up my big girl panties and walk inside only to realize I'm home alone. Dammit. I wash my face, change into some pajamas, and fall asleep in no time.

THE DAY OF THE WEDDING

As soon as the front door closes, I'm awake, and my mind is reeling. I can't believe today is the day my best friend is getting married. The coffeemaker is dripping, and I try to push away how much Drew has poisoned my thoughts with that text. He's home, and I'm half tempted to ask him about it, but I don't.

Instead, I take a quick shower and change into some comfortable clothes before grabbing my dress. Viola has us scheduled for hair and makeup at eight thirty, and I'm going to be a great best friend and maid of honor and stop by

Starbucks before I head over. If I bring her favorite coffee, she won't say a word about the way I'm dressed. God, I'm evil.

I grab my dress and shoes and slow down to glance at Drew as I walk past the kitchen. He's making a protein shake, shirtless, and all I can see are his tattoos and muscles cascading down his back. The man is total sex on legs, and he's so blind he can't even see what he does to women, but that's my bestie. Oblivious.

Drew turns around and smiles at me staring, and I own it.

"Hope you're ready for the party of a lifetime," I say, shooting him a wink.

"I'm more than ready, Bishop."

I laugh and head out the door.

On the way to the salon, I stop and pick up a venti white chocolate mocha with an extra shot for Viola and three shots of espresso for me. On the way to the salon, I see a donut shop and decide to stop and order twelve donuts with icing in all different pretty colors. I'm sure I'm not the only one who could use it after yesterday. If Viola smells carbs, she's going to give me the same look that Drew always does.

I arrive ten minutes early because I hate being late, and as I walk in, I can tell Viola's nervous.

"I got coffee because I love you. Do you have any idea how crowded Starbucks is on a Saturday morning?"

I walk across the room and hand it to her with a sly smile.

"You know me too well. But donuts? Ugh. I can't," she says because she's given up carbs for the wedding.

"Oh, all the donuts are for me. I'm not sharing." I shoot

her a wink, and Kayla grabs a pink frosted one with sprinkles.

"She was just complaining about needing coffee," Kayla says.

Viola glares at her.

"It's true," Ashley says.

Viola smiles and takes a sip of her coffee then dramatically sighs.

"Did you just have an orgasm? Because I'm pretty sure you did." I laugh.

"Starbucks does it to me every time," Viola says.

I'm placed in a salon chair across from her. The woman that does my hair has it washed and blown out quick. The girls are already getting their makeup done and soon I'm joining them. I could get used to this type of treatment. Contouring has never looked so easy.

The bridesmaids dress first, and then we all help Viola into her layers of Spanx without messing up her hair. I help touch up her lipstick and mascara just before we head down to the chapel. I can tell she's nervous, but she has nothing to be nervous about.

"You look stunning," I tell her. "Travis is going to have a hard time keeping his hands off you."

"How's that different from any other time?" She laughs, completely serious, though. Their love is intense and has been since the first day.

"Well, hopefully, he can keep it in his pants until you two are back home behind closed doors."

She snorts. "Doubt it."

The bridesmaids pair up with their groomsmen except me. Drew is already standing next to Travis as he waits for his bride. They both look so handsome in their tuxedos and vests. Viola wanted yellow and maroon colors, after her Potter house, but Travis wasn't on board, so they compromised on red and black. The guys have red vests under their black suits with a matching red tie. They're fitted nicely and shows off their muscles, or rather, Drew's muscles because that's the only person I'm staring at.

Viola had all her bridesmaids wear matching red dresses to match the tuxedos except for the maid of honor. I wore the same style dress but in black. At first, I wasn't sure how it'd look all together, but once we all were dressed and standing in line, it looks really elegant.

"Ready?" I turn to Viola just before it's my turn to walk down. The music is soft and slow, but will soon change when Viola starts walking down. "If I trip, just let me fall. Don't even try to save me," I tell her, hoping it helps her smile.

It does, and she laughs, her face visibly relaxing. She nods, adjusting her bouquet for the hundredth time. The wedding coordinator motions for me.

"I love you," I mouth to her.

"I love you, too," she mouths back.

I turn and start making my way down the aisle. The church is filled, and I'm happy so many people have come to celebrate their love. They deserve this more than any other couple I know.

CHAPTER EIGHT

DREW

WATCHING my baby sister walk down the aisle in a wedding gown toward my best friend is the most surreal thing I've ever witnessed. I know she's a grown woman and mother, but I still see her as my annoying kid sister who would fling grass snakes at me.

She's beaming, smiling ear to ear and staring straight into Travis' eyes. I glance at my best friend, standing at the front of the aisle, waiting for her. He smiles right back at her as he wipes a tear from his cheek. I've never seen him so happy.

Everyone is standing and watching as she glides to the altar with our father escorting her. Our mother and Larry wait patiently in the front row with Ginny, the flower girl, and James, the sleeping mini ring bearer. The minister steps forward and asks who will give her away. Dad turns and stares at Viola, her smile not faltering one bit. She tells him she loves him and he says it back.

"I do," Dad finally says, his voice shaking with nerves. He kisses her cheek and releases her hand into Travis', who steps forward and accepts his bride, which is just as corny as it sounds. I've seen enough romance movies in my day to know how this works.

I stand proudly at Travis' side and smile at my sister. She's beyond giddy, her face glowing as she squeezes Travis' hand. The minister says a few words and then gestures to the guests to take their seats.

Glancing around them, I study Courtney and see her beautiful smile. She's even more stunning than I realized before, and I can't help but think of all the thoughts that have surfaced since that one night. She's so full of life and sweetness that I sometimes wonder if she ever imagines what life would be like after we stop being roommates. Not that I plan to move out anytime soon and I know she doesn't, but what's going to happen when that time comes? I went from moving out of my parents' house to college dorms to moving in the house with Travis and then Courtney. I like consistency, and things are good the way they are now, but watching Travis and Viola make their commitments has me thinking long-term more than ever before.

I've wasted the last three years on a woman who runs circles around me and has no real goals for what she wants. For years, I've played her games, and I've allowed her to play me. It's safe to say I don't do well with change.

Travis side-glances over at me with one eye, and I take that as my cue to hand him the ring. I listen as he confesses his love to her, promises to love and take care of her, and teases her when he makes a reference to Harry Potter and love spells. She chuckles, even though her eyes are tearing up. He slides the ring on her finger and places a sweet kiss on her hand.

Courtney is holding Viola's bouquet and staring at the couple. She's been over-the-moon about the wedding since they first got engaged. Their journey was definitely not an easy one, and it's no secret I wasn't exactly on board with it the first time I found out about their relationship; but looking back, I should've seen it coming. They were always at each other's throats growing up. Viola despised him, and he lived for taunting her right back. It was the classic *If he picks on you it means he likes you* scenario, except their hatred was mutual. Once I came to terms with it, I couldn't have been happier that Viola was with him. I knew he was a good guy and would treat her the way she deserved to be treated. I didn't have to worry about some loser treating her like shit. I know she's in good hands now.

I listen as Viola tells Travis how much she loves him. She tells him that even when she hated him, she was crazy about him, that sometimes hate disguises love and that she's loved him all along. There's no doubt in my mind that what she's saying is true.

Once Viola slides the ring on Travis' finger, she smiles wide and we all wait for the final words.

"I'm beyond excited to finally announce you as husband and wife. Ladies and gentlemen, for the first time ever, Mr. and Mrs. Travis King!"

Travis doesn't wait for permission and pulls Viola to his chest and takes her breath away as he dips her. She squeals loudly, earning a round of applause as she wraps her arms around his neck, the guests continuing to cheer them on.

Travis finally lets her up for air as the orchestra begins playing again. My mother places Ginny on her feet, and we all watch as she runs to the middle of the altar and Travis swoops her up into his arms.

He takes Viola's hand and guides her back down the

aisle. Courtney and I meet up in the middle, and she links her arm with mine as we follow them.

I study her face and smile. Leaning into her, I whisper, "I saw you crying."

She turns her head faster than I can back mine away and our faces are inches apart as we continue following the new bride and groom.

"Tears of happiness, Drew. Their love is real. It's so beautiful," she says, passionately.

I flash a small smile and nod. "Yeah. It is, isn't it?"

Cheers and whistles surround us, the noise growing louder as we exit the church for the receiving line and pictures. Lucky for them, it's a gorgeous fall day today. There's a light breeze, it's a comfortable seventy-five degrees, and the sun is shining between the clouds.

It really couldn't have gone any better for them.

COURTNEY

I'm seriously a crying mess.

Weeks and months of planning all finally coming together for two of my favorite people. It's hard to not think about your own future when you witness your best friend finally getting her happily-ever-after. Although they've been together for years and have two kids already, this finalizes it for her. I know Travis will always take good care of her.

Drew looks incredibly handsome in his tux, but his mannerisms are different today. Since the breakup with Mia— *again*—he's been keeping himself over-the-top busy. Between working longer shifts and staying at the gym longer, he's been by Travis' side, helping him prep and party his nights away to becoming a married man. I can tell he's hurting, but he won't talk about it, which I guess I'm mostly happy about since she's the last person I want to talk about, but he needs to get it out. He needs to heal, and once he finally does, he can move on from that heartbreaker and forget about her completely.

...Only in my dreams.

Although he's avoided me most of the week, I get it. I wasn't exactly Team Mia, but I want him to know he can talk to me about those things, even when I wholeheartedly disagree with it.

"You okay?" I lean in and ask Drew as we line up outside the church. Viola and Travis are at the front of the line with Ginny and James and their parents.

He turns to look at me, but with the four-inch heels I was forced to wear, we're almost eye level. "Of course."

"I can't believe they finally did it," I say with a smile.

"Yeah, it's been a long time coming." He looks away, watching the rest of the wedding party take their places behind us.

"Logan looks as comfortable as a whale flying in coach." I chuckle at his stance. Broad shoulders, groomed facial hair, tense facial features. He looks like he's ready to jump someone at a moment's notice.

That finally gets a smile out of Drew, but he doesn't look at me.

"Yeah, he's known for being a hard-ass, but he's really a gummy bear in disguise."

I stare at Logan again. His arms are crossed over his chest, and if his eyes weren't blinking, I'd have to check for a pulse. "Somehow I doubt that."

"He didn't bring a date?" I ask, intrigued. Stance aside, Logan's a good-looking guy.

"I guess not."

"Hm...interesting," I say mostly to myself, but I can tell Drew overhears me. He stays silent, and I'm still left wondering why he's acting so weird.

Half an hour later, the receiving line finally comes to an end. Apparently, everyone in the Fisher-King family is a freaking hugger. It reminds me of home and the Brooks-Bishop family reunions.

I finally get a moment to grab Viola and hug her.

"Oh my God!" She chuckles. "You scared me!"

"Sorry! I've just been bombarded by strangers and needed to hug my best friend before you got away for pictures."

"Lord, tell me about it." She rolls her eyes slightly. "My Great-Aunt Esther decided it was the perfect time to give me the birds and the bees speech for our wedding night and our 'first time' together. Apparently, the birth announcements of our kids got lost in the mail." She inhales a deep breath. "I didn't even know I had a great-aunt."

I laugh at her expense, and she narrows her eyes at me.

"I can't even tell you how happy I am for you all right now." I begin tearing up again, and she pulls me in for another hug.

"I wouldn't be here without you," she says, and I blush. "Seriously."

"You two deserve it." I kiss her cheek just as the photographer begins shouting for the bride and groom. "Go," I say, grabbing James from her arms. "You don't want to be the bride that has baby puke on her wedding gown."

"It wouldn't be the worst thing that he's done to me," she

says with a sly grin. She presses a soft kiss to his cheeks and catches up to Travis.

James is sleeping peacefully, somehow. Although we're outside, the chatter is loud, and cars are zooming out of the parking lot. Most are meeting up at the reception to take advantage of happy hour before the party officially begins. Viola's mom walks over with the diaper bag and offers to release me.

"Are you sure? I don't mind holding him."

"Okay, dear. We'll be called for pictures soon, so just let me know if he begins to fuss." She smiles down at him, and I can tell she's a super proud grandma.

"He's not a fusser," I say in a soft voice, rubbing my finger along his smooth cheeks. "He's just the cutest baby ever."

"I thought you said baby talk annoyed you?" I hear Drew say as he walks up to my side. I might've said that a time or two…

"Only when it's not being said around a baby," I clarify. Mia's nasally voice comes to my mind, and I have to shake my head to rid of it. "It's cute and totally appropriate when there's a wittle baby," I coo at James who isn't the least bit amused. Or awake.

I glance up, and Drew is staring at me with both of his brows raised.

"What?" I ask. "Like you've never spoken that way to Ginny." I roll my eyes at his attempt to pick at me.

Drew is the biggest sucker when it comes to Ginny, whether he wants to admit it or not. Ginny has her Uncle Drew wrapped around her little fingers.

"Not the same," he proclaims and glances down to James.

Kayla walks up with a beaming smile and glowing eyes.

"What's wrong with you?" I ask with a knowing smile.

"We're at a wedding. Am I not supposed to be happy?" she asks, defensively.

"Exactly," Drew interrupts.

"All right, if you two say so, but I know happy, and I know *happy-happy*. Something's up."

"You make no sense," Kayla says, directing her attention toward Logan as he walks across the lot to his car.

Mm Hm. *I knew it.*

CHAPTER NINE

DREW

ONCE PICTURES at the church are finally over, my face feels numb. They wanted the traditional church photos and then outside in the garden photos. Wedding party pictures, couple pictures, family pictures, best man pictures, groom's party photos. I thought it'd never end.

Our parents take Ginny and James as the rest of us all climb onto the party bus. Champagne and beer are passed around as we're driven to the reception hall. Travis and Viola are laughing and smiling, taking selfies, and kissing every five seconds. It still feels surreal, but I couldn't be happier for them. I just wish I wasn't hung up on someone who clearly isn't the one for me.

"Come on, roomie," Courtney grabs my attention and places a beer in my hand. "Weddings are for free alcohol and bad decisions!" She clinks her glass against mine, and I gladly take a drink.

"How many have you had already?" I ask into her ear.

"Hm…" She pinches her lips together, pretending to count. "What's after seven?"

"Courtney!" I scold, knowing damn well she can hold her liquor but she needs to slow it down or at least wait until she's eaten something.

"Relax, Deputy!" She giggles. "I was teasing. It's only my second."

I release a breath and give her a pointed look.

"I'm over twenty-one, officer, I swear!" She puts her hands up in a mock surrender stance and chews on her bottom lip as she fails at holding in her laughter.

"Funny, Court. Very original." I grab the champagne glass out of her hand and before she can reach for it, drink it down. "Problem solved."

"That was rude," she huffs. "Now how will I find Mr. Right?"

"*What*?" Her question takes me off-guard. "Who are you talking about?"

She shakes her head as she grabs another glass full. "No one. I was joking." She sips it down, and I'm left wondering what she meant by that.

There's no way she can know about that dream. I hadn't told anyone, and unless she's suddenly mastered the talent of reading minds, she can't know. *There's no fucking way.*

I pinch the bridge of my nose, willing myself to clear the visions of her from my mind. It would only lead to a huge disaster. I mean, not the act itself, but the aftermath. I should know better than to think of my roommate and one of my best friends like that.

"Come on," Courtney shouts, grabbing my hand and linking her fingers. "First stop!"

She forces me up, and once we walk off the bus, I understand what she means. We're barhopping before heading to the venue, and as much as I try to get into it, I can't stop the thoughts of her from running through my mind.

Once we're inside, everyone rushes to the bar to order, so I escape and find a bathroom instead. I wash my face and hands, hoping the cold water will shock my brain enough to get my shit together.

"Hey, there you are," Travis says as he walks in. "You doing okay?" He hands me a towel.

I wipe my face and hands dry. "Yeah, just overwhelmed a bit, I think. Lots going on."

"Tell me about it. I can barely wrap my head around everything that's going on at once, but I'm glad you were standing up there with me." He flashes a smile, and I can feel the happiness radiating off his cheeks.

"Me too."

"Come on." He nudges his head toward the door. "Time to loosen up, man. It *is* a party, after all."

I walk with him to the bar and order another beer. And then two more before we pack up and get back on the bus. Twenty minutes later, we're being dropped off at the venue. Courtney grabs me and links her arm in mine and rests her head on my shoulder.

"Feeling okay?" I ask.

"Fabulous!" She squeezes me tighter. "We have to walk in together," she says, wiggling her arm. "So, you have to escort me one last time, Deputy."

I narrow my brows at her because I have no idea what she's talking about.

"It's tradition," she begins to explain. "The DJ announces the wedding party and then the bride and groom as we walk to the head table."

Oh. Right.

"What's your drink count now?" I ask, knowing damn well she didn't stop at two.

"Oh, I'm totally fine. I ate some saltine crackers I had in my purse. It has to hold me over at least until I give the maid of honor speech."

I laugh. "I'll be sure to record that."

She playfully smacks me. "Don't be a douche. You have to say one, too."

"I know, but I can hold my alcohol, *unlike* someone."

"I have no problem holding my alcohol," she says with amusement, raising the glass in her other hand. "See?"

I swipe it from her and sniff it. "Clearly," I deadpan. "C'mon, let's go." I escort her, and when we walk inside, she slides her arm out and grabs ahold of my hand, linking her fingers through mine. It's no big deal, and I know it's all for show right now, but it does something unexpected to me. She's held my hand dozens of times, never meaning anything, but this feels different, and I'm not sure why.

Once we're seated and the food is served, I'm ready to give my speech. Travis is so much more than a friend, and although I know he knows that, it makes me emotional just to think about how far we've come and how much we've been through together.

I stand up and grab the microphone that was left on the table. Clearing my throat and grabbing everyone's attention, I begin.

"There isn't a time in my life I can remember when you weren't in it. From our awkward teen years to our college years sharing a house together to you falling in love with my sister, you've always been there for me." I stand there looking down at Travis and Viola, who are both looking up at me from their seats. Their fingers are tightly weaved together, and wide and gleeful smiles fill their faces. Seeing them so happy together causes me to feel an overwhelming amount of joy for the two of them. I love that my childhood was filled with memories of us.

I continue my speech and end with a joke because he did marry my sister, after all.

"May your invisibility cloak save you when you need it the most." I chuckle, knowing they'll get the reference.

"Good speech," Courtney whispers over my shoulder from behind me. I hadn't seen her coming, but I'd been in my own little world so I could've missed the President with how much my mind is racing.

"Thanks," I say as I turn around and face her. "Yours wasn't too bad, either." I chuckle, amused by her too-honest speech.

"Hey," she says defensively, "I had people crying they were laughing so hard." She smiles proudly and so do I. It's true. Courtney blew it out of water. "I thought your grandma was going to have a heart attack; she was snorting so loud."

"She was choking on her water because the last time she heard the word *fanny* — "

"What?" she interrupts me. "Fanny is a very suitable term to describe your sister's ass. I was only trying to keep it PG."

I shake my head at her and laugh. Courtney's always been good at putting a smile on my face. "If we were in England, fanny would mean something much different."

"Do you think your grandma is British?" Her eyes widen in fear.

I bust out laughing at how genuine her voice sounds. "I think you're safe."

Her head falls back as she groans and images of her in

my dream immediately surface in my mind. I blink, hoping it pushes them away, but it does nothing to erase them. I need a distraction.

"Logan looks like he needs a wingman. I'm going to grab a drink and rescue him from the middle-aged woman who hasn't left his side since dinner." I smirk, knowing damn well he's capable of getting away, but I can't breathe with Courtney right next to me, not with the way my head is persistent on reminding me of what I can't have.

"What's Logan's deal?" she asks, following close behind me.

"What do you mean?"

"He just stands there like he has a stick up his ass."

Her blunt words make me stop and turn. Looking at her, I can tell her guard is down.

"He's just a little—"

"Wound up tighter than a virgin on prom night?" She giggles, sipping from her drink that is probably all tequila, and my plan to escape her goes out the door.

"Jesus Christ, Court," I groan, brushing a frustrated hand through my hair.

"Oh, come on!" She yanks on my arm. "It's a wedding, for God's sake. Loosen that tie and dance with me!" she pleads, her eyes staring into mine, making it impossible to deny her. I know how she gets when she's been drinking, but this time feels different. I never pictured her naked or imagined the sound she'd make when she came or wondered what her breasts under my hand would feel like until now.

Shaking the images from my mind, I grab her hand and lead her to a nearby table. "I think maybe you need to set the drink down and—"

"Oh my God!" she screams, stopping everything I was

just about to say. "I fucking love this song!" My heart nearly jumps out of my chest at the urgency of her tone, and I'm pissed when I find out it was due to a damn song.

"Court—"

"Come on, Deputy! Dance with me!" She grabs my hand before I can pull away and something inside me follows her anyway. I'd rather be the one she's clinging onto than some random guy just looking for a one-night stand.

I make sure to keep as close to her as I can. Viola and Travis are nearby, but they're in their own little world with each other. Several of Travis' and my friends from college showed up for the reception and are on their way to getting just as wasted as Courtney is right now. They're only looking for a quickie, and although I know them, I don't trust them around Courtney one bit.

"I warned you she was a handful," Viola shouts over the music as she dances in front of me.

"Oh, I know."

"She's just having fun, you know?" She smiles, but I can tell she's exhausted. It's been a long day for all of us.

"I can see that; however, every guy in here is looking at her like she's a piece of meat." My jaw clenches, and I'm sure Viola takes notice.

"Chill, Drew," she says casually. "Courtney can take care of herself." Viola's pulled away by another bridesmaid before I can respond. I take another look and see Courtney surrounded by other chicks, so I walk back to the bar where Logan is sitting.

"Quite the party," he mutters, taking a sip of his whiskey.

"So I've been told," I say, grabbing the bartender's attention. "Brings you back, huh?"

His lips pull back into a sly grin. "College was an

experience, that's for sure."

I order my drink and turn around to face the dance floor. "I think that one chick is into you," I say, making conversation. "The petite brunette." I nod my head toward one of the bridesmaids.

"No time to date."

"I wasn't suggesting you propose. But one dance? Or a drink?"

He shrugs his shoulders, uninterested, so I drop it.

"What about that roommate of yours?" he asks, staring a little too intently at her.

"What about her?" My jaw ticks again and I take another swig of my drink.

"She hasn't taken her eyes off you all night."

I chuckle into my drink. "Courtney's my best friend."

"That's it?" His brows raise, and I know he's testing me. *Bastard*.

"Yeah."

"So, you'd be okay if I asked her to dance?" His lips tilt up, and I know what the fucker is doing.

I shrug as if it doesn't bother me one bit. "Go for it."

He swallows down the rest of his drink and sets it down on the bar. "Good." He pushes off his stool and begins walking toward her.

Before I can think twice, I follow right behind him and grab his shoulder, stopping him immediately. "Get the fuck out of here."

He chuckles with a knowing grin and lets me walk ahead of him.

"That's what I thought, Fisher," he calls out.

"Fuck off, Knight." I grin, although he can't see me, but dammit, he got me this time.

CHAPTER TEN

COURTNEY

"DANCE WITH ME," I hear from behind. I recognize the voice, but it sounds deeper than usual. Once I spin around, I smile as I see Drew's perfect face.

"Finally in the dancing mood?" I ask, letting him take my hand. My body presses against him, but since I took my heels off about seven songs ago, we're no longer at eye level.

"I guess you could say that."

He's looking down at me as if he's waiting for something. As if right on cue, the song changes to *Fallin' for You* by Colbie Caillat—which is quite fitting, considering—and everyone around us starts slow dancing. Figuring Drew won't want to slow dance, I take a step back, but he pulls me right back into him.

"Where do you think you're going?" he asks.

I tilt my head and see his lips spread into a sweet grin.

"You owe me a dance."

"Says who?" I tease.

"Are you resisting, Ms. Bishop?" He arches a brow as if in warning.

YES! YES, I AM, OFFICER, I scream to myself, but my mouth goes dry even without saying a word.

"You couldn't handle me if I did," I say without thinking. He mutters something under his breath, but I don't quite catch it.

He wraps his arm around my waist and places his hand in mine. He pushes our bodies close as we begin to move to the music. "You're drunk." He narrows his eyes at me, and I'm pretty sure he's not happy about it.

"Is that why they pay you the big bucks?" I quip. "So observant."

"Good lord, Court." He shakes his head at me, and I can tell I'm getting under his skin.

"You miss her," I say, realizing that he must be hurting even if I hate her guts. He was supposed to be here with her and now being here must be making him think about it even more. "I'm sorry. I should've realized."

"It's not your fault," he reassures me. "I don't know if I miss *her* or just the idea of her."

I furrow my brows, not understanding. "What's the difference?" I ask, our bodies still flowing in motion to the very song that I could've written myself.

"I don't really know. We've been together for so long that I've just gotten used to being with someone and having someone to care about. I've forgotten what it feels like to not have that." He blinks and looks down at me. "Does that sound crazy?"

I shake my head because it really doesn't. "No, we all get stuck in our routines, even if they aren't good for us. I remember feeling that way with Toby. I was so used to us being together that anytime we weren't, I was fighting for us to be even when it no longer made sense. That didn't stop the pain, though. Once I figured out how to live life without him, I no longer needed that relationship validation. I learned that being alone was okay. It's hard, though. We're affectionate creatures by habit."

"Yeah, but you didn't go sleep around after you and Toby broke up." *Unlike Mia.*

"No, instead I cried myself to sleep every night as I listened to One Direction and Taylor Swift." I wrinkle my nose. "And baked."

"So, if I listen to pop songs and eat sugar, I'll feel better?" he playfully asks.

I shrug with a smile. "It hasn't let me down yet."

"Good to know." He wraps an arm around me and pulls me tighter to his chest. "Thanks for being my best friend, Court."

Another piece of my heart shatters at his words. *If only he could see what's right in front of him...*

I sing the lyrics that talk about falling in love in my head and wonder what it would feel like to just have him for one night, for him to see me the way I see him.

The song fades away, and I expect him to release me, but he doesn't. His grip tightens, and I inhale his earthy scent.

"Want another drink?" His words break the tension, and reluctantly, we break apart.

"Sure," I say. Watching as he heads to the bar, Logan leans against the bar top waiting for Drew with a smile. Looks like the guy does know how to loosen up, after all.

"Isn't he dreamy?" I hear Kayla next to me sigh as she stares at Logan. "Too bad he's barely looked at me."

"I know the feeling," I mutter, mostly to myself.

An hour passes along with several drinks before we prepare to send off the happy couple. The crowd hasn't died down; they're rowdier than before, but it's late, and my bed is calling me.

Before they leave, Viola finds me and wraps her arms tightly around me. "I love you, Courty. I wuv you so much! Thanks for being the bestest maid of honor *ever*!" She presses sloppy kisses on my cheek as she slurs her words.

Chuckling at her being a lightweight, I squeeze her back. "I love you more, Lola." I smile as I pull back and look into her eyes. "Use protection," I warn in a stern voice. "You're the most fertile person on Earth I know."

She snorts and nods in agreement. "Don't worry, *Mom*. I've tied, twisted, and taken every action possible to make sure no more babies."

Travis comes and pulls her away just as Drew wraps his arm over my shoulders.

"One more dance?" he whispers, the closeness of his lips sends shivers down my body. I know he thinks it's harmless, but every time my body reacts to his, another part of me wants to die.

"The DJ is packing up all his equipment, Drew. There's no more music," I tell him, realizing he's drunker than I thought. "We should call for a cab."

"Courty, don't be a Debbie Downer," he teases, leaning up against me.

I shake my head and chuckle. "C'mon, Deputy. Time to go."

"Court! Drew!" I hear Kayla shout as she runs to catch up to us.

"Hey!" I shout a bit louder than necessary as I lean into Drew's side. "Want to share a cab with us?"

"No, Logan offered to *drive* me home," she exaggerates, her eyes as wide as her cheeky grin.

"Well, then." I smile right back. "You two *drive* home safely." I flash her a wink, and she winks right back.

"Will do. I'll give you a call tomorrow." She gives me a hug and skips off.

"Well, I gotta give your friend credit," Drew says, pulling me back to reality, his body still against mine.

"For what?"

"She's been tracking him all day long."

"Yeah, I know. Looks like she's pretty persuasive." I shake my head in agreement, anticipating hearing all about it tomorrow.

Drew grabs us a cab just as the rest of the guests follow out. The air has a chill to it and Drew wraps his suit coat over my shoulders. "Thanks," I say, pulling it tighter, enjoying the way it feels against my bare skin.

We hop in the cab, and he lets me rest my head on his arm. It feels natural—like home—when he wraps his arm around me, and I lean against his chest.

"I'm so hungry," I mutter, my eyes falling closed.

"Any chance you have any of your baked goods lying around?" he asks, making me smile. I knew he secretly wanted my muffins.

"I always keep a stash in the freezer for emergencies."

"I knew I liked you," he teases, and I smile.

We finally arrive back to the house and immediately start binging on my homemade blueberry muffins.

"These are so damn good," he says between chewing. "You really know what you're doing." He leans against the kitchen counter and moans as he takes another bite.

I laugh, knowing it's the alcohol talking. Drew wouldn't eat them under normal circumstances. Between his morning protein shakes and lifting weights, the sugar in a blueberry muffin would put his body into shock.

"Well, I'm an emotional baker. When Toby and I broke up, I obviously didn't handle it well. Viola was there for me as much as she could be, but when she wasn't, I needed to keep my mind busy. I started baking, anything and everything, to get over the pain. One thing led to another and I had fourteen dozen muffins and cookies piled in my apartment."

I laugh just thinking about it. Not about losing Toby, but about how irrational I was at the time.

"Sounds like you made a good stockpile for yourself."

"I handed out baked goods for weeks to anyone who would accept them. After a while, I'd gotten pretty good at hoarding them."

"Well, bonus for me then." He smirks as he takes his last bite.

I put the rest back in the freezer and grab the milk. "Want a glass?" I hold the gallon up for him to see. "They taste better with milk," I try to convince him because we've both been binging on beer and tequila shots the last six hours.

"No, but you know what I *do* want?" he asks, his voice low and unpredictable.

"What's that, Deputy?" I tease, knowing he hates it when I call him that, but the alcohol rushing through his veins is too strong to take notice.

"One last dance." He flashes me one of his infamous looks that always helps him get his way. He leans forward and stretches his hand out to me. How could I ever say no to him?

"It's like two in the morning, Drew. Plus, there's no

music," I try to make excuses, but he ignores me and grabs my hand anyway.

"Don't make me stuff a muffin in your mouth." He presses a finger to my lips and pulls me into his chest. "I'll hum you a song if you need music."

I chuckle, shaking my head at him as my heart flutters. If he wants to torture me and let me inhale his scent while slowly killing me, who am I to resist?

"One song."

He grins and accepts my counteroffer.

Placing one hand on the small of my back, he pulls me against his chest and my entire body buzzes. His other hand cups mine, and soon his body begins rocking back and forth.

My body moves with his, and it feels like a dream come true. Even with his humming off key, everything about this moment is perfect.

"Dance skills aren't so bad," I say. He pushes us apart, grins, and spins me around.

"I've learned a few things along the way. This isn't my first rodeo."

"Oh, really? Are we about to two-step or do the polka?" I arch a brow.

"Let's not get crazy." The corners of his lips tilt up slightly. "I know you probably learned to hoedown before you could walk, but the rest of us non-Southerners shouldn't attempt it while boozed up."

I wrinkle my nose and laugh. "Good point. Plus, it's not really a rodeo without some good ole fashion cowboy hats and boots."

He spins me again, except I trip and nearly tumble into the wall. He catches me on time, and we both laugh.

"Good thing no one can see what an awful dancer you are." He flashes his pearly whites at me.

"Maybe if my dance partner knew what he was doing," I tease right back as he repositions us and soon my back is pressed against the wall. Our eyes lock, and all I can hear is the panting of our deep breaths. The energy between us changes, and I wait for him to back away once he realizes it.

Except he doesn't.

Just when I think he's about to step away and leave me brokenhearted, he takes me completely off guard and leans forward, pressing his lips to mine. His hands cup my cheeks, his tongue glides over mine, and soon I'm lost in him. His movements are fierce and passionate, desperate and greedy. *I want it all.*

My hands are tangled in his hair as he continues, my body on fire, but preparing for ice because it feels too good to be true.

Drew is kissing me.

Drew Fisher.

Part of me wants to overanalyze what the hell is happening while the other part—the mostly still drunk part —tells me to shut up and go with it. His lips and hands on me feel amazing, and I never want him to stop.

He releases a throaty moan and slides his tongue in deeper. Fuck, he's a goddamn good kisser. His arms wrap around my waist tighter, and as I rise on my tiptoes to feel more of him pressed against me, he pushes our bodies harder against the wall.

Groaning, his lips move from my mouth down to my jawline and neck where he sucks on my collarbone. I release a satisfied moan of my own, which encourages him even more. His body against mine, I can feel how hard he is and my body responds almost immediately.

I had no idea it could feel this good with him, but it does. It feels like forever was meant to happen with him and after fighting the urge, he finally came to his senses, and I don't ever want to break away.

As if reading my thoughts, he grabs underneath my ass and picks me up. My legs wrap around him as he spins around and places me on top of the kitchen counter. Thoughts run through me, and before I can comprehend any of it, his lips are back on me and they're everywhere. I hadn't even taken my bridesmaid dress off yet, but that doesn't seem to be an issue for him. His tie is already loosened, and the top of his collar is unbuttoned. He fights with my zipper until it releases and slides down my back. I tighten my legs around him, wanting to feel him against me again.

"Court..." He says on a moan, and I nearly die at the way he says my name, although he's called me that thousands of times, it's the first he's ever said it like *that*. "I should stop..." he whispers, and I'm ready to beg him not to when he continues, "...but I *can't*."

DREW

I don't know what's come over me, but I can't stop. All those times denying those thoughts that would sometimes flood my mind have all finally come to a halt.

Courtney.

Smart. Beautiful. Funny. *Tastes incredible*.

I know I'm not thinking clearly, but I don't want to. I

unzip her dress and pull it down her body, letting it sit at her waist. Just as eagerly, she undoes the buttons of my shirt. My tie flies off, and before she can finish unbuttoning, I say screw it and pull it over my head.

"Careful, it's a rental," she teases as I press my mouth back down on hers.

I smile against her lips. "The damage fee would be worth it."

"I'm sure it wouldn't be the first time." She chuckles, wrapping her legs back around my waist. I brush my fingers through her blonde hair and pull it until her head falls back, pushing my tongue deeper inside, loving the way she's just as eager as I am.

I brush my lips across her jawline and look down at her. "I'm sure it won't be; however, I'm more worried about this contraption piece." It holds up her breasts nicely and goes all the way down to her hips. Whatever the fuck it is, it needs to come off. "Do I need a special code to break through this thing or what?" I attempt at removing it, but it's so tight, I have no idea how she can even breathe with it on.

She licks her bottom lip and grins. "It's a strapless corset bra."

I furrow my brows because she lost me at corset. "Are you attached to it?" She gives me a look. "Not physically. But if it gets torn," I try to explain, but she pushes our lips back together before I can finish.

She nods, giving me all the permission I need.

"Good, I wasn't feeling very nice anyway." I wrap both arms around her, fist the bottom of the material in both hands and pull as fast as I can. It finally rips apart, and as it falls off her body, her breasts are completely exposed. I inhale sharply, unable to control myself any longer. *She's fucking beautiful.*

"A good cop gone bad?" she asks, my palm wrapping around her and squeezing her taut nipple. My tongue traces along her bottom lip, and I'm dying to taste her breasts next.

"Bad cop?" I ask, amused by her tone. "You want to role-play, huh?"

She moans, her head falling back as I make my way down her chest. She leans back on the counter, giving me exactly what I want. Her body is pure perfection, and I can't stop touching every part of her.

"Handcuff me and find out, *Deputy.*" Her breathy tone comes out as a plea, and I know she's begging for it.

"What did I say about calling me that?"

"The consequences are worth it," she says matter-of-factly.

"If I get my handcuffs out, it's to benefit me, sweetheart. You don't get to be the boss this time," I warn, knowing she'll want to argue.

"We'll see about that." Her head falls back, and I inhale deeply.

"You smell like blueberries and buttercream," I say, pulling the bottom of her ear in between my teeth.

She chuckles and leans back even farther. "Is that your version of dirty talk, Officer Fisher?"

I smile in response. "You always smell like something I want to eat."

Laughing, she reaches for my slacks and begins unbuttoning them. "Duly noted."

The alcohol rushes through my veins and the throbbing in my pants is more evident than ever before, especially with her body so close to mine. Once she successfully undoes my top button, I pull her off the counter and watch as the rest of her dress finally falls to the ground. I remove the piece of lace she calls her underwear and slide it down her legs. She keeps both eyes on me, intently staring as I unzip my slacks and push them down.

My heart is pounding against my chest, and I wonder if she's thinking the same thing I am. Her hands and mouth are back on me before I can even think twice about it. I begin leading us out of the kitchen and down the hallway to my room. We stumble along the way, but eventually make it to the bed.

Collapsing on top of the mattress with her underneath me, it takes me a moment to really wrap my brain around the fact that Courtney, my best friend and roommate, is naked and in my bed. I feel like an adolescent again—nervous and overwhelmed. She's absolutely beautiful as her hair sprawls over my pillows and her body shivers on contact. My tongue traces down her neck and as she releases another moan; I don't know how much longer I can wait to feel inside her. She's awakening something inside me I hadn't realized was missing.

Screw the *what ifs* and overthinking my feelings for her. I want her.

"So, handcuffs, huh?" I ask, grinning as I twirl my tongue around her nipple and feeling her shiver against me. "Is that what you'd like?"

"Unless you'd be willing to give me a plea deal?" she teases in a seductive tone, and I swear to God her voice will be my ruin.

I kiss back up her neck and part her legs with my knee. "You give me what I want, and I'll see what I can do for you,

Ms. Bishop," I tell her in a deep tone. "However, things don't look so good for you."

"No?" She willingly parts her legs for me and arches her hips up to greet mine. "Perhaps we can work something else out then…"

"I think you might be onto something…" I smile, bringing our mouths together and giving into desires I hadn't even realized were there.

Her hands explore my chest and back, moving everywhere and touching anywhere. The way she acts as if she can't touch enough of me drives me insane. I'm tempted to grab my spare cuffs in my desk drawer and do exactly as she asks, but I can barely find the willpower to break away from her.

I lean back just enough to pull my boxer shorts down. We scramble together to move the covers out of the way, and before I can process anything, she climbs on top of me and holds both of my hands above my head.

"Well, Deputy, looks like you're not as quick as you think." Her smile is wide as she gloats. I love the way she thinks she's won the game.

I break away from her grip and grab ahold of her hips. "I'm not so sure, sweetheart. You might've made the rules, but you aren't going to win this one."

She bites her lower lip and smiles above me. "I was hoping we'd both win."

And with that, I flip her over, part her legs, and finally give in to what we've both been seeking. I slide inside her, and my world tilts on its axis. The moment I hear her first moan, I nearly lose myself. The joking, the playfulness, the teasing; it all vanishes the moment we connect, and there's nothing funny about it. *It's perfect.*

CHAPTER ELEVEN

COURTNEY

**PRESENT DAY
THE MORNING AFTER THE WEDDING**

I PEEL my eyes open and see the sun glaring through the window. I hate that damn sun. And fuck that window, too. Jesus, I feel like I ran a 10k marathon last night. My feet are most likely swollen from wearing those damn shoes Viola made the bridesmaids wear, and I can feel the pins jabbing into my skull from having my hair done. Being Viola's maid of honor was a blast, but between the over-drinking and the too-tight shoes, I'll be paying for it for at least a week.

It takes me a minute to clear my eyes and realize I'm not even in my own room. I'm in Drew's room, which could only mean one thing.

Last night wasn't a dream.

Once I sneak out, I head to the bathroom and look at myself.

Oh, God.

I drop the sheet and hop into the shower. The warm

water beads hard against my back as I try to come to terms with how I woke up this morning. Naked. In Drew's bed. *With Drew.*

Memories flash through my mind, and as much as I enjoyed, like *really* enjoyed, last night, I can't help wondering how this changes everything. You can't just sleep with your best friend and have everything stay the same. Especially when you *live* with them. There's no escaping it. I'll have to face him and then what? Will it be weird? Awkward? Will he break my heart the same way Toby did?

Could I even bare it if he did?

I can't stop the questions from flooding my brain, but I can make a plan. Yes, that's exactly what I need. A plan.

I just need to figure out what that should be.

As soon as I'm out of the shower and wrapped in a towel, I grab my phone. I can't text Viola because she's on an airplane headed to London, but even if I did, what would I say? *So, hey, I slept with your brother last night. The one I've been crushing on for the past three years and now I'm freaking out. Any advice?*

I send her a text anyway, knowing she won't receive it until she's connected to Wi-Fi.

I groan to myself and smack myself in the forehead. *How the hell did this happen?*

That's a rhetorical question, by the way, because I know exactly what happened.

Alcohol and zero inhibitions.

I stare at my reflection in the mirror, beating myself up, when I remember the other half of the equation. It wasn't just me, obviously, but Drew. He wasn't a one-night stand kind of guy. Hell, he was barely a 'moving on from Mia' kind of guy. *Oh my God.* I start panicking as I put it together.

Was I his rebound? Sleep with someone else to get over the girl you really love?

Just the thought makes me nauseous. Drew wasn't that kind of guy, but who's to say this wasn't the start of a new habit for him?

I feel sick.

The self-doubt and uncertainty are eating me alive, and I don't know how I'm supposed to go out there and face him.

Finally, I decide to text Kayla. Desperately, I hope she's awake and can give me some sound advice before I stay in the bathroom forever and hide.

Courtney: I did something crazy last night. I'm freaking out a little.

Kayla: Well, that makes one of us. Logan was a bust.

I try to keep calm, but my fingers fly across my phone faster than my thoughts, and I can barely keep up with them.

Courtney: After Drew and I cabbed home, we ended up in his bed and now I'm hiding in the bathroom freaking out because OMG what the hell did I do?!

Kayla: Wait… WHAT!

Courtney: I KNOW! Help me! I've NEVER done this before, Kay! I don't even think I can look at him.

Kayla: Why are you freaking out? You've been after Drew forever. Isn't this a good thing?

One would think…but I'm not so sure.

Courtney: We both had too much to drink! What if he tells me it was a mistake and he regrets it and I'm left looking like a moron and feeling even worse than before. I don't know that I could handle it if he tells me 'we need to talk'. I WILL DIE.

Kayla: Well maybe it took some liquid courage for him to finally come to terms that he has feelings for you and doesn't regret it at all.

Courtney: Because that would mean fate is on my side and that bitch is NEVER ON MY FUCKING SIDE.

Kayla: Ok, calm down!!! Just breathe. Let's talk this out…

Before I can respond, a loud knock at the bathroom door makes me nearly piss myself. "Court? Are you almost done?"

His voice doesn't give anything anyway. I don't know what to do or say, so I just swallow and nod.

Then I remember he can't see me.

"Sure, just a minute!" I shout back, trying to take deep breaths.

Courtney: OMG he just knocked on the door. He knows I'm in here.

**Kayla: Well, who else would be in there, Court?
You live together.**

I roll my eyes at her obvious statement. Fuck. What am I going to do?

Courtney: I'll text you later. If you don't hear from me, I probably died from embarrassment. Promise me you won't let anyone look in the top drawer of my nightstand when they come to clean my room out.

Kayla: You'll be fine!!

I shake my head because I'm not so sure I will be.

I open the door, and when I see Drew standing against the wall with his arms crossed, I have a mini heart attack. He's been waiting for me.

"Finally," he says, pushing off the wall and walking toward me. "I was about to piss in the kitchen sink."

"Sorry," I mutter, getting out of his way so he can walk into the bathroom. He shuts it without saying another word, and I'm left wondering *what the hell?*

Walking to my bedroom, I tighten my grip on my towel and start to overanalyze everything that happened last night. If I hadn't woken up in his bed, I would've sworn it was a dream. *A very detailed, sexy, hot type of dream...*

But I did wake up in his bed—naked and hungover. I know we both probably drank too much, but it's not like it was the first time. We've hung out plenty of times, watched movies together on the couch, cooked and ate together, went out to the bars and came home together—but *never ever* has that lead to ending up in the same bed together.

After getting dressed and combing through my hair, I decide I'm just going to walk out there and wait for him to bring it up. If I act all weird, he'll sense it and then everything will be awkward.

As I walk down the hallway, slower than normal, I hear him banging pots and pans around in the kitchen. It echoes in my head, and that's when I realize I'm still feeling the effects of last night's tequila shots. I'm not sure how he's standing after all he drank, let alone, in the kitchen cooking. I round the corner and see him standing by the oven, shirtless—go figure—and cracking eggs into a pan on the stovetop. My eyes widen as I study his back and notice the claw marks across his broad shoulders. It all started in this kitchen...

Oh my God.

Looking down at my nails, I realize they're scratched down. Taking even a better look at my wrists, I notice the red marks the handcuffs left behind. Swallowing, I pull my long sleeves down and cover them up. If I hadn't come out for a drink this morning before hopping in the shower, our clothes would still be all over the floor in here.

"Making breakfast?" I ask, trying to think of the last time Drew made eggs. He's normally a fruit and protein shake kind of breakfast guy.

"Yeah, I figured after last night, we could use some real food in our systems." He looks over his shoulder and flashes me a smile. I'm confused as hell by his demeanor. Mostly because he's acting as if nothing happened at all.

"After last night?" I inquire, wondering if he'll actually be the first one to say it. I lean against the other wall, making sure to keep just enough distance between us.

"Yeah, after all those drinks and shots, I think our stomachs could use some real food." He turns the heat down on the stove and covers the pan. "Especially since I can't remember most of it."

I gulp.

"What?" I ask, not meaning to say the word aloud, but it just came out.

He turns and faces me, leaning up against the counter. "I mean, I remember the wedding of course, but once the binge drinking started, things get a little fuzzy."

"Oh, right. Yeah, me too," I spit out, but it doesn't sound convincing at all. I shuffle to the fridge and open the door.

"We took a cab home, right?" I hear him ask.

"Uh, yeah. We did." I grab the jug of orange juice and shut the door.

"Let me know if I owe you half for it." He shuffles around some more. "I mean, unless I'm the one that paid for it." He chuckles, and I want to sink to the floor and become invisible.

How doesn't he remember?

I grab a cup from the cupboard and pour myself a glass, trying to remain calm and act normal. "You did," I say. "I owe you half actually."

I take a drink and nearly spew it out when he stands right next to me and pats me on the shoulder. "I'll add it to your tab."

I manage to swallow it down and flash him a smile. "Sounds good."

He grabs two plates from the cupboard and sets them

down next to the stove. He splits the eggs evenly on each plate, and I don't have the courage to tell him I'm not hungry, but I also can't sit across from him and pretend I'm fine.

Because I'm not.

Absolutely, positively am not fine that Drew Fisher has no memory of sleeping with me last night.

DREW

Once I finish eating and clean up the kitchen, I head to the shower. Last night was rough, but I've had worse. College life with Travis gave me many unwanted experiences, and I don't party like that anymore. My baby sister's wedding was just an exception.

My shift starts at three and goes for twelve hours. Four days on this week and then three days off. It's not the best schedule, but I've become accustomed to it. Those twelve hours usually go by pretty fast, and by the last day I'm ready to sleep for a week, but guys like Logan help the time pass.

Dressed and ready to head out, I knock on Courtney's door before leaving. She's used to my long shifts, but I still like to let her know before I go.

"Come in," she shouts, and when I push the door open, she's sitting on her bed with her laptop. I can tell she drank a lot last night too by how flushed her face looks. She threw her hair in a messy bun on top of her head, and she's in her casual comfy clothes. There are three bottles of water on her nightstand and I can definitely tell she's nursing a hangover.

"Just letting you know I'm off to work. I won't get in till after three in the morning, so if you hear noises, it's only me."

I grin, remembering the time she nearly stabbed me with a pencil when I walked down the hallway, and she heard footsteps that 'sounded like a murderer's.

"Okay, well have a good shift," she says with a small smile. She's not as giddy as usual, but that's to be expected after last night. I imagine she'll be sleeping it off the rest of the day.

I nod and take a step back, but before I can shut the door, she speaks up again. "Drew." I push the door open. I arch my brows and wait. "Stay safe."

"Always do." I wink and shut the door behind me.

After only the first few hours of my shift, I pull a car over, and the driver reeks of alcohol. I radio in for backup since Logan is off today, and wait for another officer before giving the driver a sobriety test.

He fails miserably, and the other officer and I take him in. Paperwork and a meeting with my supervisor fill the time until midnight, and then I'm left patrolling my area until my shift's up.

Walking into the house after 3 AM, I'm always worried I'll wake Courtney up, but I also think she might be used to it. Or she sleeps like a rock.

It usually takes me an hour or so to unwind before I can fall asleep, so I turn the TV on in my room and start flipping through channels. A commercial ad for an upcoming Halloween movie has me thinking of the first time Courtney and I watched a scary movie together and how it led to our yearly tradition.

"Is there a reason every light in the house is on?" I asked, walking into the living room. She's settled on the couch with a bowl of popcorn.

"Not every light is on," she argued. "I'm watching *The Conjuring*."

"Ahh…" I said, sitting on the couch next to her. "So, you're afraid."

"I am not! I just don't want to watch it with the lights off."

"Because that makes it less scary?" I teased, grabbing a handful of popcorn.

"Well, it makes it less likely I'll pee myself. So, either be a friend or get the hell out." She scowled at me.

"Geez, okay. If you're so scared, why are you even watching it?"

"Because it's Halloween season," she explained. "It's my favorite time of year."

"You want a soda or something?" I asked. "This is some salty popcorn."

She nodded without taking her eyes off the TV. I grabbed a couple sodas from the fridge and decided to creep up on her from behind just as an intense scene was playing.

"BOO!" I gripped her shoulders with my hands, and she jumped, dropping a hand full of popcorn.

"Drew!" she shouted. "You're an ass!"

I laughed, her reaction priceless.

"You're pretty skittish for someone who isn't scared," I teased, taking a seat next to her.

"You scared me, not the movie." She scowled at me and pulled the bowl of popcorn out of my reach as I went to grab some. "No popcorn for you either."

I chuckled, reaching over her lap and nearly touching the edge of the bowl. "Don't make me pull your hair and call you a name to get what I want."

She laughed, her head falling back as the sweet sound released from her throat. I always did like her laugh, but she was having a full-out laughing fit.

"Oh my God," she said while laughing. "You're like one of those bullies on the playground."

"Only when you withhold food from me on cheat day." I reached for the bowl again. "I will pull your hair," I told her.

She scoffed. "I'll pull your hair right back. What are we? Seven?"

"You tell me. You're the one who won't share." I glared at her, and she was still laughing so hard, she snorted. Now I'm the one laughing.

"I hate you so much right now," she said through laughter and more snorting.

I grabbed a piece of her hair and tugged it lightly. "Share!"

"You're such a baby!" She swatted at my chest, pushing me away. "Here." She poured the bowl over my head and laughed as kernels fell down my shoulders and chest.

I took a piece that fell and tossed it into my mouth. "You're cleaning that up." I smirked.

Once we finished the movie, I started to get up, but she stopped me. "Wait."

"What?"

"I have to watch something happy first before I can go to bed." She took the remote and started playing with it.

"Something happy?"

"Yeah, like a sitcom or something. It flushes the scary movie out of my brain."

I burst into laughter. "So, let me get this straight. You watch scary movies, alone, with all the lights on, and then afterward you watch something 'happy' so you can go to sleep?"

"Precisely, yes."

"So why even watch the scary movie then?"

"It was always a tradition growing up. My brothers watched scary movies every Halloween, and because I was so much younger I wasn't normally allowed to watch the same movies as them, but on

Halloween my parents always let it slide. It became my favorite tradition."

I smiled. "All right. Let's pick out another one."

The following two years, we'd watch a marathon of scary movies, and it inadvertently became my favorite part of Halloween ever since.

CHAPTER TWELVE

COURTNEY

I WAKE up as soon as I hear the shower come on, and I breathe easy knowing Drew is home because I worry about him each time he puts on that uniform and walks out the door. Though it's almost four in the morning, my body's wide awake, but my eyes are screaming out in protest. I'm half tempted to burst into the bathroom and demand we talk about what happened, but considering he doesn't remember, how would I even start the conversation? As I run each scenario through my head, they seem ridiculous, so I stay where I am and try to go back to sleep, but it's useless.

I don't do one-night stands. I'm not that kind of girl and never have been. One-night stands are meaningless, purely physical and that night was neither of those things to *me*, which is what scares the shit out of me the most. I felt an overpowering stream of emotions as we connected on the most intimate level two humans could.

The nagging feeling comes back in full force and I somewhat feel like what we've done is wrong. He's my best friend. He's my roommate. For all I know, he's still hung up on Mia, and I was exactly what I never intended to be—*a one-night stand*.

For the next two hours, I toss and turn thinking about it. When I close my eyes, I feel the ghost of his lips and tongue kissing the softness of my neck. I can almost hear his moans as his warm breath grazes gently across my skin. Now that I've had a taste of him, one that still lingers on my lips, there's no forgetting it. Pretending it never happened may be easier, but honestly, it seems impossible.

It's crazy to think how much my life has changed over the past few years. If someone would've told me I'd be living with Drew Fisher or that we'd slept together and had the most amazing sex of my life, I would've looked that person in the face and called them a liar. If this same person continued to say Drew didn't remember a lick of it, I would've immediately asked what I did in a past life to deserve the torture. Because it is torture. And it's driving me crazy.

My alarm goes off at six, and I'm physically and mentally exhausted. Any other Monday, I'd show up at eight, but since Travis is out of the office this week, it's my responsibility to make sure the group doesn't completely go crazy. But honestly, we all act the same if he's there or not, because he's one of the best bosses around.

After I get dressed, I make a pot of coffee and fill a travel mug full before heading out the door. I walk into King Marketing, and everyone is shocked I'm there before eight on a Monday. It's not something I usually do. Though I'm punctual, Travis gives us flex time so I can show up whenever really, as long as it's before 8:30.

"I'm learning to be a morning person," I say to Jayden, a new intern Travis hired last week. No one believes me. Heck,

I don't even believe myself. But if I have to get up early, I can do it no problem.

I walk into my office and sit at my desk. I open my phone and type a big long, detailed text message to him, read it, and immediately delete it. Texting is not the place to talk about something so personal, and he's sleeping after working twelve hours. I answer a few emails and fix a networking problem and before I know it, half the day is gone. Before I lock my computer, I see an email from Viola.

To: Courtney Bishop
From: Viola King
Subject: No fucking way!

We landed safely. I'm so excited to be in London that I can't help it, but I'm tired and jet lagged. On the way over, I asked Travis why we couldn't have invited you. He reminded me it was our honeymoon. But I miss you. Oh also, WTF! YOU AND DREW? Travis and I literally high-fived when I connected to Wi-Fi and received your text. It's about time. Oh yeah, are you pregnant with my nieces and nephews yet? Too soon? :)

P.S. Please spare me the details. I just had a croissant and I'd like to keep it down.

Love you,
Lola

My heart begins to race. I totally forgot I had sent her that panicked text message when I was in the bathroom. And I just remember she hadn't responded yet. I hurry up and type back just in case she's still around Wi-Fi.

To: Viola Fisher
From: Courtney Bishop
Subject: Yes fucking way!

Lola….

Oh, you're going to get details whenever you come home. Maybe you can tell Drew because he doesn't remember a thing. He told me that and I died inside. I don't know what to do. I want to talk to him about it, but I don't know where to start. I'm freaking out over here. HELP ME. FREAKING OUT. WORST THAN WHEN TOBY BROKE UP WITH ME FREAK OUT.

P.s. The only person who gets pregnant the first time they do it is *you*.

P.S.S. It's called birth control.

P.S.S.S. I hope you were surprised about London!

Love you & miss you,
Court

I hit send and stand and start pacing. It's crazy how much Viola gets me and when I need her the most she's off celebrating the most important day of her life. My email refreshes and I sit and smile.

To: Courtney Bishop
From: Travis King

Subject: GET TO WORK

NOW!
P.S. Congratulations.

Travis King
Owner, King Marketing

Travis makes me laugh out loud, the jerk. I give him a quick reply that says NOPE right as an email from Viola floods in.

To: Courtney Bishop
From: Viola King
Subject: WTF?

What do you mean he *doesn't* remember? People don't just forget about things like that, do they? Oh, Travis just informed me that if a person drinks enough it's possible, then I gave him evil eyes because he probably knows from experience. Okay I'm sure that doesn't make you feel any better. Please don't freak out. It'll make me worry about you. Why not text Kayla and ask her to hang out with you? She'd probably be all about it. Ice cream hath no fury when you're losing it and she's a sweets junkie like you. Also, I was on birth control, remember? But I won't jinx you. Too much.
London is amazing but all I want to do right now is sleep. We're waiting for a cab to drive us to the hotel. I love you. Email me at any time. Just remember: everything is going to be okay, always.

Sending virtual hugs,
Lola

I let out a breath, but I don't feel any more relaxed. I'm wound up tighter than a wind-up toy. I decide to leave work and grab lunch. It's a beautiful day so I put the top down and blast Adele's latest CD, and sing the sappy words at the top of my lungs like I'm dedicating them to Drew as the wind blows through my hair. Obviously, I need to get a grip. I go to a drive-thru deli and grab a quick salad and coconut water. While I'm waiting in line for my order, I pull out my phone and text Kayla.

Courtney: Busy tonight?

Kayla: Not really. Just another rerun sesh of Friends with Ben & Jerry.

Courtney: S.O.S.

Kayla: What's wrong? Drew?

Courtney: You guessed it.

Kayla: I'll bring Ben & Jerry. They're good company.

Courtney: Bring their friend, Vodka, too.

Kayla: I'm on it.

I smile as I drive back to the firm. While I'm working, I

pick at my salad, but barely make a dent in it. Knowing I need more coffee, I get up and swiftly walk to the break room. On the way there, I run smack into the office secretary Kelsey, and she loses her footing. "Oh, my goodness. I'm so sorry, Kels," I say.

She turns around and sweetly gives me a smile. "No biggie. I know you've been out of it today."

Her words catch me off guard. I scrunch my face and give her a look. "Huh?"

"You've just been in la-la land. It's obvious something's up."

I playfully roll my eyes at her and give a laugh, but I'm really dying inside and apparently on the outside too. I walk in the break room and grab a Styrofoam cup from the cabinet and pour a huge glass of coffee.

"Hey, Court," Jayden says behind me, and I knock the coffee off the counter and spill it down my skirt. He rushes over and starts putting paper towels all over the counter and floor.

"Are you okay?" he asks.

And as soon as I open my mouth, I realize how much truth begins flooding out of my mouth. His eyes go wide, and he's staring at me like I've lost my mind before I realize I've told him I slept with my roommate and best friend, who everyone at the firm just happens to know.

"I was talking about the coffee on your skirt," he says with a smile.

"Oh, right." I swallow hard and know I'm slowly breaking and should probably not talk to people before I get my thoughts together. Yes, I'm known for keeping calm and cool, but when it comes to my love life—completely different story.

"It's cool. Your secret is safe with me," he says, and I really hope he's telling the truth, but I don't know him well enough to know. Drew comes to the firm every Friday and delivers lunch, and as soon as he walks in, it'll be way too obvious for those who haven't heard me blab if I can't get my shit together.

The rest of the day I stay in my office and try to concentrate while avoiding everyone. Once the clock hits four, I grab my things and head out. On the way home, I stop by the grocery store and before I know it my basket is full of enough ingredients to feed muffins to a small army for a week, but it doesn't even faze me. It's like I don't even know what I'm doing. I'm a self-diagnosed stress baker. When life throws you lemons, squeeze them into a margarita and make muffins. At least that's what I do.

I pull into the driveway and see Drew's already gone. It's not uncommon for us to not cross paths with each other when he's working swing shift. I'm not sure if I'm happy or sad we haven't seen each other. Perhaps it's best.

I bought so much stuff it takes several trips for me to bring it all inside. There's barely room on the counter, and I start organizing it in order as I preheat the oven and pull out muffin tins. I grab an extra mixing bowl and the one from my professional mixer that's always set up in our kitchen and start adding flour, baking soda, and salt. In another bowl, I add the sugar and eggs until they're foamy, then I add my secret ingredient—butter. I laugh as I think about Drew eating my muffins like he was starving and then my mind wanders to what happened right here on this counter.

My heart begins to race, and the oven starts beeping. I place all the ingredients together slowly and begin pouring the batter into the tins, forty-eight muffins and forty-eight to go. I place them in the oven then lean against the counter like I just successfully made the fastest batch of muffins on Hell's Kitchen and Gordon Ramsay himself is going to be eating them. I take a deep breath and release it and basically scream when I hear Kayla say 'hey' behind me.

"Holy fucking shit." I press the oven mitt against my chest and pant. "You scared the crap out of me. Seriously, I nearly saw my life flash before my eyes."

She's laughing. "Sorry! You left the door unlocked." Drew always flips out when I do that. She steps farther into the kitchen.

"What's all this mess?" Her eyes go wide as she looks around. There's sugar and flour on my face and the floor. Mixing bowls and ripped open bags. Actually, it does look like a mini disaster area.

"I'm baking." I shrug.

She slowly nods. "I can see."

I pull out more mixing bowls to whip up more ingredients, and just as I'm pouring more sugar in, the oven goes off. My hands are full, and Kayla jumps into action, pulling cupcake tins out of the oven, one after another and setting them on the stove.

"So, what's the occasion?"

I start laughing as I shove the other four pans of muffins in the oven like it's no big deal. "Some people are stress eaters. I'm a stress baker."

"So, you're making one hundred muffins for nothing? Who's going to eat all this?" she asks, curiosity written all over her face.

"It's only ninety-six muffins. You can have some. I'll bring them to work. Give some to the neighbor. Make Drew bring them to work. They disappear, trust me," I say, knowing one time I was able to pawn three hundred muffins on different people in one day.

"I'll deliver them to Drew's partner for you."

I give her a side-glance.

"I'm sure he'd be all for it." I encourage her.

She rolls her eyes. "Enough about him. The last thing I heard you woke up in Drew's bed and I've been left in suspense ever since. So, spill it," she says with a sweet smile on her face.

"Well, there isn't much to tell since he doesn't remember *anything*. I'm scared that maybe Drew's ashamed or embarrassed. I'm afraid I was nothing but a one-night stand. What if I'm a rebound fuck? Or maybe he's not over Mia and thinks it was all one giant mistake and it's easier to pretend it didn't happen than to talk about it. I don't want it to be awkward, but I can't straight-up ignore him. He's going to have three days off, which happen to fall on a weekend, which means I'll be off. And we always hang out on our weekends off when Mia's not in the picture."

Kayla just shakes her head as she listens, disagreeing with every word I say. "It's good to get out your fears, but I don't think you have anything to worry about. Do you know what will solve all of this?"

"What's that?"

"Talk to him."

I sigh.

"You need to pull up your big girl panties and see what he has to say. Maybe he thinks it was a mistake. If that's the case, it's better for you to know where you two stand than for you to slowly lose your mind thinking about it. And what if he doesn't? You won't know until you talk to him."

"Wow. You're like Viola 2.0."

She smiles. "I'll accept that. I love her."

"I do, too," I say. "But honey, I have plenty of room in my heart for more friends."

"Southerners," she says, shaking her head with a smile.

The oven starts beeping with the second round of muffins, and Kayla grabs the mitts as I place cork cooling boards down on the counter. Carefully she places each pan on top. She's a natural at this.

"They smell delicious."

"Wait until they cool and we have them with milk. We might eat all ninety-six ourselves." I give her a big smile.

"I'm okay with that! So, you're going to talk to him, right?" she asks as I begin removing the cooled muffins from the baking pans and placing them on a tray.

"I don't know. I'm not even sure what to say."

She starts helping me pull the muffins from the pans, and I give her a small smile.

"Just say what's in your heart. You can't go wrong with that."

"I'm worried I'll end up losing one of my best friends, but I know I can't keep pretending it never happened. It'll eat me alive."

"Or baking dozens of muffins in the meantime."

I laugh. "Oh, I'm already there." I brush my hands on my apron and turn to give her a big hug, regardless if I have flour all over my clothes and face. I already know we're going to be best friends.

CHAPTER THIRTEEN

DREW

AFTER FOUR LONG days of working twelve-hour shifts, I'm more than ready for a day off. After several months of working various rotations, my body's schedule gets messed up regularly. Working out helps me blow off steam, but sometimes I just need to sleep it off.

Getting home at 3 AM Thursday, I'm ready to pass out before I walk in the door. Relieved to have the next three days off, I can't help thinking about Courtney and what she's been up to this week. We normally catch up over the weekends when we're both off work, but I have a feeling this weekend isn't going to be like the others.

I sleep later than I mean to, but once I'm up, I drink my shake and head to the gym. It'll get my head back on track even when it feels like a tornado has blown through it. I've been overthinking everything that's happened lately and the blowout with Mia over two weeks ago. I've refused to call her like I normally would after an argument. I'd beg and plead for her to talk to me over her voicemail, and when she'd finally call back—on her terms—she'd dangle the carrot in my face just long enough until I cave and say what she wants to hear. She held all the cards, and she knew it, but that's the last time that'll happen. I haven't attempted to call or text her, and I bet it's driving her absolutely crazy.

When Mia and I met, I felt it instantly. I felt the pull, the rush, the need to speak to her. She had this energy around her that just spoke to me. On top of her being gorgeous, I thought we had a lot in common. The harder I fell, the stronger the hold she had on me became. I'd dated in high school and college, but it never led to anything serious. Not until Mia.

That was over three years ago.

Things have changed between us since then, and I can't pinpoint exactly when they did, but it's as if I've just woken up and realized all the bullshit she's put me through and how toxic our relationship became over the last few years. I wanted to believe she'd change, that we could make it work, and our relationship become what it was before, but once she gave me an ultimatum of not living with Courtney anymore, that's when something inside clicked. I hadn't realized it right away, but after taking the time to think about it and what she was asking me to give up, Mia was no longer the person I could see spending the rest of my life with and that was a big slap in the face for me. I had made excuses for her behavior in the past, but I won't do that any longer. I can't.

For the first time in three years, I'm finally seeing things as they really are.

Being at the gym helped unclutter my mind, but no matter how many weights I lift or repetitions I do, it does nothing to take away the nerves of seeing Courtney today. She needs to know how sorry I am for even considering her moving out and what a jackass I am for even letting Mia put the thought in my head. We haven't had a chance to really talk about it yet with the wedding, and I'm not sure how much of the conversation she really heard, but it's been bothering me. Randomly, I think about the look on Court's face as Mia acted out.

I wish Travis were home, although I know he's having the time of his life in London with Viola right now. He wasn't Mia's number one fan either, but he's a good listener and is good at giving sound advice, even when it's advice I don't want to hear.

After this past week with no Mia, no drama, no anxiety— I feel free. She put this hold on me for so long that I forgot what it felt like to feel this way.

Once I return home from the gym, I hop in the shower and think about how I'll apologize to Courtney for all the drama Mia brought between us. I know she was hurt by Mia's comments even if she didn't show it. It was a dick move for me to even say I'd think about it. Courtney is one of those people that come into your life with no expectations, no agenda, and no idea of how they're going to change your life by just being present. She's been distant, and just the thought of losing her as my best friend makes me sick to my stomach.

Once I've fully processed what I plan to say to her, I turn off the water and step out of the shower. As I'm drying off, I hear movement in the house, and I begin wondering if Courtney is home from work early.

Wrapping the towel around my waist and slicking my hair back, I walk down the hallway and see grocery bags on top of the dining table. Courtney should still be at work, nevertheless, have time to go shopping.

When I round the corner and turn into the kitchen, it's not Courtney I see.

"What are you doing here?" I ask, pissed Mia just walked in and made herself at home in *my* house. I almost forgot I had given her a key because she rarely used it.

"Hi, darling," she says in an overly sweet tone. She walks over to me and places a hand on my cheek. "You look good. I missed you."

"Cut the bullshit, Mia. What are you doing here?" I jerk my face away from her.

She drops her hand but continues smiling. "I'm making you dinner tonight. Thought you could use a home-cooked meal after your long rotation."

"What the hell are you talking about? We aren't together. You don't just get to come into my house whenever you want and pretend nothing happened." I hold my stance, crossing my arms over my bare chest, and tightening my lips. She needs to go. I cannot deal with her today.

"Oh, Drew..." she says as if I said something hilarious, shaking her head at me. "That was just a little fight. You know we can't stay apart. We've both been stubborn, and it's time for us to move on."

"Exactly. Move on, Mia. It's over." I take a step toward her, grabbing a bag off the counter and pushing it against her chest. "Go home."

"How can you say that to me? After everything we've been through over the last three years? After everything I've done for you?"

Her words hit me like a brick, and I have no idea how I ever put up with her shit before. "Everything you've done for me? Are you insane? You've been toying with my emotions and dragging me along in your little web of lies since the start, and it's ending now."

"You can't mean that, Drew." She puts the bag back on the counter and steps in front of me. "I love you, baby. I know you love me, too. Sure, we've had our problems, but they aren't anything we can't work through. Look how far we've come. How could you just walk away from us and everything we have together?"

It's the most genuine thing I've ever heard Mia say, but that doesn't mean I'm falling for it.

"Because it's time, Mia." Sounding sincere, I don't know how else to break it to her.

"I don't believe that," she says firmly.

"Well, you should. I'm sorry."

She lowers her eyes, and I worry she's going to start crying. After a moment, she surprises me and plasters a smile on her face. "Well, that doesn't mean I can't cook for you still. You've been living off shakes and bars all week, I'm sure. Let me make you a decent meal."

Mia is a lot of things, not all good and not all bad, but she's always been skilled in the kitchen. I don't want to send her away considering she already brought all the food here, but I don't want Courtney walking in on Mia being here either.

What the fuck am I going to do?

COURTNEY

I have never been so nervous to come home after work in my life.

It's Thursday, and Drew will be home for the next three days. And I know we need to talk. After going through every possible scenario in my head, I've decided two things: I'll humiliate myself by telling him we had sex—the very sex he doesn't remember. I'll tell him I'm moving out because there's no way to come back from something like that *or* he'll say since he doesn't remember, perhaps I should remind him and we get naked in his bed. Since that's the most *unlikely* version of what's to happen, I'm preparing for the worst, but I know either way, I can't hold this in anymore.

The sinking feeling in my gut returns the moment I pull into the driveway and see Mia *Fucking* Montgomery's car. I don't know what to make of it, especially since I haven't spoken to Drew and the last time he mentioned her was at the wedding about how he missed her. I know they have a history and now I feel like a fool for thinking anything would ever change.

Parking my Jeep behind Drew's, I stay in and sit, willing myself to keep the tears away. I knew this was always an option—that he'd take her back, and I'd be wondering *how*.

"Hey, what's going on?" Kayla answers the phone. "Are you getting cold feet?" We've talked about this all week, and she knows tonight was the night.

"She's back," I say, my voice low.

"Who?"

"Who do you think? Mia."

"She's back? They're back together?" Her voice is high-pitched.

"Her car is here, that's all I know, but I can piece two and two together." I frown.

"You have to tell him, Court." She lowers her voice.

"What? No way!" I shout.

"He deserves to know," she tells me. "It might change his mind whether or not to take her back."

"Or he'll think I'm a jealous, crazy person." I inhale deeply. "I don't want to be that girl who begs a guy to pick her. Mia's a snake, but she always wins. She says jump and Drew asks how high."

"You don't know that. She could be over to get her things, for all you know."

I sigh, wondering if that could actually be the case. Somehow, I doubt it because she doesn't really have any personal belongings at the house. I know better.

"Fine, I'll go in, but if they're in there doing it, I'm moving out," I say seriously.

"For your sake, I hope not; and if they are, key her car."

I chuckle. "Got it."

We hang up, and after several deep breaths, I get out of the Jeep and head inside. I pretend as if it's any other day and that whatever I see won't bother me.

Oh, how wrong I am.

Drew is sitting on the couch, shirtless and facing away from me, and Mia is straddling his lap, looking at me as soon as I walk in. The smile that spreads over her face is a devilish one, letting me know she's won, and that there's nothing I can do about it. Drew turns his head to look over his shoulder, but he can't see me from that angle. The moment he exposes his neck, she keeps her eyes locked on mine as she sucks on it like she needs his skin for air. *Nice play, bitch.*

The table is set for two with candles in the middle. Apparently, she's already setting up house for their romantic night together.

I decide to ignore them and walk toward my room. I hear commotion as I walk down the hallway, but it doesn't take a genius to know what's happening. Once I'm in my room, I change into my sweats and a t-shirt. I grab my headphones and plug them into my phone, putting my favorite playlist on repeat. It's a mix of The Chainsmokers, Boyce Avenue, and Maroon 5, and by the time I get to the third song, I'm angrier with myself than anything.

I'm mad I let myself think this time would be any different. This is Drew's pattern. Every single time they have a fight and break up, a few weeks pass and they get right back together. I should've known, and because I thought otherwise, I'm the one left feeling like an idiot.

Kayla sends me a message and it takes me a few minutes to think of a way to respond.

Kayla: So what's the verdict?

Courtney: Based off the way they were on the couch and Mia was on top of him, I would guess they're back together. (Broken heart + knife emoji)

Kayla: SHUT UP!! OMG, I hate them both right now.

Courtney: Join the club.

Kayla: You need to tell him.

Courtney: Why? So the knife can jab into me deeper? He'd end up saying something about how it was a drunken mistake and would make everything between us even more awkward. Forget it, Kay. The bitch won.

Kayla: I can't believe what I'm hearing, Court. DON'T

LET HER WIN! March in there and tell them both what happened!

Courtney: *eye roll* I'm too busy sulking.

I turn my phone on silent and lie back in bed while Adam Levine seduces me with his voice. I have no intention of getting out of this bed for at least the next four hours.

I fall asleep, thankfully sleeping through whatever the hell they were doing in the living room. On the couch. On the same damn couch I sit on.

I cringe.

God, I hope she got her crabs taken care of. I'm not dry-cleaning that sofa cushion.

I decide to email Viola for an update. It's been awhile since I've heard from her and I guess now would be the appropriate time to tell her what's happened.

To: Viola Fisher
From: Courtney Bishop
Subject: Future Cat Lady

Lola!

I haven't heard from you in a few days and wanted to check in! I'm sure you've been pretty *busy* so I won't take it too personal that you haven't emailed me. But here's an update on my end: Your brother has severe brain damage. He's hit it one too many times on the headboard while Mia sits on top of him and cracks her whip while he moans *harder...harder...harder.*

On that note, your future sister-in-law is back and

let's just say, I'm feeling pretty fucking stupid right
about now. Kayla helped me prepare all week for how
I was going to approach the subject and what to say
and it was all for nothing.
So how was the tour? What house did the Sorting
House put you in?

Hufflepuff, right? :)
Did you make it to platform 9 ¾ yet?
Can you tell I miss having you around?

I hope you're having the time of your life, but come
home soon. I need the Selena to my Taylor back.

Love you!
-Court
P.S. Tell Travis he can cancel Drew's weekly lunch
deliveries. They won't be needed any longer.

As I press send, I frown, thinking of our Friday
tradition ending. It's been something he's done for me since
day one, back when my crush was eighth grade Nick Carter
level.

My stomach growls, and I'm going to have to go out
there to find something to eat and risk seeing them together
again. I should be used to it, but knowing Mia and her love
for PDA, means I'll probably lose my appetite before I even
make it to the kitchen.

Just the thought of seeing them together again makes my
heart pound harder. It starts to really sink in that I wasn't
even a rebound. We had a drunken one-night stand, one that
he doesn't even remember, and now it means nothing.

Absolutely nothing. I've slowly been falling for my best friend, and he's in love with another woman.

And he'll never know it either.

I bravely walk out into the hallway, bracing myself, but it's completely quiet. The table is still set for two, and once I get into the kitchen, the grocery bags are still sitting on top of the counter. Knowing Drew, he probably wants to organize it all alphabetically. He has a special kind of OCD where cans and boxes all must be in certain places.

I've always enjoyed messing with him. Viola taught me that trick long ago just in case I ever needed to get back at him for something. Too bad this isn't something I'll ever come back from. Perhaps moving out is the only option, after all.

Once I finish microwaving a bag of popcorn, I head back to my room. Since they aren't around, I guess I don't have to hide out anymore, but I'd rather not risk seeing them together again tonight. If they didn't get to the dinner portion of their evening yet, that can only mean one thing: they skipped it and went right into the bedroom.

I pause at my door and see his door is shut. He only closes it when he's sleeping, and since it's only eight o'clock, I highly doubt he's in bed for sleeping reasons. Needing to know for sure, I walk back to the front door to check for their cars in the driveway, but I stop just before I grab the knob.

Some things are just better not knowing.

Walking back to my room for the second time, I grab my phone and text Kayla.

Courtney: I hate myself.

Kayla: Is it self-loathing time? Do we need a pep talk?

Courtney: Nope. But any chance I can sleep on your couch till I find my own place?

Kayla: He's kicking you out? That asshole!!

Courtney: No, I mean, he might be if Mia is back in the picture, but I've made the decision myself. I can't be around him when he's all into her, and I'm fantasizing about him in the shower like a teenage girl. Our night together will continue to haunt me forever, and I'll die an old cat lady.

Kayla: I see we've moved to the overdramatics portion of this self-sabotage episode. Let's go out.

Courtney: But it's Thursday.

Kayla: Exactly. So get your hoochie boots on and let's go.

Courtney: It's Ladies' night. Drew and I go out every Thursday after his rotation is over and get cheap drinks. It's our drunken tradition.

Kayla: Well, now it can be ours. I'm picking you up in 30 minutes. Get dressed.

Courtney: Ugh…

Kayla: And by dressed, I mean out of your sweats and into something decent. Don't forget to tame your hair, too.

I roll my eyes and smile because she's gotten to know me pretty well.

Courtney: Fine. But you're buying me a Bahama Mama.

Kayla: Deal. Don't forget your lucky underwear ;)

CHAPTER FOURTEEN

DREW

As I sat on the couch with Mia, I told her exactly what she needed to finally hear, even if it was hard to say. She continued talking, holding onto hope that she'd change my mind, but for the first time, I was standing my ground and refused to buy into her bullshit. I knew she wasn't going to take it well, but the moment she heard Courtney's Jeep pull into the driveway, she hopped into my lap and pinned me down with her legs. By the time I threw her off, Courtney had already walked in and left the room.

Once Mia realized I wasn't caving and allowing her to have her way like usual, she had a complete meltdown. This included me being called every name under the sun along with being accused of cheating. I couldn't handle another word from her and forced her to leave. Never had I ever cheated on her, and unfortunately, I'm not so sure she could say the same. Regardless, I refused to allow her to spew lies and hate in my face. It wasn't worth arguing over, and I refused to take her bait. I think she finally understood I'm really done this time. The realization that we were truly over was written on her face.

Once she peeled off in her Mercedes, I stood outside and stared at the dark clouds moving in. Truthfully, I don't know if I ever expected us to break up indefinitely. I thought Mia was the one I'd spend the rest of my life with, but after taking time away from her and focusing on myself, I realize how wrong I was. At one point in our lives, we wanted the same things, or maybe I was manipulated into believing that. I'm not sure if that was ever the truth because the reality of us was so blurred. Each day, the stress of being with her and making sure she was constantly happy fades away. Along the way over the past few weeks, I've found pieces of myself that I don't plan to ever give back to her.

A cool breeze sweeps across my chest and before I step inside the house, my cell phone buzzes, and I'm tempted to leave it in my pocket just in case it's Mia's calling. Allowing curiosity to get the best of me, I unlock my phone and see it's not Mia, but a text from Logan.

Logan: Busy tonight?

I know I have unfinished business with Courtney, and I shouldn't leave until we talk. Before I reply to his text, I walk back inside and stand outside of her door. All is eerily quiet, so I crack it open and peek inside. She's sleeping peacefully with her headphones on. Her hair cascades around her soft features, and I can't stop staring at her, which is new for me. I can almost hear the lyrics of the song she's listening to it's so loud, and I have no idea how she's able to fall asleep with all that noise, other than she may be exhausted from getting up so early all week since Travis is gone. Though I'm tempted, I decide against it because I'm not in the right state of mind after dealing with Mia. Instead of waking her, I close the door and text Logan back.

Drew: No plans. What's up?

Logan: I need a wingman tonight.

I halfway wonder what he's up to because Logan isn't the type to go out unless asked, but I don't question him and agree to meet him at Good Times for cheap drinks and music. At least it will give me time to think about what I'll say to Courtney.

After I change into some blue jeans and a button-up shirt, I hesitate outside of Courtney's room. It's one of our Thursday traditions when my days off fall on a weekend. There were many Fridays where she's played wingman and had to literally drag her ass to work hungover, but she refuses to call in, and she's never late. I smile thinking about all the good times we've had together over the last few years and realize that each time I've gone out with her, I've never left with anyone. Isn't that the purpose of a wingman? We've never had a real argument, and she's never tried persuading me to think a certain way about a specific topic or people. There's zero manipulation when we're together and I can actually be myself without worry or care. There's no comparison between her and Mia. Courtney puts me first and will always be there for me just as much as she's been there for Viola. That's one thing that will never change—no matter what.

I grab my keys from the counter and glance at the groceries that are sitting haphazardly in a paper bag on the kitchen table. Before leaving, I put the perishables and chicken in the refrigerator and the canned goods in the pantry where they belong. It looks like Mia was going to make some sort of chicken parmesan and that's when I realize I haven't eaten dinner. I grab some prepped chicken out of the fridge and pop it in the microwave for a few minutes. After I eat, I head toward Good Times and the only person who's on my mind is Courtney. She's taken hold of me, and I can't seem to shake her from my thoughts, and weirdly enough, I don't want to.

When I arrive, the parking lot is full, which isn't surprising considering it's also ladies' night. I walk into the building and see Logan sitting alone at the bar, and I can't help but laugh because he looks awkward as hell, like a tiger surrounded by sheep. He's sitting up straight and rigid, his back facing the room, and there's an underlying message telling everyone to leave him the fuck alone. That's the ex-marine in him speaking.

I walk up and place my hand on his shoulder, and he turns around like he's going to break my neck.

"Whoa, chill," I say.

"Just making sure you weren't some prick who wanted his ass kicked," Logan says, and a small smile hits his lips before he takes a drink of his whiskey.

"You need another drink and to relax just a bit. Everyone in here is scared shitless of you."

He looks around, then pops an eyebrow up at me completely unamused. That's when I lose my shit and burst out into hearty laughter. He's used to my antics. It causes him to smile, and I sit down beside him, considering there are a handful of free stools on both sides.

Logan orders another whiskey and doesn't really say

much, but I'm all smiles. He's the worst wingman ever because he's scaring everyone away, even the women.

"How's the roommate?" he says, glancing over at me.

I narrow my eyes, knowing where this is going. I haven't told anyone about the night of the wedding, not even Travis. But Logan has a sixth sense or some shit, and he's always using it to his advantage. Honestly, he's just good at reading people.

"She's good," I say, ordering a drink.

"Yeah?" He's smiling when he notices I stiffen just slightly.

I give him a side look and shoot down the whiskey in one big gulp.

A woman sits down next to me and tries to make small talk.

Logan leans over and speaks over the music. "Hey babe, he's taken."

Her cheeks go pink, and she awkwardly walks away.

"I'm not with Mia anymore," I say, ordering another drink.

"I wasn't talking about Mia," Logan says, turning around, actually acknowledging he's in a bar with music, dancing, and people.

I give him a confused look, and he grabs his new drink from the bar top and twists back around.

Before taking a sip, he shoots me his signature smirk and looks me dead in the eyes, speaking just loud enough for me to hear.

"I was talking about the roommate."

COURTNEY

Kayla isn't going to let me sit around to swim in my feelings, and I'm thankful for her friendship. After my nap, I realize how stupid I was to ever think there could be more between Drew and me, especially considering he doesn't remember a lick of the best sex I've ever had. I let out a laugh because it's my luck.

After Toby broke up with me, I'd become numb to my heart being broken almost to the point where I can say it doesn't faze me anymore. *Almost.*

Toby and I started dating at the end of my senior year of high school. He was the first boy that I ever allowed to steal my heart. I say boy, because I had a curious side and had to make sure girls weren't for me. Living in a small town meant being secretive about dating someone of the same sex. Violet, the first and last girl I ever dated, wanted to run away together, but after a few months, I realized that while I thought women were beautiful creatures, I was more sexually attracted to men. It wasn't a phase or something I did for attention because I truly cared for her. Though we were just stupid kids, the breakup was messy. The rumor mill started, and I later found out Violet was the one who told everyone about us sneaking around and being together. We weren't best friends like everyone assumed, but were more than that. To this day, my parents still don't know, and I'm not sure they'd believe I kissed and dated a girl anyway.

After Violet and I broke up, Toby was there. He was tall and handsome and said all the right things at the right time. He'd always had a crush on me, but I never gave him the time of day, until my senior year when he asked me to the fall dance. He willingly took my heart and kept it.

When I found out I was accepted to the California State University on a full scholarship, he was upset. Everyone hoped I'd go to the University of Texas and then Toby and I would get married and start a family, but I had no desire to stay in Texas. I wanted to experience something different and be someone other than the Bishop boys' little sister. When I told him I'd taken the opportunity, he was pissed that I didn't allow him to make the decision for me. After a year of doing the long-distance relationship thing, Toby decided to attend a college that was close by so we could be together again. I was so consumed by him and I loved having him around because it was like having a piece of Texas in California with me.

I knew after graduation he would be going back to El Dorado. It was always the plan. He made it very clear that California wasn't for him and I'd wished I was enough to make him stay. I had limited time with him already so when I heard the Brooks family reunion happened to fall at the same time of spring break and it'd be in Dallas instead, my heart sank. It meant we wouldn't be together for two weeks. Though I loved Toby, he never got along with my brothers, and they made sure to give him hell every chance they could. Anytime I hinted about him meeting me in Dallas for the reunion, he'd have an excuse. Though our spring breaks fell at different times—I had two weeks and he had one—we decided to go our separate ways. It was the first time since he'd moved to Cali that we had been apart for a significant amount of time.

Before I flew to Dallas, he came over, and we made love on the floor in front of the fireplace. He'd told me he'd love me and I believed him. He'd told me I was the only woman for him and I believed him. I told him I couldn't wait to plan our future together after college and how I would do anything for him, even though it wasn't always reciprocated.

The next morning when my brothers picked me up from the airport, they gave me so much shit for Toby not coming with me, but I ignored them like usual. After the reunion, I booked an early flight back to California because I wanted to surprise him before he left for home. He'd been so distant while I was gone that I really should've gotten the hint. When I checked Facebook, I was annoyed by the amount of pictures of him and this girl that he was tagged in, but even then, I made excuses for him. He really didn't use his Facebook that much anyway. In my eyes, he could do no wrong, and he would never hurt me. I believed the good in him because I loved him with all my heart.

Courtney: Baby! I'm home! Surprise! I missed you.

Toby: Packing up to fly home.

Courtney: Can I come see you? Thought I'd catch a flight back to San Angelo with you. It can be our own little secret.

Toby: That's not a good idea.

We'd been together for years, and the shortness he had with me was new. I didn't know how to react or what to say, and all I could think of were the pictures of him with another woman on his Facebook.

Courtney: I'm coming over anyway. :)

There was a long pause before I received a response. I had enough time to get dressed and put the top down on the Jeep. Right as I was backing out of my driveway, a text message blinked on my phone.

Toby: I think we should break up, Court.

My heart dropped, and I was in so much shock I sat there reading the words over and over. We'd been together for years. He knew everything about me, and I knew the same about him. Sadness was followed by anger, and at that very moment, I realized I'd been played and replaced by another woman. From that point on, I wasn't sure if I'd ever be good enough for anyone.

But I can't deny it's different with Drew. He's not just anyone; he's my best friend and roommate—for now. As much as I hope it's not the case, I feel as if my eviction notice could be coming since she's back in the picture. Considering how crazy she is, she might just tell him to stop talking to me altogether.

After I get dressed in a sexy little skirt and halter top, I pack an overnight bag with work clothes to stay with Kayla. She may have thought I was joking, but I was dead serious about sleeping on her couch tonight. I need time away, I think, especially with Drew being home for the next three days, though we really do need to talk. Even if he doesn't believe me, or thinks it's a big mistake, the conversation needs to happen. But I have to decide if it's worth bringing up or not since he and Mia were a little too cozy on the couch. My heart says yes, but my head says no, and I'm not sure which one will win yet.

I let out a deep breath as I put on my high heels and grab

my keys to the house, forcing the thoughts of her kissing him away. As soon as I shut the door, I exhale, seeing both of their vehicles are gone. I swallow hard, allowing my mind to wander. He probably went to her house so they could be alone. My stomach twists in knots thinking about it.

Right on time, Kayla pulls into the driveway in her cute little cherry red Mustang convertible. The top is down, and her hair is as wild as her glitzy outfit that's reflecting moonlight.

"We're going with the top down?" I ask as I throw my duffle into the backseat and climb inside. "You told me to tame my hair!"

"Yes, top down! I'm pretty sure you're the one that told me the bigger the hair, the closer to Jesus," she says with a giggle and reverses once I'm buckled. The girl has a lead foot just like me, and I think I'm in love with her car already.

"That's what we say in Texas. I don't think Cali is ready for big hair and well, big everything." I give her a wink, but she doesn't put the top up. Honestly, I wouldn't either. The weather is way too nice to waste it, regardless of how long it took me to fix my hair. There's a brisk coolness in the air that makes me shiver, but I love every second of it. She turns up the music, and it's blaring as we speed through the neighborhood. It reminds me of all the good times Viola and I have had in the Jeep during summer breaks. Happiness is allowing the wind to blow through your hair as you speed down the highway, plus it always helps me clear my head.

After we park, Kayla turns and looks at me and gives me a big smile. "Are you ready to dance your ass off?"

"You have no idea," I say, trying to comb my hair down with my fingers.

We walk into a dance club called Toppers, and I'm

shocked we're here because it's been years since I stepped foot inside this place. Kayla orders us drinks, and we're vastly traveling down a one-way road to Margaritaville when she decides she wants to leave and go to Good Times. I don't argue, but neither of us is in any position to drive, so we Uber across town because the drinks are cheap and it's ladies' night, so the place will be full. The Uber drops us off in front of the main entrance and Kayla and I walk inside laughing about something I can't remember.

"The goal for tonight is to forget about it all and have a good time, okay?" she says.

I nod and give her a big hug. "Yes! Girl Power!" I say and begin to laugh because I've had so much to drink that the silly ridiculous side has come out to play.

"I'm going to get more drinks. I'll be right back," Kayla says.

"I'm going to dance!" I say to her, pointing to the dance floor as soon as I hear *Love Me Down* by Britney Spears come on. When my feet hit the dance floor, men flock around me, and I quickly become the center of attention. I ignore them and shake my ass, hoping to get lost in the music. It's one thing that's never changed, my love for music and dancing.

After a few songs play, Kayla returns *without* our drinks and begins dancing and smiling big and pointing behind her. That's when I notice she has Logan's hand in hers and she's pulling him behind her. I laugh because I can't even get mad about it. But I'm really confused he's here until I feel strong hands grab my hips and pull me back.

"Court." Drew's warm breath crawls against the soft skin on my neck and my lips slightly part. It takes everything I have not to lean back into his touch. I'm grateful my back is against his chest and he can't see my face because I'm completely shocked and it shows. I genuinely thought he was with Mia, but he's not, he's here, with *me*.

I move my ass against him, and he tightly grabs ahold of my hips. I allow the alcohol to take control and forget about what I saw tonight. Once the song ends, a slow one comes on. I'm so confused by him being here that I barely recognize the song, but I can feel the mood of the room change. Couples walk onto the dance floor, and I don't have the courage to look him in the eyes, so I try to walk away, but Drew grabs my hand and pulls me to his chest. For the first time in days, we're face-to-face. My eyes flutter closed because I can't look at him as he tucks loose strands of hair behind my ear. He's done this a million times before, but now it feels different.

"Just one dance," he says, and memories of our night together flood in and I try to push them away, but it's impossible.

"Dancing is what got us into this predicament in the first place," I say under my breath. Drew pulls me even closer as we slowly move our bodies in sync to the music. He smells so damn good, like fresh soap and aftershave. I swallow hard, pushing my feelings aside.

It's okay. He doesn't remember a thing; at least, that's what I keep telling myself over and over.

"What predicament?" He gives me a little side grin before he spins me around and pulls me back to his body. The closeness is making me nervous, and I don't know what to say, but the liquid courage takes control, and my truths all spills out.

"The one where you handcuffed me to your bed and then forgot about it," I blurt out. As soon as the words leave my mouth, I go into internal freak-out mode because Kayla and I had gone over the scenario time and time again over the last few days. I knew exactly what I was going to say and here I am spilling my guts in the middle of a crowded place, talking about something so personal like it meant nothing. Heat rushes to my cheeks, and I smile to cover up my nervousness.

Drew stills for just a second then relaxes and interlocks his fingers with mine. I'm taken aback, struggling to breathe, because it's all so unexpected. His chest is rising and falling, and we stop moving, but neither of us breaks the closeness. As I stand there staring into his eyes in the middle of the dance floor, my heart flutters and I swear he feels it too. Flashes of light slowly sweep across his face, and in that moment, we're lost together in a stream of unspoken words. Not being able to continue staring because I'm flustered as hell, I look down at the floor.

Drew grabs my chin between his fingers and removes the inches between us. His mouth is so close to mine that if I moved forward just a tad, they'd touch, and I'm not sure I'd be able to stop. Being here with him like this is reckless, especially in my current state. My heart is racing so fast, that it matches the beat of the dance remix that starts playing.

Drew leans in, the softness of his lips outlines the shell of my ear. "Court," he says lowly, "that's not a predicament I'd ever forget. But let's not talk about it when you've been drinking."

Realization sets in and my eyes go wide and when I take a step back, Drew bites his bottom lip. He's looking at me with hooded eyes, and a small smile plays on his lips.

Oh my God!

My throat goes dry as I instantly sober up, regardless of all the margaritas I drank. I don't know what to think or say as I'm studying his face. My mouth gently falls open, and I understand now. He doesn't have to say a word or confirm anything because his eyes gave him away.

He never forgot a damn thing.

He remembers, and by the way he's looking at me at this very moment, I'm pretty sure he remembers *everything*.

CHAPTER FIFTEEN

DREW

SECURING Courtney's hand in mine, I lead her out of the bar and toward my truck. The air is cooler now, and I notice her shoulders are bare, so I shrug out of my jacket and place it over her. "Were you trying to catch pneumonia?"

She wrinkles her nose at me. "It's not even that cold."

"Tell that to your chattering teeth," I say, unlocking my truck. "Get in."

As soon as she's in and settled, I shut the door and round the front to the driver's side and hop inside. I turn the engine on and start the heat. California is nice this time of year, but once the sun goes down, the breeze from the water drops the temperature.

"You lied to me," she finally speaks, keeping her head down.

"I didn't lie."

She whips her head at me, narrowing her eyes. "You said you didn't remember anything after the binge drinking. So, do you, or don't you?" Her voice is demanding, and I know she wants answers. I'm just not sure I can explain them to her right now.

"Court, we should really talk about this when we're both sober," I begin, hoping she understands.

"We didn't get into your bed sober, so why start now? Just tell me. I need to know."

I bow my head and crack my jaw, thinking how to word it right. "I didn't forget. I woke up, hungover as fuck, and when it dawned on me that the night before wasn't another dream about you, I turned over, and you were gone. I figured you woke up, realized where you were and what had happened, and bailed before I was up. I thought you felt regret and I didn't want things to be awkward between us." I finally look at her, and she's staring at me, emotionless. "I was afraid to lose you."

"You've had dreams about me?" Her brows raise.

"You caught that little bit, did you?" I smirk, and for a moment it feels normal between us again. But her lips tilt down, and I know it'll never be normal between us again.

"You made me believe you didn't remember anything," she states, anger forming in her voice. "You made me believe it meant nothing and that you were back with Mia."

"That wasn't my intention. You have to believe me," I tell her genuinely.

"My heart was shattering. I was so angry with myself for even *thinking* you'd be interested in a girl like me and that only girls like Mia get guys like you." Our eyes meet. I can see how hurt she is right now, and it's killing me inside to see her like this.

I reach for her hand, but she pulls it away. "I'm so sorry. I swear, I've wanted to tell you all week, but with my work rotation, I wanted to wait until we had a night together."

"A night that turned into Mia and you on the couch," she mutters.

"I had nothing to do with that. She and I are over."

She cocks a brow at me. "Does she know that?"

I shrug, because who knows what Mia is thinking. "It doesn't matter because she's not the one I want." I reach for her hand again, and this time she lets me hold it.

She looks down at our hands and licks her lips. "And it took you this long to figure that out?" She looks back up at me, doubt in her tone.

I bow my head and nod. "I didn't want to admit it to myself. I categorized you as just a friend, someone I share a house with, and one of my sister's best friends. I didn't allow myself to think of you as anything more than that, but once I did—once I let my guard down—the feelings I always blocked came rushing in and there was no more denying it. Bringing you lunch every Friday was the highlight of my whole week. Our Thursday night Ladies' night traditions, our Saturday night movies, and even our Sunday morning pancake feasts—they were always more than just two friends hanging out together; I just never wanted to admit it."

"If that's true, then why didn't you acknowledge us being together? Why pretend you were too drunk to remember?"

"Courtney, I was worried you'd think it was a mistake, and I needed time to process it all. It consumed my mind all fucking week long. Between telling you the truth and wondering what you'd say about it all, I figured either option meant I'd lose you."

Our eyes lock, her soft features studying mine. "You forgot the third option."

The corner of my lips tilts up, feeling hopeful. "What's that?"

"You could kiss me."

I smile, so fucking happy over the way she's looking at me right now. My heart beats harder because kissing Courtney is something I've thought of nonstop all week.

"I like that option." I cup her cheek and bring our bodies closer. "I like that option a lot, actually," I say against her lips. She smiles, and my whole world tilts.

Kissing Courtney feels like the most natural thing in my life. My tongue glides with hers as our lips connect and arms wrap around each other. She lets out a small whimper of a moan, and I feel my dick hardening in my jeans. I won't lie and say I've always felt this way for her, but something buried inside me came alive the moment our bodies connected while dancing with her at the wedding. Once one thing led to another, feelings for her flooded my mind I hadn't realized were there.

She twists her body, allowing my hands to wrap around her waist and pull her closer. The awkward position of sitting in the front seat is becoming uncomfortable, but I can't find the willpower to release her.

Her hands explore my body and chest, wrapping a palm around my bicep and holding on tight. She moans deeper, pushing her body closer to mine and gripping her fingers into my hair. I want to do much more than kiss her, but right now, her lips are the source of my oxygen, and I want to breathe all of her in.

"Drew..." she releases on a moan.

"Mm?"

"Your wand is stabbing my groin," she says against my lips.

Our lips part as I burst out in surprise laughter. "Excuse me?"

She leans back and grabs something on the seat. "Your police wand." She holds it up.

"Shit. Sorry." I take it from her and throw it in the back.

"Any other police equipment hiding in here?" she asks, biting her lower lip.

"No, which I'm *highly* regretting right now."

She chuckles, and I see a faint blush rise on her cheeks.

"I could never forget something like that, but let's say I did. Would you refresh my memory?"

"Well, Deputy," she drawls in her Southern accent. "I think I could do that for you."

Arriving back to the house, it's pitch black inside, and neither of us reaches for the lights. My hands and lips are back on her before the door slams shut. She reaches for my shirt and pulls it up, tossing it to the floor. We collide once again, and she stumbles over her heels, and before she can throw them off, I lift her up and wrap her legs around my waist.

I blindly walk through the house, careful to avoid the kitchen table and bookshelves. She giggles as I trip over one of her boots she left out.

"This is exactly why I tell you to put your damn shoes away," I mutter, kicking them away.

"Sorry, I didn't realize they'd be a sex hazard." She chuckles, arching her hips and feeling the hard growth between us. *She's fucking killing me.*

"Tripping and falling on our asses hazard," I correct.

She tightens her grip, and I can feel my cock pressing against her leg. Walking into Courtney's room, I set her down on the bed when I feel the side of the mattress against my knees. She scoots back, allowing me to lean over her as our lips meet. Her hands explore my body, and as much as I want to do the same, I can't let this go too far.

We lie on her bed, our legs tangled together when she reaches for the button on my jeans.

"Court, wait," I say, grabbing her hand in mine. I press my forehead against hers and inhale. "Please don't take this the wrong way, but we can't have sex tonight."

Her hand drops. "What?"

I'm so kicking myself in the balls for this.

"We can't rush this," I say, hoping she'll understand. "I just got out of a relationship, and I don't want this to be a rebound or mean any less because of it."

"Drew, we've been friends for years. Roommates for almost two. I don't think you can really suggest that we rushed it."

"This—whatever this is between us—is brand new. We were drunk when we first jumped into bed together, and believe me, it was fucking amazing, but if we're going to try and make it work between us, I want it to be based on something other than sex."

"Are you willing to counteroffer?" she asks, pressing her lips against my neck, making me second-guess myself. "Or perhaps a compromise?"

I groan. "There's really no compromising when it comes to having or not having sex."

"Well, what kind of sex are we talking about? Oral? Penetration? Anal?"

"Jesus Christ," I choke out. "All kinds. Well, maybe not oral." I grin.

She pulls back, and from the glow of the moon and streetlights, I can see the outline of her face. "You're killing me here."

I tilt my head and smile. "It'll be worth it."

She sighs. "If I were a guy, I'd have the biggest case of blue balls right now."

Nodding, I say, "Trust me, I know. My whole body feels fucking blue right now."

She laughs and we lie back on her pillows, her head resting under my chin. She places her arm over my chest and begins tracing over my tattoo.

"I've always wondered about this one," she says, following the music notes that run from the top of my shoulder down to the middle of my pec. "Is there a significant meaning to it?"

I nod, smiling as I remember all the work that went into the finished product. "A buddy of mine sketched it out for me junior year of college." The treble clef is formed into a crazy eight design with four sets of notes on it. "He was obsessed with the song Highway to Hell and played it constantly when he would study for a big test, and at first it was annoying as fuck, but then it started amping me up and making me feel really good. Once I started training harder in the gym, I'd play that song to get fired up. It was the first time music inspired my decision to go to the police academy after graduation. So, I told him I needed a music drawing for a tattoo, and once he finished, I had it done."

"I've never heard you play that song before," she says, tracing her finger over one of the notes.

"I only listen to it when I'm lifting weights at the gym or running. It's a good song to get pumped up to."

"Hm...good to know. Maybe I'll play it when I'm doing my yoga."

I chuckle, part of me certain she's still tipsy. I move to my side and face her, brushing the hair off her forehead and seeing how tired her eyes look. "You should get some sleep. Tomorrow's a workday, after all." I grin.

"And it's Friday," she adds, looking up at me. "You still going to bring me lunch, Deputy?"

"It's my favorite part of the week." I kiss her forehead. "I wouldn't miss it for anything."

COURTNEY

Waking up in Drew's arms is a feeling I can't quite describe. We stayed up talking, and when we weren't talking, we were kissing and touching, and when things got too heated, he'd pull back and redirect us. I understand the reasoning of not wanting to rush things; I don't want to feel like a rebound considering they were dating just a couple weeks ago, but being around him makes me want to do things to him. Bad things.

But I trust him, and the logical part of me knows we're being smart. However, the not so logical part of me wants to rip my clothes off and test his true willpower.

I know in my heart that if this is what it takes to build a solid relationship with him, I'll play by his rules. *For now.* But that doesn't mean I have to make it easy for him.

Getting out of bed for work is nearly impossible. Drew's hair is sprawled over my pillow, and his body is so close to mine, I can feel the warmth from his skin.

"You're going to be late," he mutters, his eyes staying closed. His lips turn up into a knowing smirk.

"I hate you so much right now," I groan, crawling back into his side.

"Lies," he teases. "You're thinking of ways to get me naked right now."

"Well, I've been doing that for the past three years," I admit. "However, a joint shower wouldn't break any rules." I glance at him and grin. "You said no sex. You never said we couldn't be naked at the same time."

He coughs out in laughter and rolls over to his side, facing me. "I figured it was implied."

"Well, implied or not, there were no rules saying *I* couldn't be naked." My lips tilt up as he arches a brow at me. I sit up, kneeling on the bed and pull my shirt off, revealing the black lacy bra underneath. He lays on the bed, his arms folded behind his head with ankles crossed as he enjoys the show.

"There. Now we're even," I say. We can both be shirtless and suffer.

"All right." He begins unbuttoning his jeans. "I can play this game, too." He pulls them all the way off and kicks them to the floor.

"These were *your* rules, Deputy. If you want to play, I'm all in," I say with a wide smile, then remove the rest of my clothing until I'm only in my panties and bra.

"You saying I'll be the first to crack?" He raises both of his eyebrows and watches me gaze down his chest and abs.

"I've abstained from sex for *months*. I have some pretty strong willpower. Not to mention, I've lived in the same house as you for years and held back on jumping your bones every time you walked around in only a towel."

"You say that like it's a bad thing." He smiles.

"You could've covered up once in a damn while. Or actually, no, I'm glad you didn't." I laugh. "I still have more willpower than you."

"Is that so? I've seen you devour a six-pack of donuts in less than two minutes."

I burst out laughing. I push him onto his back and straddle him, feeling him hard underneath me. I really should've thought this through.

I lean over until my lips almost touch his. His hands grip the outside of my thighs, holding me tightly. "That's not the only thing my mouth can devour in two minutes."

He flips us over so fast, I scream as he towers over me and pins me down to the bed.

"Damn you and that mouth of yours."

I suck in my lower lip and try to hold back my laughter. "It's known for getting me in trouble."

He presses his lips to mine and wraps his arms around me, lowering down my back and underneath my panties. He releases a moan as he squeezes my ass cheeks, and I arch my hips to press against him. Feeling his cock rub against me drives me insane.

Pushing his hips against mine, he makes sure I know just how aroused he is right now. Our tongues and hands go wild, desperate to feel the other, both fighting our self-control.

Grinding our bodies together, his cock presses against the fabric of my panties and the way my body shivers in response makes it impossible to back away.

"You have to tell me to stop," he murmurs against my lips. "I want to fuck you so bad, Courtney." *Good God…yes!*

"I'm not saying no," I remind him.

"You have to." His mouth moves down my jaw, and he sucks on my neck. "You feel too good."

I lower my hand down his body, feeling the hard edges of his stomach and slide my hand into his boxer shorts. He's so hard and thick; I can feel the veins bulging against my fingertips.

"You aren't exactly persuading me when you're carrying around a weapon this size in your shorts."

I feel him smile against my neck as he moves his lips to my ear. "I knew it."

His words confuse me. "Knew what?"

"Your willpower sucks." He chuckles. "You lose, sweetheart."

He's still hard and throbbing in my palm. If this is how he wants to play, I'm game.

"I don't think so, Deputy." I look up into his lust-filled eyes. I stroke his cock in my hand, feeling it pulsate faster as I move my hand up and down his shaft. "You come, *you* lose."

"No fucking way." His eyes roll as his head falls back. "There's no man on this earth that wouldn't come with you touching it like that."

I move my hand faster, increasing the pressure on the tip.

"Fuck, Courtney. You have to stop," he growls, arching his hips. "Fuck it." He grabs my hips and slips his hand inside my panties, finding my clit within seconds. "You come before me, *you* lose."

"Or we could find a way for the both of us to win?" I suggest, hopeful. His mouth covers mine in a heated battle of who's going to crack first.

The alarm on my phone goes off, making both of us jump. "Dammit," I mutter, reaching to turn it off. It slips off the nightstand and continues its loud assault on the floor.

I roll over and reach for it, my body falling off the bed just as Drew grabs my thighs and catches me. "That was close," he says, attempting to pull me back.

"Damn phone fell under the bed." I pat my hand on the

floor, trying to reach underneath. I finally grab it and hit the snooze button. "Got it."

He doesn't help me up, rather he pushes my legs apart and begins kissing up my thigh. My hand releases the phone as his kisses make their way up to my panty line.

"What are you doing?" I whimper, my eyes fluttering closed as I try to regain my balance.

"Just marking you with my mouth," he says, sliding a finger inside my panties and rubbing along my slit. "You always wake up this wet in the morning?" I hear the amusement in his voice.

"This isn't playing fair," I moan, pressing my hips down on his hand. "You can't touch me if I can't touch you."

"Those weren't in the rulebook."

"Rulebook?" I groan. "You're making it up as you go along."

He laughs, pressing a finger against my clit and making small circular motions. "And so far, it's working out in my favor." He slides his finger inside, and I feel his lips closing in on me. He's repositioned his face underneath my hips, giving him the perfect angle at my pussy.

"You're a damn cheater," I hiss, grinding my hips down on his mouth. He wraps both arms around my legs and positions my body so I'm practically sitting on his face. "You're one of those dirty cops, aren't you?" I taunt.

I feel his lips smile against me and shiver. "You say that like it's a bad thing."

Before I can respond, he slides his tongue inside, and I lose all my coherent thoughts. His mouth devours me as he releases a throaty moan. I fist my fingers in his hair and clench my jaw as he takes complete control. His tongue is doing things to me that make me grind my hips on him harder and faster until I can no longer take it. I lose myself in him as my body shakes against his lips and I release on his tongue.

Once my heartbeat finds a steady rhythm again, we lie on the bed together.

"Guess I won't need to make breakfast today," he says with a guilty smirk.

"You're a smug asshole." I pretend to pout.

"For a girl who just screamed out my name and came on my face, you're a little moody," he quips.

"I so hate you right now."

"Don't be a sore loser. Better luck next time." He turns toward me and presses a sweet kiss on my lips.

I shake my head at him with a knowing smile. "I see how we're playing now."

Brushing the hair away from my face, he wraps the loose strands behind my ear. "Does that mean you'll be bringing your A game?" He cocks a brow, mocking me.

"You may have won this round, Deputy. But don't count your chickens just yet."

I'm over forty-five minutes late for work, and I'm so pissed about it. I'm never late, but considering the reasons, I think today can be an exception. No one dares to say anything about it, but I see the dirty looks they're giving me. But I can't even care today because I woke up with Drew Fisher in my bed.

Once I get settled in, I check my email and see Viola has

responded to my last message. *Shit*. I'm going to have to update her. *Again.*

To: Courtney Bishop
From: Viola King
Subject: Future Dead Man

Court,

Sorry it's been a few days! It's ahhh-mazing here! They also have *really* comfortable beds here, if you get what I mean. So, first things first. Drew is a Grade A idiot for going back to Mia. He's also mental if he's claiming he can't remember. I'm going to kick his ass so far when I get back you'll need to find a new roommate. I just might tell Mia where she can stick that whip.

Okay, more on that later.

The tour was incredible. And I'm 100% Gryffindor, you bitch. Don't insult me like that. I'm bringing back the best souvenirs for you, too. (Harry Potter themed, of course)!

I miss you, too. We'll have a catch-up date when I get home!

Love you!

-Lola

P.S. I'm truly sorry he hurt you. I hate him for you.

Shit. Shit. Shit.

She's going to have my head for not emailing her back

172

with a proper update, but I'm afraid if I don't, she'll send an owl to claw his eyes out.

To: Viola King
From: Courtney Bishop
Subject: Hold back the torches!

Lola,
There are so many reasons I love you and being so protective of me is one of them, so thank you for always having my back, even when it has to do with your brother. However, there's been a *teeny* misunderstanding on my part. (Who said I was rational?)

The **GOOD** news: Mia is out of the picture! FOR GOOD! (Fucking finally!)

The **BAD** news: Your brother still won't have sex with me. (Okay, this is really just bad news for me, not you.)

The **GREAT** news: He did remember our night together & now we're seeing where it goes. I guess? Basically, I threw myself at him and he said he wanted to take things slow since he just ended a relationship. (Seriously, my poor vagina has been so neglected it's taken up crochet as a hobby.) I feel like I can't really be mad about him wanting to take things slow and really making sure it works out between us, but Jesus Christ. Every time I look at him, my body is ready to launch at him like a spaceship.

So with all that, we will be picking you up from the airport Sunday morning! I can't wait to hug you! I hope you can still walk after all the sex you two have been having. I'm not carrying you.

See you soon!!

Love you

-Court

Once I hit send and finish up a few weekly projects, Drew is due any moment to bring us lunch. I hope whatever it is, it's injected with ten pounds of caffeine so I can actually stay awake to finish the rest of my shift.

When he arrives, his hair is down to one side, showing off his long, dark locks in the middle. I love when he pulls it up, but my panties nearly combust when he leaves it down.

"Are you gawking?" He tilts his head to one side, eyeing me.

"I'm looking at you like I've always looked at you," I reply with a smirk. "You've just never noticed it before."

He smiles as he unloads the bag. Inside are two pieces of cake.

"You brought us cake for lunch?"

"I brought *you* cake for lunch. The other one I plan to save for later."

"For later?" I ask with hesitation.

"Remember when I said you smelled like buttercream?"

I nod.

"Now you'll taste like it, too."

I take a longer lunch than normal, but I can't even feel guilty about it today. As I'm sitting at my desk, Jayden comes over and stares at me with a big cheesy grin on his face.

"Yes?"

"Girl, did I just see you locking lips with Drew Fisher?"

I smile, not meeting his eyes. "You sure did."

CHAPTER SIXTEEN

DREW

I DELIVER lunch to Courtney and can't stop smiling the entire way home as the sweetness of her lips linger on mine. I wished I could've captured her and spent the rest of the afternoon together, but I know she'd never skip, especially with Travis gone. Later that night, I cook dinner, and it becomes a battle of the wits. It's hard to keep my hands off her body when she's wearing little shorts and a sports bra.

Throughout the weekend, we're too busy teasing and enjoying each other. Randomly when I'd look at her, my heart would beat a little harder. Each time we'd touch and when our lips pressed together, my body would instantly react. With Courtney, it's different, and as hard as it is, I don't want to rush this. But she's determined to watch me crack under pressure.

Saturday night, we decide to stay in and watch action movies with tons of explosions, but this time I hold her in my arms. It's almost frightening how right it feels. All this time, she's been right here waiting for me, supporting my choices, regardless if they were the right ones or not. Eventually, she falls asleep in my arms, and I carry her to bed. I lay her down against the mattress, and she lets out a little moan when her head hits the pillow.

"Don't go," she whispers sweetly and reaches for me. I lean down until our lips connect and smile. I don't want to go, and it's hard to say no to her. Already I'm ruined.

"I'm not," I say, crawling in her bed, and she lays her head against my chest as we fall asleep.

Sunday comes early, earlier than I expected, and I wake up without an alarm. I feel like I'm dreaming as I glance over and see Courtney. I'm not used to being like this with her. I let out a yawn and press my eyes tightly together before opening them again. I'm not thrilled to be awake because I have to be at work at three. Then again, I did promise Viola I'd be at the airport when she and Travis arrived home.

"Court," I whisper, "we have to get going so we're not late."

"Mm, just twenty more minutes. My alarm hasn't gone off yet." She moves her body close to mine and her eyes flutter open. "I'm not dreaming, right?" Her hand trails down my stomach until she has me in her hand. "Nope." She smiles, stroking my cock.

I release a groan, knowing I've got to take control before I lose it completely.

"Now who's not playing fair?" I ask, pulling her tighter into my arms.

"Your rules aren't fair, so we're even." She gives me a smirk before wrapping her leg over mine and pinning me down.

I dig my fingers into her hips, and she lifts an eyebrow before slowly rocking against me.

"You don't want to play this game, trust me," I say.

She laughs before bending down and kissing me. "You'll lose every time."

She holds back a smile knowing she's already won because every minute I'm with her, I'm ready to throw my logic out the window.

"I'm going to shower; you're more than welcome to join me, Deputy...if you can handle it." She stands and turns and looks at me with a smile on her face before strutting to the bathroom. Before walking out of the room, she turns around and bites her bottom lip. I shake my head at her but can't hold back the smile that fills my face.

"You're so bad!" I say loudly enough for her to hear as she walks away and her laughter echoes down the hallway. My body is begging me to go to her, but my head is saying no. It's hard enough to keep my hands off her, and just the thought of her wet little body makes me hard. As the water comes on, I know there's no use fighting the urge. I stand up, walk to the bathroom and open the door. She instantly laughs. Steam from the shower rises to the ceiling, and the bathroom mirror is already fogged.

I slide my jogging pants down my body and step out of them. Courtney peeks around the side of the shower curtain then glances down at my hardness.

"You're fully loaded, Deputy." She smirks; her wet, blonde hair is slicked back. I take a few steps forward, peel the curtain back, and step inside. The hot water cascades down my back, and I can't take my eyes from her.

"Damn, you're so beautiful," I praise. Her blue eyes meet mine, and I'm lost in her gaze for a moment. "And I've never been so fucking jealous of a bar of soap in my life." Soap suds spill across her breasts and I realize now that I'm in the shower with her, my willpower is dwindling.

"Oops," she says, dropping the soap on purpose and bends over, ass toward me, taking her time picking it up, teasing me to the extreme.

"*Goddammit*," I whisper, and she knows she's getting to me when she looks over her shoulder at me and pulls her lip into her mouth. Once she stands, I grab the soap from her and rub it between my hands then begin to wash her back. I massage her shoulders, wash down the length of her back, and she lets out a small moan.

"Your hands… They feel so fucking good," she says, turning to face me. She takes a step forward, walking completely over the invisible line I've drawn and glances down at me. Confidently, she grips her hand around my shaft and slides up and down. The sensation of her touching me is almost too much to handle. She's so fucking perfect and sexy, and I love how confident she is in her own skin.

"You can tell me to stop," she whispers, her eyes trailing up my body until they meet mine. Those are the same eyes that have looked at me over the years, and the message has always been the same. *I want you.* Only this time, I recognize that look and welcome it because I'm looking at her the same way. Without words, she begs to please me. I should tell her to stop, that we shouldn't, but the words don't come. It feels too right to be wrong, and I find myself questioning everything about us. Courtney is my best friend, my roommate, my partner in crime, and now she's *mine*. I don't know how this happened or how we got here, but I don't want this to end.

Courtney starts slow, using the water of the shower to her advantage, as she slides her hand up and down my cock. I let out a moan, and she increases her speed, rolling her thumb across the head. My breathing increases, and it's all the permission she needs to continue. She cups my balls in her other hand and continues to stroke me until I'm close. Before I can even say a word, Courtney drops to her knees and places me in her mouth.

"Court …"

She pulls me from her mouth and licks the tip, driving me fucking crazy. "What's that, Deputy? You want me to stop?" she purrs, knowing the answer to that question. I grab a fist of her hair and gently tug it where I can look into her baby blues.

"I want you so fucking bad," I growl. *"Christ."*

"Mm." She cups my balls in her palm and doesn't hesitate to place me back in her warm mouth.

I'm teetering on the edge, and she knows because my entire body tenses. She runs her hands up my thighs, and that's when I lose it. Courtney takes me deep in her mouth. Her eyes flutter closed, and she moans against me, swallowing me down.

Once she stands, I pull her into my arms. I've never experienced anything like that with anyone. Emotions soar through me, and they are almost too much to comprehend. Wrapping her arms around me, I hold her until the water cools down.

"God, Court…where have you been all of my life?"

She pulls back and looks up at me. I run my fingers through her wet hair and rest my palm against her cheek. Moving in closer, she speaks against my lips before I can kiss her. "I've been waiting for you."

COURTNEY

Is it bad that I'm falling hard for Drew? I know we're supposed to be taking this slow, but I want to be with him every free minute I have. I've always loved hanging out with him, but having no boundaries, being able to touch him and say whatever I want whenever I want feels like a dream. For years, I've imagined what it would be like to be with him on a more emotional level, so each day that I am, I wait to wake up from this dream, but fortunately, I don't.

After our little fun in the shower, we get dressed and head to the airport. We take the truck because Viola and Travis—plus their giant suitcases—would be squished in the Jeep. The whole way to the airport, Drew holds my hand in his, and it feels so natural. Goosebumps cover my body each time his thumb brushes against mine.

We pull up to the airport, and I keep glancing down at my phone waiting for Viola to text me. As soon as the text message arrives, I squeal.

"They just landed and are getting their bags," I tell Drew and he smiles at me. "Oh, and I told Viola about us."

His eyes widen. "You did what?"

At first, I think he's going to be upset, and I worry if he wanted us to be kept a secret. Before my insecurities take over, Drew cracks a smile and laughs. "Actually, I figured you would. I'm not ashamed of you, Court. I don't give a fuck who knows."

"Even Mia?" I ask, calling his bluff.

"*Especially* Mia."

My heart leaps with joy, and I scoot closer to him. Leaning over, he gives me a slow, sensual kiss, pulling my bottom lip into his mouth and sucking. His tongue brushes against mine, and when I close my eyes, I'm lost in the taste of him. I climb onto his lap and feel him harden beneath my ass as his hand trails up my shirt and grabs my breast. Before it gets too hot and heated, Viola and Travis open the passenger doors, and we both sit there with wide eyes. Drew nonchalantly removes his hand from under my shirt, but it's a little too late for that.

"You said you wouldn't believe it until you saw it," Viola says to Travis. "So, now you've seen it."

Travis laughs and mumbles something to her. She blushes, and I'm sure it's something dirty.

I crawl off Drew's lap and can't stop smiling. I get out of the truck and so does Drew. Viola gives me a big hug and Travis and Drew load everything into the back.

"I've missed you so much," she says out loud, and then whispers, "and you have to tell me *everything*."

"I plan on it. Even the parts you don't want to hear," I whisper back.

We release our embrace, and she gives me a death glare then smiles so big. I know she's happy for Drew and me. It's what we've always wanted.

On the way to Travis and Viola's house, they tell us about the trip. London sounds amazing, and I make them promise to bring me the next time they go. We hear about the castles and Universal Studios and how they took a train to Paris to see the Eiffel Tower. They're both gleaming with happiness, and I'm overly happy for them and excited they're finally home. I've missed Viola and Travis being a smartass at work, and I even miss the kids. For a moment, I think everything will go back to normal, but when Drew grabs my hand in his, in front of them, I realize that this is quickly becoming my new normal.

Before we arrive at their house, Viola speaks up. "So, when are you two getting married? Ginny and James need a cousin, and we're not having any more children."

I turn around and glare at Viola and Drew tenses, speaking in a matter-of-fact tone. "We're not rushing, Vi. Go get those tubes untied."

Travis quickly changes the subject. "When should I bring the check by for the annual benefit?"

"Shit," Drew says and glances over at me and his mood shifts. Now I'm confused.

"What?" I say, wanting to know what his reaction meant. My heart drops, and for a split-second I think he's going to tell me something terrible like Mia will be there or he's going with someone else. Both stupid thoughts, but his hesitation is way too long.

"I kind of, sort of volunteered you to bake some of your amazing muffins." Drew gives me a boyish grin, and my heart skips a beat. I relax because it's not so bad, but after I realize what he said, my eyes widen.

"You did what?"

"I forgot to tell you last week. I'm sorry. I can call the chief and let him know you can't do it. But they all love your muffins, and he asked, so I thought…"

I let out a deep breath. "No, that's okay. I'll do it. It's just a few pans. But you're making it up to me." I give him a really evil grin, and he glances over at me knowing exactly what I'm referring to.

Nervously laughing, he says, "I actually need five hundred."

"Drew!" Viola and I say in unison.

Now Travis is really laughing hard.

"Five hundred muffins? That's going to take me days, which is going to be a lot of making up for you to do."

"I'm up for the challenge." Drew's voice is deep and throaty.

"I don't think you are," I say, forgetting Travis and Viola are in the backseat, until I hear Travis chuckle again.

"Almost reminds me of us." Travis looks at Viola.

"Yeah, but I'd be punching you in the balls for doing that to me."

"Who says I'm not going to punch him in the balls?" I ask with a laugh.

Viola gives me a high five as Drew grabs himself. "Ladies, please leave my balls out of this."

"You deserve it." Viola laughs at him.

"She's still pissed she was sorted into Hufflepuff," Travis says and Viola slaps his hand that's resting on her knee.

"You're an asshole. You know for a fact I was Gryffindor. You Slytherin!"

"I knew it!" I let out a loud laugh, and we pull up to the house giggling like teenagers.

"I'm going to *Slytherin you…*"

"You're relentless," Viola mutters, then gives him a kiss.

We all get out of the truck and help them unload everything. Drew and Viola's mom and stepdad agreed to watch the kids for the week, and I'm sure they were left with a list ten pages long. I grab a suitcase, and so does Drew, and we walk inside trailing behind Travis and Viola. As soon as their mom sees all of us she squeals with James in her arms. Viola grabs him and gives him sweet kisses and tells him how much she loves and missed him. Ginny runs up to her, and I take the opportunity to steal James from her arms. She huffs, and I tell her not to be stingy. She rolls her eyes at me and lets me continue.

"There's my little heartbreaker," I say, and he coos at me then wraps my hair in his fist.

"I've missed you so much. Almost as much as Mommy," I tell him, pulling my hair from his superhero-tight grasp. I kiss his cheek again, and he smiles.

Viola and Travis are talking about the trip, and I watch as Ginny twists out of Viola's arms and reaches for Travis. He gives her a big hug and tells her how pretty she is. Going into supermom mode, Viola rubs dirt off her face without breaking a sentence. They are such a beautiful family, and I hope one day I have the same.

Drew leans against the doorway, studying me with James. His eyes soften as he walks over to us. "Stealing my woman, are you?"

Drew is so gentle when he smooths his hand over James' head, but I can't help thinking about him calling me *his* woman.

"James loves Aunt Courty, huh. Love, love, love. Tell Uncle Drew I'm yours." He leans his head against my chest, and my heart melts.

James says gibberish over my shoulder to Drew, which causes him to burst out laughing.

"I think he just told me off in baby talk."

Viola can't stand it another minute and takes James from my arms. "Oh, my gosh. I think he just pooped."

"I have that effect on men," I say. "Look, your brother just pooped his pants too."

Drew pulls me into his arms and squeezes me tight as he laughs. "You're going to pay for that."

"I'll gladly volunteer as tribute," I say, not realizing anyone else can hear us.

Viola stops talking to her mom and turns around. "Hunger Games, Court? Really? Not in my Harry Potter household."

"When it comes to your brother, I'll always volunteer first." I give her a wink.

"Yep. Just threw up in my mouth." But Viola is smiling when she says it, and I know she's joking.

Larry and Carla walk over and give Drew a big hug.

"So, how are you two?" his mom perks up with excitement. She's always loved me since the first day she met me. Drew's arm is wrapped around my shoulder, and he doesn't hesitate or move his arm from me.

"Still roommates."

She gives him a head nod, not believing a word he's saying. But honestly, it's complicated to explain because we're on a trial run. It would be hard to tell anyone what we are exactly because we're not anything, we're taking it slow.

"Okay kids, we're going to head home. We're already packed and ready to go. Want to give the newlyweds some alone time," Carla says with a smile.

"I'm sure they've had enough of that," Drew chimes in after he gives his mom a hug and Larry a handshake before they leave.

"Never," Travis yells from the kitchen.

I give Viola another big hug. "Want to come over Thursday and help me bake all these effing muffins?"

I turn around and give Drew a glare from hell.

"You might want to call Kayla to help too." Viola glares at Drew as well.

"The both of you together are scary as hell. Seriously."

"I love you," I tell her and she tells me back. "Bye, Travis!" I yell to him.

"Bye, Court! Bye, Drew! Protect your balls!"

We walk to the truck and Drew walks over to my side. Before he opens my door, he pins me up against it. The cool metal against my back makes me shiver. Grabbing my hands, he moves them over my head until I'm pinned between his strong body and the truck. But I'm not complaining one bit.

"Oh my God," I whisper before his lips crash into mine. I'm flooded with emotions as his tongue swirls with mine. Our mouths separate and I feel lost without them, as if they are my compass. Trailing kisses up my neck, he reaches my ear and sucks and licks the shell. He has no idea how much I love that until a moan escapes my lips.

"I'm up for the challenge, are you?" he whispers, letting go of my hands and I'm instantly reminded of the five hundred muffins Drew volunteered me to make for Saturday.

"Well, you do owe me *big time*."

"I know," he kisses me again, and I don't ever want him to stop.

Wrapping my arms around his neck, I pull his mouth close to mine.

"Good. Challenge accepted."

CHAPTER SEVENTEEN

DREW

I HATE that I have to go back to work already. It was nice having a few days off and getting to be with Courtney as much as possible, but it still doesn't seem real.

By the time we return from taking Viola and Travis home, I have to get ready to leave. Courtney pouts and it's so damn cute.

"Can't I come with you? I'll sit in the back quietly," she pleads, wrapping her arms around me. "I'll keep all the criminals in check."

"I have no doubt you would." I kiss her forehead. "I'll come in and tuck you in when I get home."

"You better stay and sleep with me." She tightens her grip.

"I will. It'll be the only time I can lay with you without getting groped," I tease.

"Don't get used to it." She smirks.

I kiss her goodbye and head out, feeling something I've never felt before. I can't stop thinking about her, wanting her, missing her. I'm completely obsessed.

"So, since I hadn't heard from you, I'm guessing Thursday night went well?" Logan asks as soon as we get into the patrol car. I'd forgotten all about texting him.

"You could say that," I say with a shit-eating grin, adjusting the seat.

"So, without sounding like a chick, are you going to tell me what happened?"

I laugh at him. "Well, basically, we're together and seeing how it goes."

"Seeing how it goes?"

"Yeah, we have a history. Neither of us wants to jeopardize our friendship, but the feelings are mutual, so we're taking it slow."

"Good for you, man. I always thought she looked at you differently."

I nod. "I was an idiot."

"At least it's worked out now, though, right?"

"Yeah. I'm pretty happy about it." I smile. "So, you going to tell me how you and Kayla conned me in the first place?"

"Figured that out, did you?" He laughs. "It was her idea."

"So, what's going on with that? You guys a thing yet?"

He shakes his head. "No. That wouldn't be fair to her."

"Why don't you let her make that decision?"

"Several failed relationships allow me to make that decision now."

He doesn't offer anything else, and I don't push for more. I know he's a private person, especially when it comes to Skylar, but I wish he'd open his heart and let Kayla in.

Once Logan and I drive patrol for a few hours, we break and stop for food. I grab my phone and smile when I see Courtney's name.

Courtney: I'm lying in your bed naked right now. Just thought you should know.

Drew: You're killing me. Not fair.

Courtney: I can smell your cologne all over the sheets. It's driving me INSANE!

Drew: Maybe you should do something about that since I'm not there to do it for you.

Courtney: I just might.

Drew: Why do you enjoy torturing me?

Courtney: Because it was your idea to withhold sex from me and now you must pay for it.

I can't stop the outburst of laughter that releases as I read her message. Logan narrows his eyes at me and shakes his head. *I know, man. I'm doomed.*

Drew: I'm starting to regret ever saying the word no to you. I bet you were a handful as a child.

Courtney: I have four older brothers. No one dared to say no to me.

Drew: Should've figured. Spoiled rotten :)

Courtney: Well, since you won't do the job, I'm doing it myself.

Drew: Bullshit.

She sends me a picture of her vibrator. *Jesus Christ.*

Drew: I knew you had toys in there!

She stops responding before we have to leave the restaurant and get back to work. I drop Logan off at the station to work on some unfinished paperwork, so I respond to some calls on my own.

Courtney: Park and meet me.

It takes me a minute to figure out what she's talking about and then it hits me.

Drew: 24th behind the alley

Courtney: Be there in 10.

As long as I don't get any calls, I should be safe to park and wait for her. I'm not sure what she has up her sleeve, but knowing Courtney, I know it'll be against the rules.

"Well, hey there, Deputy," she says in a thicker accent than normal. "You look pretty good sitting here in your uniform."

I pretend to dust something off my chest. "Is that so? What's a pretty lady like you doing out in the dark anyway?"

"Came to show my man what he's been missing out on." She tilts the corner of her lip up.

Taking a step back, I then realize she's wearing an oversized coat with it tied around her waist. I watch as she slowly unties it and opens it up, revealing what she's wearing underneath.

I swallow.

She's wearing *nothing*.

"Jesus Christ, Courtney," I mutter, looking around to make sure no one else is getting the view.

She closes it back up with a sultry smile and leans over the door window. "You wanted to play the game, Deputy," she reminds me. "I'm just playing by your rules."

I wrap my hand around the back of her neck and pull her lips toward me. Kissing her never feels like enough.

"You're a dirty player," I mutter. "I'm making plans to get you back, just so *you* know."

I kiss her goodbye and immediately feel sad when I watch her walk away.

As soon as I return home, I anticipate seeing Courtney in her bed, but to my delight, she's in *my* bed asleep. I brought home an extra pair of handcuffs, and I plan on using them.

Knowing she'll hit the snooze button at least twice on her phone, I fall asleep with her in my arms and keep my handcuffs on the nightstand. Once it goes off, I know that's my chance.

She rolls over, hits the button, and rolls back, all without opening her eyes. I grin, knowing in just a moment she'll be wide fucking awake.

I slowly remove my arm from underneath her and stand on the side of the bed. Placing her arms above her head, I grab one pair of handcuffs and lock her wrist to the railing on my headboard. She twitches slightly, and I pause, waiting to make sure she doesn't wake up.

Once she settles, I grab her other arm and cuff her wrist to the railing so now both of her arms are handcuffed to the headboard. I almost feel bad for how she's about to wake up, but then I remember all the tormenting she's done to me and I know this is how the game is being played.

Walking to the edge of the bed, I lift the covers up slightly and crawl under them. I slide my hands up to her hips and pull her pajama shorts down with her panties. She begins to rustle when I spread her legs apart and begin kissing up her thighs.

"Drew..." she moans, and I smile.

I lick my tongue up her lips and circle her clit. She rustles some more and then the loud clank of the handcuffs echo off the headboard railings.

"What the hell?" she squeals. "You handcuffed me?"

I slide my tongue deeper inside her and don't come up for air until I taste her against my lips. Her hips rock against my mouth, and I know she's going insane not being able to put her hands on me.

"Dammit, Drew..." she hisses, arching her hips. "You cheater!"

I smile against her pussy and continue devouring her. The cuffs clank against the railings some more, and I know I've definitely won this round. I spread her legs some more and slide a finger inside her as I suck on her clit.

"*Oh my God*," she moans, her hips rocking fast against my mouth. "Fuck, it's too much." I know she wants to run her hands through my hair and pull my mouth away and the fact that she can't is driving her insane.

"Seriously, Drew...oh my God. I can't," she pleads for

some relief, and I smile knowing I'm just about to give that to her.

Pressing my lips to her, licking and sucking, I slide my fingers inside until her body shakes against me and she releases a loud moan. Her body goes limp as I press gentle kisses along her thigh. Finally, I push the covers back and crawl up her body.

Her eyes are closed, and she's taking in short breaths.

"That was pure evil," she says, her chest rising and falling. "But I can't even hate you for it."

I smile and lean down to press a kiss along her jaw. "You forgot just who you were playing with, sweetheart."

Her eyes peel open, and she shakes her head at me. "Let's call a truce and forget all about the rules."

I laugh, kissing the top of her forehead. "Nice try. You need to get ready for work now."

Rolling her eyes at me, she clanks the cuffs against the railings again. "Are you going to remove these, or are they going to be my new accessory?"

"Hm…that's not a bad idea, actually." I smirk. "But these are just for my viewing pleasure."

COURTNEY

Thursday finally arrives, and I can't wait to see Drew after work. Although it's the muffin baking party and four other people will be around, it'll be like our first night with friends as a couple.

Viola and Travis are the first to arrive before I even make it home. Viola is here to help me, and Travis is here to watch Thursday Night Football with Drew.

Once I walk in, Drew has me up against the wall with his lips pressed to mine before I can even speak.

"Is this what you've had to suffer through when Travis and I got together?" I hear Viola ask in the background as Drew smiles against my lips.

"Do I need to remind you of the things I almost walked in on when the two of you were sneaking behind my back?" Drew looks over his shoulder and asks.

"You can't even be mad about that anymore." She sticks her tongue out.

He shrugs and looks back at me. "I've missed you." He tilts my chin up and places a soft kiss on my lips. "Let's kick them all out and climb back into bed."

I groan, loving that idea. "We could if someone hadn't volunteered me to bake a million muffins before Saturday."

"I promised I'd make it up to you," he reminds me. "Plus, just think of how good you'll smell," he says with a boyish grin.

I roll my eyes and laugh. "All right, I need to change and get started."

He finally releases me, and that's when I notice Ginny and James are both here.

"Ahh...it's my babies!" I swoop Ginny up in a massive bear hug. "Are you ready to bake some muffins?"

She smiles and chews on her finger. "Aunt Court will have to find you a little apron one of these days, so you don't get your clothes dirty."

Setting her back on her feet, I find Travis sitting on the couch with James and grab for him. "Don't feel too sad, James. You can bake with us when you're a little older." I wiggle my nose against his.

"Don't you dare. He's here to watch football with the boys," Travis informs me.

"He can learn to bake, too," I defend. "Don't you want your boy to be able to know how to take care of himself and be able to bake muffins for his kid's bake sales?"

"No, that's why he has a sister." He chuckles, and I slap him on the back of the head.

"Kidding, geez!" He covers his arms over his head.

I hand James off to Viola who's standing next to me with Ginny at her side. "Your husband is rude."

"Well, I didn't hate him for most of my childhood for nothing." She laughs.

"What was that, Courtney? You want to work overtime next week? And Saturday?" He tilts his head and eyes me over his shoulder.

I narrow my eyes at him and scowl. "I hope Viola punches you where the sun doesn't shine when you get back home."

"I don't know how anyone works with you two at the office bickering all day," Viola says, laying James over her chest.

"I wear earplugs and just smile when she talks." Travis snickers.

I roll my eyes at him and tell Viola to follow me back to my room.

"Thank you again for coming to help me. It's kind of nice having you guys here and knowing I can be around Drew at the same time. Feels like we're a real couple now."

"Because Travis and I are here?"

"No, because we get to be together around other people. Like when couples host dinner parties and whatever," I explain, digging around my closet for something to change into.

"Well, I honestly couldn't be happier for you two. I really thought you'd be in the friend-zone for life." She laughs and so do I. "I'm glad everything worked out."

"Me too." I smile, pulling a shirt off the hanger.

"Oh my God," Viola squeals, grabbing my attention. "There's my Book Beau that I thought I lost."

"No, I think you left it here a long time ago."

"Awesome, I've been needing that." She grabs it off my dresser and kisses it. "Wait, what's in here?"

My eyes pop open as I remember I had borrowed it for something else.

"Sweet Jesus," she says while laughing. "Is this your—" She pulls it out with just the tips of her fingers.

"Whoops, sorry." I grab the vibrator from her hand and casually throw it on my bed. "Forgot I was using it as my vibe holder."

"Ew, Court. Seriously!" She makes a disgusted face.

"What? It has nice padding, and it's discrete. It even has a cute pattern on it."

"You put your sex toy in my book sleeve!" she scolds. "It's for books, not for hiding your vibrators!" She holds the Book Beau out. "Take it. I can't put my paperbacks in there now."

Rolling my eyes at her, I take it from her hand. "Fine. But considering the print, it's kind of fitting for a Vibrator Beau." I flash a sly smile at her. She doesn't laugh. "Oh, come on! It's a bunch of wiener dogs! It's literally a wiener Beau."

"Courtney, I swear to God…"

"Hey, new marketing idea! The Universal Beau. Keep

your paperbacks and sex toys safe wherever you go! Or Bullet Beau. Storing your vibrating bullets since 2017."

"I'll make sure to pass on your genius idea," she deadpans, rolling her eyes at me, but we both know I'm on to something.

Once Kayla arrives, all the girls end up in the kitchen and the boys are in the living room screaming at the TV. Logan even stops by, and soon it's feeling like a triple-date.

"So, Logan being here…" I start, eyeing Kayla's reaction. "Is that okay?"

"Doesn't bother me," she says in a flat tone as she measures out some sugar. I know something's up with them, but she claims there's not. "He's made it perfectly clear he's not in a place to date right now, so there's really nothing I can do about it."

"But you like him," I say, grabbing the blueberries from the fridge. "Have you told him?"

"No. I mean, not directly, but I think I've made it pretty obvious."

"Trust me, obvious doesn't always work." I laugh, setting the blueberries down and grabbing the mixing bowl.

She chuckles and nods. "Well, he's not dating someone else; he's not dating *at all*."

"I wonder why," Viola asks, placing the muffin cups in the tins. "Is he maybe gay?"

"No!" Kayla bursts out, dropping the bag of sugar on the counter.

"How do you know? Maybe he hasn't even come to terms with it yet," Viola explains.

"I can't believe we're having this conversation," I say with amusement. "Maybe he's career focused right now, and when he's ready, he'll date. Until then, all you can do is be his friend," I say, knowing from experience.

"Yeah, I mean, I like talking to him and being around him, and it's just hard sitting there wondering if it's you he's just not into," she says, helping me add ingredients to the mixing bowl.

"He'd be crazy to not be into you, Kay," Viola adds. "You're smart, beautiful, funny. You're the whole package."

"Sometimes being the whole package can intimidate guys. Maybe you're too much for him," I tell her with a genuine smile.

"Yeah, you look like a sweet, quiet girl from the mountains and then once people get to know you, you're really this loudmouthed, high energetic person," Viola says. "Plus, with your dance background, I would imagine you're pretty flexible," she teases.

We all burst out laughing.

"Well, I did master the split leap when I was twelve, so you could say my flexibility is pretty strong." She smiles, proud.

"That reminds me," I say, getting my hand mixer out. "My yoga skills could use a little help. You'll have to come over and stretch me so I can actually do those poses."

"Oh, yeah totally. I could use some Zen." She gives me a cheeky smile, and I start mixing up our first batch.

Once halftime comes, the boys come in scouring for more snacks and beer. Drew drags me away into the hallway and assaults my lips again.

"Can we kick them out now?" he teases.

I giggle against his mouth. "Not yet. Lots of muffins to bake still."

"Dammit." He presses a soft kiss against my forehead. "I'm digging this apron," he says, plucking it between his fingers. "However, I'd love to see you in this apron and *only* the apron."

"I could probably arrange that for you, Deputy."

CHAPTER EIGHTEEN

DREW

THE CHIEF NEEDED EXTRA HELP, and I volunteered to work on Friday. It sucks because I wanted to stay home with Court, but when you're asked if you can work, the answer should always be yes. Part of me didn't want to answer the call, but I took it begrudgingly. By the time I get off shift on Friday, there are five hundred freshly-made muffins sitting on the counter in the kitchen in containers stacked practically to the ceiling. Smiling, I unbutton my shirt and untuck it, set my gun and badge on the table, and walk to Courtney's room. Cracking open the door, I notice she's not there. Knowing all too well where she is, I kick off my shoes and head toward my bedroom.

The warm glow of the light from the side lamp illuminates her face. I stand there for a second studying her soft features, and I wonder what I did to even deserve a chance with her. After I take off my belt and pants, I remove my socks and crawl into bed with her. When I lift the sheet, she's wearing absolutely nothing.

"I missed you," she says.

"Missed you, too. You smell delicious, like blueberries and sugar." I wrap my arm around her and kiss the softness of her neck.

"Your body's cold." She stiffens when I press my chest against her back.

"Then warm me up."

She presses her ass against me and I'm thinking of all the bad things I want to do, but I can tell she's exhausted. There were so many muffins that Travis gave her a paid day off; but I'm sure Viola had something to do with that.

"You owe me big time," she reminds me with a small laugh. Minutes later, I hear her breathing become more stable, and I know she's fallen back asleep.

"You've already got my heart," I whisper.

It's hard for me to fall asleep. There's too much running through my mind. By the time my body relaxes enough to sleep, it seems like the alarm instantly goes off. I wake exhausted and to an empty bed.

Once I sit up, Courtney comes in with two cups of coffee, just the way I like it—black. She hands me the cup, and I stand up to kiss her then yawn. She's already dressed in blue jeans and a black shirt that falls off her shoulders. I want to kiss every inch of her skin, and she notices.

"Get dressed, Deputy. We can't be late."

"We don't have twenty minutes?" I give her a smile.

"As much as I want to say yes, and I want to say yes *so* bad, we can't because being late makes my brain explode and Kayla's going to be waiting for us already."

I let out a small laugh. "Okay. You're going to regret it, though."

"I already do."

I put on a pair of jeans and a Sacramento PD polo that we wear for special events like this.

Courtney's eyes widen as I walk into the living room. She saunters over to me and runs her finger across the embroidered badge with my name below it on the top left breast of my shirt.

"Officer Fisher," she says slyly.

"How can I be at your service?"

She stands on her tiptoes and kisses me slow and sensual. When we break apart, she's breathing hard and staring at my lips. My heart is racing, and for a moment, I don't care about being late.

"Damn this! Can't we just stay home?" She sticks her bottom lip out and pouts.

"And eat five hundred muffins ourselves?"

"It wouldn't be the worst thing that could happen." She grins.

I pull her back to me and kiss her one last time before we load up the muffins in the truck.

On time, we drive over to the city park where the annual benefit for fallen officers is being held. It's an emotional time and reminds me of how inherently dangerous my job can be. At the Academy, it's ingrained into us that every day we put on that uniform, it could be our last. Regardless of the risk, I willingly took the oath to protect my community. Events like this bring that truth closer to home.

We arrive, and Kayla runs across the grass with a big smile on her face and grabs as many muffins as she can carry. I'm happy she's here, and I'm sure Logan is too, although he won't admit it.

"There you two are. It took forever for you to get here," she says excitedly.

Courtney laughs and rolls her eyes. "We're ten minutes early. How long have you been here?"

"An hour. I even helped set up our tent close to the festivities near the stage."

"Any sight of *Logan*?" Courtney drags his name out, and I can only imagine what they say about me. It makes me laugh at how fast they get lost in the conversation.

We drop off the first load of muffins and Logan comes over and helps us carry the rest. Kayla instantly perks up when she sees him and tries to make small talk. Surprisingly enough, he's actually responding. She's learning not to be so pushy, which is good. Logan's a hard shell to crack on a good day.

"This is a shit ton of muffins," he says, carrying as many as he can. "You should feel guilty for forcing them to make these."

"It wasn't so bad," Kayla says, giving me a wink as she sets them down on the table.

Courtney laughs as she neatly spreads hundreds of muffins out. They smell like heaven.

"Oh, he's going to pay." Lifting her eyes to meet mine, I know exactly what she's referring to. I swallow hard, and Logan shakes his head with a smile on his face.

Several other women walk over and help Courtney and Kayla. They are naturals at getting involved and helping wherever it's needed. I make a mental note to volunteer them for double the amount of muffins next year, even though they might all kill me.

The crowd begins filing in, and I know the event will start any minute.

Right on cue, the chief pulls Logan and me away. The opening ceremony is about to start, and Logan was asked to say a few words after the introduction. A few weeks ago, he pulled me to the side and asked if I'd join him on stage as his partner and his brother in blue.

Logan's previous partner was one of the officers killed on duty years ago, and it only made sense for him to speak of his character. The families of all fallen officers were asked to attend, and we would be presenting them with plaques for the sacrifices they've endured. All the funds raised today would go toward a scholarship fund in honor of the ones we lost.

A girl sings the National Anthem, and after the introduction from the chief, we listen as a trumpeter plays taps. Every time I hear that song, it gets to me. It's hard to listen to without feeling some sort of emotion. As it's playing, we stand at attention until the song ends. I look out at the families who have tears streaming down their faces, and I begin to choke up. The park is completely silent, and the only noises that can be heard are passing cars on the street.

Logan steps up and clears his throat and composes himself. He speaks of the bravery of the man he once knew, and I proudly stand beside him. I look out into the crowd and glance over at Courtney, and her eyes never leave mine. I can tell she's touched by his words but I can also see the sadness that's written all over her face. Speaking about officers killed on duty is not an easy topic, but Logan handles it in a cool and collected manner.

Unspoken words float between Court and me, and it's hard for me not to go to her and pull her into my arms right now and tell her everything is going to be okay and that I'm going to be okay. But the risk I take for my job is undeniable.

The audience erupts into a loud applause once we hand out all the plaques and walk off the stage. Logan gives me a handshake and pulls me close and gives me a hard hug. He's not an emotional guy; hell, his wall is as thick as the earth's core, but talking about losing a partner isn't easy for him. With his background, loss is something he's become accustomed to and it hurts knowing he keeps it bottled inside.

"I've got your back. Always," he tells me, and I say it back to him. I'd take a bullet for him any day of the week, and without a doubt, I know he'd do the same for me. A few fellow officers walk up and speak to Logan, and I take it as my cue to go to Court. As I round the back of the stage, soft hands grab mine and twist me around.

Smiling, I turn because Courtney found me first, but as soon as I see brown eyes my happiness vanishes.

What the hell is she doing here?

Mia wraps her arms around my neck and places her lips against mine before I can even process she's standing in front of me. I push myself back, needing to separate her lips from mine. Seething, I grab her arms from around my neck and place them by her side. I realize for the first time that I feel absolutely nothing for her. No electricity, no love, no connection—absolutely *nothing*.

"Don't play hard to get," she whines in an annoying voice. "I've missed you."

I narrow my eyes at her and can't help my nostrils from flaring. "What the fuck are you doing here?"

"You invited me."

"*No*. We aren't together. Why would you come here?" My voice begins to rise.

"Yes, you did. It was a few months ago. I wanted to support you like I always do."

Her words catch me off guard because, over the course of

our relationship, I've invited her to all my work events and not once has she ever showed interest or showed up.

"Bullshit. This is total bullshit, Mia," I shout, infuriated that she's come on a day like today.

I study her and she takes a step closer, removing the distance between us. I cross my arms over my chest and glare at her. "You need to leave."

She places a hand on my arm as she speaks. "That's no way to treat the love of your life. I love you, Drew. I really want to try and make us work, but you've been ignoring my calls, and you don't respond to my text messages."

"And yet you didn't take the hint," I blurt out, taking another step away from her.

"Well, I've had time to think about *us*, and I want to take it to the next step. I want us to move in together and really give us a chance this time." She's smiling, completely delusional to what's happening here. I've heard her words of promised change so many times, I could recite them verbatim. Slowly she licks her lips and begins to undress me with her eyes, giving me *that* look.

"Mia…" I warn.

She steps toward me.

"Listen," I say, bringing my face close to hers. "We're over. For *good*. I'm not sure how many times I have to tell you this, but you had your chance. *Many* times. I'm not doing this anymore with you."

Before she can say another word, I turn and walk away. I'm so pissed; I can't even think straight.

"It's because of her, isn't it?" I hear her shout from behind me. "I always knew there was something going on with you two."

I spin around as she walks toward me—that smug look back on her face.

"You can deny it all you want, but I saw how she looked at you. You two were a little too close at times. I should've known," she continues.

"You have no idea what you're talking about. Courtney had nothing to do with the fact that you were a *horrible* girlfriend. I put up with you for way too long and if it took being with Courtney to realize that, then it was for the best," I throw back at her. My pulse is racing as I finally tell her off, something I should've done months ago.

"Well, I hope she doesn't mind being second best. You'll never be good enough for her in the long-term," she spits right back.

"Go get some help, Mia. You clearly need it." I walk away before giving her an opening to respond. I'm done wasting my time on her.

"This isn't over, Drew!" Her nasally voice echoes through the crowd and people turn and look at her. She's making a scene at one of my work events, and it brings me to a level of pissed off I haven't been in a long while.

Right now, the only person I need to see is Courtney, but as soon as I look through the crowd, she's nowhere to be found. I walk over to the bake sale tent and see there aren't that many of them left, which makes me happy, but then I realize she's not here either.

"Hey, have you seen Courtney?" I ask one of the ladies behind the table.

I search around and don't see Kayla so I ask about her too, hoping someone can tell me what's going on.

The woman looks at me with sad eyes. "I think they said they were leaving."

"Leaving?"

The woman shrugs, and I pull my keys from my pocket and jog across the grass to my truck. I grab my phone from my pocket and call her. It immediately goes to voicemail. *Fuck!*

As soon as I make it to the parking lot, I catch a glimpse of Travis and Viola taking the kids out of their car seats.

"Drew!" Viola says loudly, waving and trying to catch my attention. Travis looks up with a smile as he unfolds the double stroller.

"I'm sorry, I have to go. I'll tell you later. Go have fun," I yell and climb in the truck. I don't wait for a response before I drive off. I send her a quick text and hope she responds before I search all of Sacramento.

I have to find Courtney.

I have to find her right *now*.

COURTNEY

After listening to Logan's speech and truly understanding how dangerous their jobs are, I find myself getting a little emotional. Kayla is too. I've always known that being a cop is dangerous and that we should respect the uniform, but Logan's words about losing his previous partner affected me more than I thought it would. I had no idea he'd lost someone so close, and now I felt terrible for making fun of his hard shell. I glance over and see tears streaming down Kayla's face, and I wrap my arm around her. We're way too emotional at the moment.

Drew stands proudly beside Logan, and he looks so damn handsome up there. When his eyes meet mine, I smile and think about how I never want to lose him.

Every time he puts on that uniform and walks out that door is a day he may not return home to me and that single thought destroys me. Too many horrible scenarios run through my mind, and I want them to stop.

Once Logan and Drew walk off the stage, I have this feeling that I just need to go to him and wrap my arms around him. I leave Kayla behind in the tent and rush to find him as fast as I can and tell him how much he means to me.

Everything I want to say to him rushes through my head. I try to think of the right words to tell him. He's always meant a lot to me, but after the past couple weeks with him, as more than *just friends*, those feeling have intensified and overwhelmed my heart.

As I round the corner, my heart drops, and I stop moving. The smile on my face vanishes, and my mouth falls open as I watch Mia *Fucking* Montgomery walk to Drew and wrap her arms tightly around his neck. To make the nightmare more surreal, they kiss. Instantly, I feel sick and empty. I want to speak up, I want to scream out, but I have no words. My voice is stolen while the small crack in my heart spreads. Unable to watch it for another second, I turn and walk away as fast as I can. The anger inside me begs to cause a scene, but I refuse to do that here and because of *her*.

My heart races, and I need to get away. All my insecurities come rushing back, and I feel so fucking stupid. I know they have a history together and it always seems to be in the back of my mind anytime I think about Drew and me really being together. I can't help the thoughts that surface about how he was in love with her and can he just be over her like that?

Drew's told me several times they were over and I believed him, but seeing them together makes it seem like

I've been fed lies. Perhaps he believed them when he said them, but his actions speak different words now. I know deep in my heart that Drew is better than that, and he'd never intentionally hurt me, but regardless, I need to get away.

Before my emotions can spill over, I head back to the tent. I grab Kayla and ask her if we can leave. As soon as she sees the look on my face and she registers that I'm visibly upset, she doesn't hesitate and nods her head. I tell her thank you and turn my phone off. I need time to get my feelings straight before I see or talk to him again. Because as roommates, there's no avoiding him.

For several minutes, we drive in silence, and I stare out of the window trying to make sense of what I saw. Drew and Mia. *What the fuck was she even doing there?* I shake my head, running through every scenario, and Kayla doesn't push me to talk until she parks in an empty parking lot.

"Are you going to tell me what happened?"

"Mia…" I can't even finish my sentence.

Her eyes widen. "And?"

I swallow hard, making sure to articulate exactly what I saw. Kayla looks over at me with sad eyes. "I want to kick her ass." *I should've gone over there and kicked her skanky ass.*

"Get in line," she huffs.

"I knew I didn't like her from the moment I met her, but when she tried to sabotage Travis and Viola's relationship, I knew she was insane. Then after watching the way she's treated Drew over the years…" My words fade off.

We sit in an empty parking lot for minutes, and I remember I had turned off my phone. I'm sure Drew realizes I'm gone by now. Instead of avoiding it any longer, I power on my phone and wait. I've got voicemails and a bunch of texts. I suck in a deep breath and open them.

Drew: Where did you go?

Drew: Hello?

Drew: Court, we need to talk. Call or text me back. Please.

The last text message makes my heart race. Could it be possible that Mia wants back in his life and he's willing to drop everything we have? I mean, what do we have, exactly? Yes, we're taking it slow, but we never talked about being exclusive. We never discussed officially being together. I watched them kiss and maybe when their lips touched he realized how much he missed her. Deep down I was hoping she'd become nothing more than a distant memory. I wouldn't have believed it if I didn't see it with my own two eyes.

Viola: Courtney, where the hell are you? All of your muffins were sold out before I could buy any!

Viola: Great, your phone must have died again. How many times do I have to tell you to charge it!

Courtney: I'll call you later and fill you in on some BS. That's great about the muffins.

I know she's got the kids and her phone is probably at the bottom of the diaper bag, so I don't wait for her response.

"Kay, can you bring me home?" I ask.

"Are you sure?" She has a look of concern on her face.

I nod, and she cranks the car and heads to the other side of town. When she turns down my street, I see Drew's truck sitting in the driveway but no Mercedes. *Thank God.* I breathe a little easier knowing she didn't follow him back to the house. Kayla pulls in, and we sit there for a moment.

"Do you want me to wait for you?"

"He's not going to be crazy and kick me out or anything. Drew's level-headed. I just need to get my feelings and facts straight before I go busting up in there."

She grabs my hand. "If you need me to rescue you, or bring Vodka and chocolate, you text me, okay?"

I laugh. "Deal."

I suck in a deep breath and walk up to the house. Somehow, I find an ounce of courage and open the door. When I walk inside, Drew's sitting on the couch, and he rushes over to me as soon as he notices me.

"Court, where'd you go? I've been worried that something terrible happened. Are you okay?"

It pains me to look into his eyes, and I feel like the girl with a stupid crush again.

"I'm not okay, Drew."

He studies my face, waiting for me to explain what's going on, and I feel my emotions on the rise. "Mia," I choke out. "I saw you two kissing."

Drew comes to me and pulls me into his arms. "Court."

"I've never felt this insecure before, but she… What you two had for so long has me second-guessing everything. My feelings have always been there for you, and I can't stop the thoughts inside that think I'm not good enough or that your history with her is much stronger than ours. All that came to light when I saw her touching you."

I'm trying to hold back tears, and it's so damn hard. Drew doesn't let me go; instead, he does exactly what I hadn't expected him to do—kiss me. I pour myself into that kiss, hoping to God it's not the last one I ever experience with him.

He smiles and wipes a single tear from my face. "Did you feel that?"

I nod, my heart beating and emotions swirling. When his lips pressed against mine, it was like nothing in the world mattered but the two of us. That's how I've always felt.

He grabs my chin and forces me to look into his eyes. "I don't know what you saw exactly. But I have nothing to hide from you ever. Mia came to me, tried to kiss me, and I pushed her away then told her off. For the first time in years, I felt *nothing*. Absolutely nothing. It was like, as gross as it sounds, kissing my sister. I was so fucking pissed and finally found the words to tell her exactly what I should've said a long time ago. I was shocked to see her there, but trust me when I say the only person I wanted at that moment was you."

He pulls me back into his arms, and I wrap my arms around his waist.

"I'm sorry," Drew whispers. "It meant absolutely nothing. I'm sorry my ex is crazy. I should've realized it earlier."

I pull away from him and search his face. "I was coming to tell you how much you mean to me. Logan's speech…" I swallow hard. "I don't ever want to lose you, Drew. Your job is so…dangerous and…"

"Come here." Drew runs his fingers through my hair, and

I lean into his gentle touch. "Every day I put on that uniform and leave, the first thing I think about is staying safe so I can come home to you. I'm not going anywhere." He smiles. "And I've got the best partner on the force."

My heart does somersaults when he drags his lips against mine.

"Now, about paying for those muffins."

He gives me a heated look, and I give him an evil grin. "I've been thinking about that, actually." I run my fingers up his chest.

"Uh huh," he says, a cute smile forms on his lips.

"You can say no if you want to," I tease, knowing his mind is somewhere else.

"Maybe, maybe not."

I smile. "I'd like you to come to Texas with me in a couple of weeks for my cousin, Benita's wedding. Also, to meet my parents and brothers."

A big smile covers his face, and it makes me happy to know he's not shocked at all by this crazy request. My parents and brothers have heard so much about Drew that it's almost crazy I haven't asked him sooner. But I feel as if our relationship could head in a direction where he needs to meet them. Instead of him wanting an explanation, he pulls me close and kisses up my neck.

As I sigh, he whispers in my ear. "Deal."

CHAPTER NINETEEN

DREW

AFTER THE DAY we've had, I just want to lay low the rest of the night and be alone with Courtney. I know she worries about me when I'm on duty, but it's something all officers go through. The constant fear of not returning home to our loved ones never goes away, but it's a sacrifice I'd never regret pursuing.

"So, any chance you made extra muffins and hoarded them in the freezer?" I ask, arching my brow and remembering the last time we stuffed our faces with muffins from the freezer.

She blushes and then smiles. "It's like you know me well or something." She opens the freezer door and grabs a Ziploc bag that's packed full.

"Not that I'd normally eat a muffin, but since it's one of yours—"

"—that you made me bake five hundred of," she interrupts with a knowing smile.

"Yes, so I figure I better have a few of them."

She peels the bag open and sets them down on the

counter. "They need to thaw a bit. I can make some dinner first. Maybe some pasta and wine."

"You don't have to do that," I say, pulling her into my chest. "You baked all the muffins; let me make dinner."

She tilts her head up and laughs. "*Can* you make dinner?"

I tickle under her arm and laughter erupts from her mouth. "Okay, okay! I was just kidding!" Her laugh makes me smile, so I tickle her just a moment longer to hear it some more.

Wrapped up in my arms, I lean down and kiss her again. I can't stop kissing her. My lips are magnetized to hers, and they never want to be released.

"All right, Deputy. You're on chef duty tonight." She slaps my ass with a devilish smile. "Handcuffs may or may not be included."

"Mm…I like the way you think." I kiss the top of her nose. "Maybe you'd like to assist me instead?"

"Yeah, I have an idea on what you mean by *assist*."

She grabs her apron and wraps it around her waist. Standing behind her, I push her hair off to the side and press a kiss against the nape of her neck. I wrap my hand around her throat, and her head falls back to my chest. Placing a kiss under her ear, she shivers and closes her eyes. She's so beautiful and perfect; I can't believe it's taken me this long to finally *see* her.

"Keep that up, Deputy, and we won't get to dinner." She smiles as I move my lips over her jawline.

"Are you resisting, ma'am? I might have to do a thorough strip search on you."

"What exactly would you be looking for?" She smiles as I tilt her face to look back at me.

My other hand wraps around her waist and I close the gap between us. "Weapons."

"Ooh, so like wet pussy and hard nipples?"

"*Jesus Christ*, Court," I growl, feeling myself getting hard against the small of her back. "You sure don't make this fucking easy."

"You wanted to play it slow," she reminds me.

Pressing my lips against hers, I pull her bottom lip in between my teeth and groan. "I'm done playing by the rules."

I have no doubt in my mind that what Courtney and I have is one-hundred percent real. My feelings for her are so strong; I can hardly believe I ever doubted them in the first place.

I spin her around and cup her face in my hands as I kiss her deeply. Her body melts into mine, her fists grip my shirt and pulls our bodies closer together.

"I've never fallen for someone so hard, Courtney. As much as I didn't see it at first, I'm seeing and feeling everything now. It's consuming me."

"I didn't mind waiting."

"I was such an idiot."

She laughs against my mouth and nods in agreement.

I close the gap between us and bring her lips back to mine. I kiss her feverishly, and I don't know that I'll ever be able to stop. Her body pressed against mine and the way she responds to my touch drives me absolutely insane.

Wrapping my arms around her, I lift her up and cup her ass in my hands. She willingly wraps her legs around my waist as I begin carrying her out of the kitchen and down the hall. Her fingers tangle in my hair as she moans in my mouth and drives me even crazier.

"Tell me how you want it," I say, setting us both down on

her bed. Her hips arch up and grind against my cock. "I can't promise I'll hold back this time."

Her eyes go wide. "That was you holding back last time?"

I flash her a smile and press my lips back to hers. My hands run over her body, untying the apron from her waist and tossing it to the floor. Next, I lift her shirt up and toss that into the pile we've started. She rakes her hands down my chest and finds the end of my shirt before pulling it up and letting it fall. I wrap my arms around her and unclasp her bra, fumbling with it down her arms and throwing it behind her.

"New rule: no more wearing so many layers," I tease as I fight with the buttons on her jeans.

"Is this how you pat down all your civilians? Or just the lucky ones?" She grins.

I cup her breast in my palm and shake my head. "Just you, sweetheart."

She smiles as our lips collide again. I pick us up and spin her around so she's lying on the bed and I'm hovered over her. I kiss down her neck, chest, and stomach. I finish undoing her pants and slide them down her legs. Kissing up her legs, I get an idea.

"I know you have a toy in here. Where is it?"

"*What*?"

"Viola told me about your little hiding spot," I tell her, placing kisses along her underwear line. "So, where it is?"

"I don't know if I can trust you with it." She smirks, arching her hips.

"Courtney," I warn, sliding her panties aside and kissing the sensitive flesh there. She releases a moan, her hands gripping my shoulders as I circle my tongue around her clit.

"In my nightstand," she finally confesses.

I smile. "Perfect."

I devour her and slide my finger inside her tight cunt. She's wet and begging for it.

"Ride my fingers," I tell her, pushing two deep back inside her. I suck her sensitive nub as she grinds against me. "That's my girl."

She takes exactly what she needs, and I taste her on my tongue as she comes—hard. I flick her clit with my tongue once more before crawling back up her body and circling her nipple. Her little begging whimpers make me even harder, and it takes all the willpower I have not to pound into her right now.

Leaning over, I reach for her nightstand and dig out her vibrator bullet. She blushes as I turn it on and my eyes go wide.

"Would you believe I've never touched one of these before?" I say with a grin.

"That gives me more relief than it probably should." She laughs, taking it from my hand. "Do you need an instruction manual?"

"Oh, sweetheart," I growl. "Let's see how you're talking once you're cuffed to this bed and I use this sweet little thing on you."

"That sounds a lot like a torture chamber," she says. "But I'm not a hundred percent opposed to it."

"Fuck, had I known you were such a vixen in bed, I would've climbed in here a long time ago."

"You're awful!" She laughs again, and soon I'm covering her mouth with mine. She's lit something inside me that has me craving more of her every time we're together. It feels uncontrollable right now, but I don't want to control it. I just want her.

She wraps her legs around me again, pressing our bodies together just enough to drive me completely insane. I lift her body up as our lips stay connected and run my hands over her body and chest. She moans and rubs her pussy against my cock that's threatening to burst out of my jeans any moment. I know I won't be able to hold back much longer.

"I want you so fucking bad," I growl, her body moving against mine. "I didn't know it was possible to fall in love with my best friend."

I cup her face before she can respond and kiss her in a heated frenzy. I can't stop wanting her mouth on me. Our bodies rock together, and this time it feels different. This time I know my feelings are real and that makes this even more special. Losing her would end me.

Laying her back down on the bed, she looks so fucking beautiful. I kiss between her breasts and all the way down her stomach. I find her clit and suck on it as my fingers slide inside her. Her body immediately responds, so wet and greedy. I love how she tastes.

She moans and screams for relief, and I'm eager to give her exactly what she needs. Her body tenses and her back arches as her head falls back and she releases on my tongue.

Leaning back, I undo my jeans and slide them off along with my shorts. She impatiently waits, rubbing her clit as she teases the fuck out of me.

"That's so fucking hot," I growl, towering over her body and placing a kiss on her lips. "Use the toy," I demand.

She grabs it and turns it on. I watch as she pleasures herself and it's enough to get me off right then. Her head falls back, her free hand reaching up and squeezing her breast.

"*Goddammit*, Courtney," I hiss, stroking my cock. It's so hard in my hand, I can barely stand it.

She continues rubbing the vibrator over her sensitive spot, and I can tell she won't be able to hold on much longer. I take it from her and set it on the bed.

"So fucking hot," I murmur, pressing kisses along her pussy.

She moans and I know I have to have her now.

Leaning over her, I kiss along her neck and jawline. "You're so goddamn beautiful, sweetheart."

I position my cock against her pussy and slide inside her. Heart pounding, chest rising and falling, body aching. She's all-consuming.

"Oh my God," she lets out in a breath. "*Yes.*"

Her hands tighten around my arms as my lips melt into hers. Our bodies find a rhythm and they're completely synced; I can't stop wanting to feel every inch of her.

"So fucking good," she cries out.

I take her hands in mine and raise them above her head as our bodies move together.

"You feel so incredible," I tell her as our lips connect. "I'll never stop wanting you, Courtney. You've completely stolen my heart, and for the first time, I don't want it back. It's yours."

"Good, because I hadn't planned on ever giving it back anyway." She smiles. "Giving you my heart was the hardest thing I've ever done, but I trust you."

"I'll never hurt you again, Courtney. I promise."

Licking her bottom lip, arching her hips, and smiling, she says, "Good. Now fuck me as promised, Deputy."

COURTNEY

As soon as the words leave my mouth, Drew flips me over on my stomach and presses his fingers into my hips. He pushes my ass out and begins rubbing my clit.

"Is this what you want, sweetheart?" he leans over and whispers in my ear. "You liked it rough, didn't you?"

I nod, biting my lip to hold back.

"That's what I thought," he says, pressing a kiss on my neck with a smile. "Don't hold back, Courtney. I want to hear you."

He spreads my ass cheeks and presses his cock against my pussy before sliding back in. I feel him right away, and I can't stop the inaudible moans that release from my mouth.

He fucks me from behind and the harder he goes, the faster my heart pounds against my chest. I fist my fingers in the sheets and spread my legs for him. Just when I think I can't take anymore, he pushes even deeper inside me.

"Ah, *yes*." My eyes squeeze tighter, and my body shakes as he wraps his hand around my waist and finds my clit.

I'm a lost cause and cry out when my body tenses and releases. Drew groans as he feels me tighten around him.

"Holy fuck," he growls. Once my body relaxes, he repositions us and places me on my side. With his chest to my back, he hands me the vibrator and tells me to hold it.

He pushes my leg up and slides back inside me. Wrapping his arm around my thigh, he turns the vibrator on and holds it against my clit.

It's the sweetest torture, and I can't help being greedy for more.

His lips are on my neck and then move to my shoulder. Everything this man is giving me is pure perfection, and although I've fallen for him long ago, I can feel those strong feelings resurfacing all over again.

The vibrator against my clit is almost too much and just when he pounds into me deeper, he speeds his rhythm, and soon I'm crying out his name.

"That's the most beautiful sound I've ever heard," he says against my ear before tossing the vibrator and positioning us face to face. I wrap my leg around his waist and pull him closer back inside me.

As he passionately kisses me, his movements are no longer rough, but sweet and tender. He makes love to me, and as much as I love it when he's rough, I love him this way too. It's the most vulnerable I've ever seen him, and I love being a part of it.

His body tenses and I know he's close. I deepen our kiss and tighten my legs until he shakes against me. He releases a deep moan against my neck and relaxes.

"Fucking hell," he mutters, chewing on his bottom lip.

"What?" My eyes narrow.

"I'm completely addicted to you."

I smile and kiss him. His fingers rub over my cheek, pushing loose strands of hair back. "Thank you."

His words take me off guard. "For what?"

His lips tilt up in a genuine smile. "For waiting for me."

We end up falling asleep for hours. When I wake up, he's holding me in his arms and looking at me.

"Creep," I joke. "How long have you been watching me?"

"Just a few minutes," he says, but by his devilish grin, I don't believe him.

My stomach growls, and I quickly remember we skipped dinner.

"Hungry?" he teases.

"Well, someone was supposed to be cooking dinner…"

"Oh? So, next time things get heated in the kitchen, I'm turning you down so you can't yell at me for starving you," he says with a shit-eating grin.

"Like I could get you off me even if I did," I fire back, wrapping my arm around his chest.

He shrugs, unapologetically. "Probably true." He rubs his thumb over my shoulder, making me shiver.

"Good thing there's always muffins." I smirk.

"Blueberry muffins to the rescue," he jokes.

I laugh. "And to think all this time you've been resisting."

He arches a brow, and the corner of his lips tilt. "Are we still talking about actual muffins?"

I burst out laughing and shrug.

He tilts my chin up, bringing my lips to his. "I meant what I said before."

I blink, thinking back.

"I've fallen in love with my best friend," he says, reminding me. Not that I could ever forget those words coming from his lips.

I bring my hand up to his that's resting on my cheek. "It's about damn time. I've been in love with my best friend all along."

He presses his lips to mine again, and all the butterflies swarm back into my stomach. This feeling will never get old.

Once we finally make it out of bed and get dressed, we make our way to the living room and order pizza.

"I can't wait for you to meet my family," I say as we sit on the couch with our plates. "Just be prepared, though."

He glances over at me. "Prepared for what?"

"It's another world down there, so just be prepared."

"Are you trying to scare me out of coming with you or something?"

"No!" I say, laughing at his wide eyes. "It's just, it's not California. Imagine big hair, cowboy boots, thick accents, and lots of hugging. Texas is a different world."

"Will I get to drink moonshine and eat fried alligator tail?" he asks with a wicked grin.

"Do you always have to be a smartass?" I narrow my eyes at him.

"You're worrying for nothing," he says in a calming voice. "It'll be great." He leans over and presses a sweet kiss on my lips.

"Yeah, I can't wait to see them all, even if they drive me crazy sometimes."

"Well, if you can handle Viola and our crazy family, I'm sure I'll be just fine."

His words give me reassurance, and I can't wait to spend time with him for four days without having to worry about work schedules. I know they'll all fall in love with him just as I have.

CHAPTER TWENTY

DREW

I TRADED a few shifts so traveling to Texas to meet Courtney's family would be possible. She's so happy and keeps cracking jokes about it, but I'm nervous as hell. I've heard too many stories about her big bad brothers, and all I can hope is they don't beat the shit out of me. To make it worse, she randomly mentions how she's never brought a Californian home to meet her parents.

We wake up at the butt-crack of dawn to fly to San Antonio to connect to San Angelo Airport. I've been given warnings on how much she hates connecting and how the small planes make her nervous. Once we land, we'll have an hour drive to El Dorado.

In the airport, I can't keep my hands from her and vice versa; otherwise, it feels awkward. Knowing she's mine makes me so fucking happy. No words can explain the way I feel when I'm lost in her eyes, her mouth, and the smell of her skin. I feel this is the way it should've always been—us together. It took years to get to this point, but without all the bullshit, I'm not sure I would've appreciated being with her as much. To feel the same way someone feels about you is surreal.

We board and Courtney lets me sit by the window, but she conveniently leans over my body to look out. I'd let her sit on my lap but it would be highly inappropriate, and I'm sure the flight attendants and the little old lady on the other side of Courtney wouldn't appreciate it.

"I want to go to the bathroom and join the mile-high club with you," I say into her ear.

"How romantic and a little gross." She snorts. "People poop in there."

I playfully pout, and she smiles.

"Okay, fine. Add it to our sex bucket list."

She leans over and says dirty things into my ear and instantly I'm hard. She giggles, knowing and feeling exactly what she's started. I try not to picture her naked, sitting on my face, but she's the one who put that thought into my mind in the first place.

"You're going to pay for this," I glance down at the bulge that's visible and discretely try to adjust myself.

"I look forward to it." She quickly smacks her lips against mine. The smell of her skin and soap are almost too much, but I try to push all the dirty things I want to do to her right now out of my mind. I wrap my arm around her body. My hand brushes the smooth skin on her back, and we stare out the window until the plane lands. Quickly we connect to the smaller plane and are in the air for all of forty-five minutes. Every bump, she grabs my hand and squeezes.

Once we land again, we impatiently wait for our turn to exit the plane, grab our carry-ons and head to the front of the tiniest airport I've ever flown into, where her brother Jackson will be picking us up.

"He can sometimes be an asshole; just a warning," she says as we wheel our suitcases through the miniature terminal.

"Travis is my best friend. I'm used to it."

We walk outside, and the dry, hot air rushes across my face. Courtney lets go of her carry-on, and I grab it before it rolls away. She takes off running across the pickup area where Jackson picks her up and swings her around then sets her on the ground.

I can hear her talking about the flight and he leans his muscular body against the big truck with his arms crossed, eying me and sizing me up like any big brother would do. But I'm not the slightest bit intimidated because I've given that look to some of the guys Viola's brought home to meet me. As I walk closer, I see he looks like Courtney with their matching blonde hair and blue eyes, but he's much taller than her. Still, it's obvious they're siblings.

"Hey there," he says drawing out his R. His accent is thicker than Courtney's. If I didn't know better, I'd say he was faking it, but I know it's one hundred percent authentic.

"Jackson, this is my boyfriend, Drew. Drew, this is Jackson."

He takes my hand firmly in his, and I match the hardness of his handshake. He almost looks surprised, and I see him stretch his hand out before he throws Courtney's bag over the tailgate. I put my suitcase with hers but keep my suit bag with me. Courtney and I climb into the backseat of the truck and sit beside each other for the hour drive to the ranch. I stay quiet, listening to them chat and it all seems so strange.

"John, Evan, and Alex are waiting for you at home. Benita is there with a few friends because she and Aaron have vowed not to see each other 'til the weddin'. Of course,

Aunt Charlotte and Patsy came over when she heard we were gettin' together. Mom made a big thang of potato salad and gumbo. Dad was movin' cattle from the back pasture to the front when I left, knowin' it would take him a few hours. I think he was just tryin' to avoid the commotion." Jackson rolls his eyes.

"Why didn't she just invite the entire family?" I can sense the sarcasm in her tone.

"They might all be there by the time we show up. News travels fast 'round here." He laughs, knowing Courtney is annoyed.

"So, Drew, whatcha do for a living?"

"I'm a police officer."

"Well, I'll be damned," he says, patting his knee. "Court-Court went and snagged herself a man that can shoot a gun and wrestle bad guys. Didn't you say that's what your dream man would be able to do?"

"*Oh my God.* You're so embarrassing," Courtney leans forward and tries to slap Jackson in the back of his head, but he's too quick.

"Did she tell you how good of a shot she is? Straight shooter, that one. Gotta watch her."

I turn and look at Courtney, arching my brows and smiling. "You can shoot a gun?"

"Don't look so surprised, geez. I grew up on a ranch in Texas, remember? Everyone here has guns. And there's probably a lot of things about me you don't know *yet.*" She looks back at Jackson, threatening him with her eyes as she speaks to me. "You'll probably know a little too much by the time we leave."

Instead of responding, he just keeps chatting away. "Oh, she's got a knack for rifles, handguns, pistols, shotguns, you name it. She can filet a fish. Help deliver baby calves and herd cattle. Drive a tractor…"

"That's enough," Courtney says, the tone of her voice is scary and serious.

Jackson keeps talking as if he didn't hear her. "…Put up a barbed-wire fence, saddle a horse with her eyes closed, bale hay, vaccinate pigs, change the oil in a pickup, chop firewood, and shovel shit out of a stall like I've never seen before. She's a pioneer woman hiding in California behind the fake tans and surfboards. Glad you're home, lil sis. Now don't be forgettin' where ya came from."

"As if you'd ever let me," Courtney huffs, but I'm impressed. I had no clue she could do all of that. We're going to have to have a little talk later, and she's going to tell me everything.

Jackson continues and soon we're pulling off the freeway and turning down a paved road with no shoulder. We drive up tall hills and around curbs so fast I almost ask him to slow down, but don't want to seem like a pussy. The 'safety first' motto has been drilled into my head. Soon I realize we're in the middle of nowhere. He takes a hard right and turns down an old gravel road, and I can see dust kicking up in our wake.

Land stretches out for as far as my eyes can see. Every half mile or so Jackson slows down to roll over metal piping, and everything in the truck shakes and vibrates. I look out the window to see what it is. Courtney bursts out laughing. "It's a cattle guard, so the cows don't get out. They take a little getting used to."

"This place is huge," I say, looking out at the vastness.

Jackson speeds up, and I look out the windshield as we roll under a big iron sign that says Circle B Ranch. "We've got around fifty-four hundred acres of land, and it's been a working ranch since the early nineteen hundreds. At the other entrance, we've got a nice bed and breakfast setup for people to come and stay throughout the year. It's a little ole Texas retreat," he says, answering my question before I can even ask. "It was my brother, Evan's idea. He's the brains of us all; well, except Court. She's got the IQ of Einstein."

"He really does talk too much, doesn't he?" Courtney says, eyeing Jackson. Somehow, I don't doubt the Einstein comment, considering she's best friends with Viola and they both graduated with high honors.

"Don't make me tell him embarrassing stories about you," he warns, and she quickly stops talking.

"Not going to call his bluff?" I laugh.

"Hell no, she won't! I got too much dirt on her," Jackson says.

In the distance, I see a large, two-story farmhouse with a big porch wrapped around the front. Beside the house is a red barn and I feel like we're driving up to a movie set. Cars and trucks, all covered in dust, are sitting in the large circle driveway.

"Looks like Mom did invite everyone," Jackson says with a sneaky smile on his face.

"Fuck!" Courtney whispers.

"I'm tellin' mom you're cussing. Hopefully, she'll wash that mouth out with soap," Jackson says as he puts the truck in park.

"I want to punch him," Courtney says between gritted teeth, and all I can do is laugh.

Jackson turns around with his arm stretched out on the seat wearing a big cheesy grin. "But she knows I'll punch her back. She swings like a man."

As if the entire family heard the truck pull up, they start rushing out of the house to see Courtney. She can't even grab her bag before they take turns pulling her into their arms. She has to tell each and every one of them hi, introduce me, and we all exchange hugs, hellos, and howdys. I feel like I'm back at Viola's wedding, but this is just a typical get-together in Courtney's family.

Most of them have sandy blonde hair and blue eyes. The older women wear their hair big, like the Texans on television shows, and a few of the men have on cowboy hats and boots. Some of their accents are so thick, I can't understand a damn word they say so I just nod and smile. They all walk inside and Courtney grabs my hand and leads me back to the truck so we can grab our bags.

"I'm fixin' to scream. I don't want to entertain anyone. And I'm warning you, they ask stupid questions."

"You've given me a lot of warnings today," I tease. I grab her face between my hands and place a soft kiss on her lips. She sighs and slightly relaxes. "I'm having a good time already. But you Texans are *weird*."

Finally, she laughs, and we walk down the sidewalk, up the porch, and into the house. They're all loud, and I don't think one of them talks at a level lower than a ten.

Jackson walks up to me and Court and gives Courtney a big hug. "I missed you so much."

"John. This is Drew, my boyfriend," she says confidently once he releases her.

"John?" I ask, really confused now.

"Oh," she says with a laugh. "This is John, Jackson's identical twin. He's the nice one, though. That's the only way to tell them apart these days."

"I'm better looking than him," he laughs. John gives me

a handshake and doesn't try to break my fingers, and already I like him, but it's going to be hard as hell to tell them apart.

Their mom rounds the corner from the kitchen and pulls Courtney into her arms.

"Mom! I missed you."

They are spitting images of one another all the way down to the frilly apron she has on. She gives me a big smile. "And you must be Drew Fisher."

I hold out my hand to give her a handshake, and she pulls me into her arms. "We're huggers 'round here, son. So nice to meet you finally. I'm Rose, but you can call me Mom or Mama Rose—whatever you'd like," she says genuinely with a Southern twang.

Another one of her brothers comes around the corner with a bowl of potato salad in his hand. He's muscular and tall too, and still has that Bishop look, but I can tell he's older than me by a few years. He walks past us without saying a word.

"Evan, come here," Rose says, and he immediately turns around. "Meet Drew, your sister's boyfriend."

He wraps his big arm around the bowl and stretches his hand out with a smile. "Nice to meet you, Fisher. Hurt my sister, and I'll drive to Cali and break your neck."

Rose glares at him. "And I'm going to break your neck if you don't show some manners."

"Evan!" Courtney hisses.

"I'm just kiddin'," he says, but when he looks into my eyes, I know for a fact he's not, but I smile anyway.

"Don't plan on it. But nice to meet you, too."

He nods and walks into the dining room.

"Well, I'm fixin' to pull the gumbo off the stove in about

ten minutes if you want to get everyone together," Rose says to Courtney.

"I need to go upstairs and put my things away, please," she tells her mom.

"All right. Alex! Alex, get in here, please," Rose calls out. It's a miracle he could hear her over everyone's laughter in the other room.

Alex walks in, and I can tell he's not much older than Courtney.

"Can you get everyone together in about ten minutes? It's time to eat," Rose asks nicely.

Alex nods. "Sure. Oh hey, I'm Alex, it's nice to meet you. Heard a lot about you."

"Hope it's all good," I say, looking over at Courtney, who's smiling.

"Yeah, nothing too incriminating at least. Anyway, I'll see ya around." Alex turns and walks away, and Courtney lets out a sigh. "Can we please get out of here before we have to talk to anyone else?"

"Ten minutes, Court. We're eatin' as a family tonight," Rose says sternly, and I know that I don't ever want to cross her.

Courtney smiles, grabs my hand, and we break away as fast as we can. As we walk up the stairs, I catch glimpses of family photographs they've taken over the years, and I'm tempted to stop and look at every single one, but Courtney isn't having it. When we reach the top of the stairs, several doors line the hallway. We walk into one at the end, and as soon as she closes the door, she pushes me up against it, and our lips crash together.

"I've been waiting for that all day," she says breathlessly. "Now the bad news."

I look at her, confused.

"You'll have to sleep in the guest bedroom. My parents are way too traditional to allow anything else unless we're married." She rolls her eyes and throws her suitcase on the bed.

"I can respect that." I look around and see pictures of her and friends pinned to a corkboard, and she looks so young. There's a poster of a young Justin Bieber, and I can't help but laugh. "Is this the room you had when you lived here?"

"Yeah, but don't laugh at my poster. I hung it up last time I was home." She gives me a wink but I know she's lying by how faded it is.

"I can only imagine all the trouble you got into as a teenager."

"Oh, I gave them hell. It was so easy to sneak out that window and climb down the tree—or have people sneak in."

"You did not." I take a few steps closer to her.

"What else was there to do in the middle of nowhere, other than cow tip and have pasture parties?"

The warm glow from the evening sun splashes across the hardwood floor and she looks so pretty standing there with sun kissed skin and wild hair. If I could take a picture of her right here at this very moment, I would.

"Have I told you I love you today?"

She shakes her head and looks up into my eyes as I remove the space between us.

"I love you, Court," I say between passionate kisses. My hands memorize her body, and soon our mouths are so greedy, that neither can get enough of the other.

"I love you too," she says, between pants. "I've always loved you."

I unbutton her shorts and slip my hand inside her

panties, and she gasps when I touch her clit. Her eyes flutter closed when I dip my finger inside.

"You're so wet," I whisper, swirling my thumb against her hard nub and she lets out a small moan.

"I want you so fucking bad," she says, melting into my touch.

A knock rings out on the door, and I hurry and remove my hand from her panties as she buttons her shorts.

"Come in," she says.

Evan opens the door and eyes me as he speaks. "It's dinnertime, little sis. Get your ass downstairs."

He shuts the door without waiting for a response.

She stands on her tiptoes and pulls my bottom lip into her mouth and sucks. "You're going to have to finish what you started later."

"I plan on it."

Before we walk downstairs, I pull her into my arms and kiss her one more time. She grabs my hand, and before we walk out of her bedroom, I ask if her brothers are always that scary.

She lets out a laugh. "Yeah, and you haven't even met my dad yet."

CHAPTER TWENTY-ONE

COURTNEY

I LOVE how my family is determined to embarrass me as we eat dinner, but I'm used to it, and Drew seems to enjoy their stories, even if they are at my expense. There are so many of us; we've set up a folding table so we could all eat together in the same room. As much as my brothers annoy me, I've missed them, and I'm happy to be home. I'm sure by Sunday when we fly out, I'll be happy to be back to Cali.

"And there was this one time she got on this little pony, and it bucked her from here to the pipeline until she fell off and landed flat on her stomach," Jackson says. "I watched her for about thirty minutes bucking away, holding on to his mane for dear life."

"It wasn't a *pony*. Casper was a full-sized horse for a kid," I argue with him.

"He was about ye high." Alex stands, showing that the horse barely went up to his waist. "Casper was a Shetland pony."

Everyone is laughing, and I can't help but laugh too because that horse was a little shit and we never got along, but I was determined to break him, which by the way, never happened.

As Patsy gabs on about wanting to open a winery, I can't help but notice the empty seat next to Mom. I glance out the window and see the sun is starting to set over the horizon and begin to worry about Dad. As I stand to go figure out where he is, the front door opens and my father walks in, muddy and stinking of sweat, but a big smile fills his face when he sees me. I don't even care. I get up and run to him and give him a big hug. "Daddy!"

"Hey pumpkin, I missed you. So glad you're home, even though it's only for a few days." He always gives me a hard time about staying in California. When I told them I wasn't moving back to Texas, that's when he decided to stop funding my adventures, which is how Drew and I became roommates. So, in a roundabout way, I can thank him for bringing us together.

"Go wash up, Scott. I'll make you a bowl." Mom stands and laughs.

Dad looks over at Drew then back at me. "That's your boyfriend I need to threaten?"

I give him a stern look, and he smiles. "I know you're growing up and you won't always be my baby girl."

"Yes, I will, Dad. No matter what."

"Is he treating you right?"

I nod. "He loves me. He'll protect me. And if he doesn't, I'll kick his ass."

"That's my girl." He gives me another hug and heads up the stairs. Dad was never one for big crowds though his family was huge. When he married Mom, it doubled in size. Growing up, we always had get-togethers, and somehow he'd always find a way to get out of them. But he's a true rancher at heart. He loves working the land, being with the animals, providing for his family, and enjoying the smaller things in life like sunsets, oak whiskey, and sweet tea. He has a hard exterior at times because there's no crying in ranching, but it made me into the woman I am today—strong, confident, and not afraid to get my hands dirty.

I return to my seat at the table and Drew places his arm around me. Every single one of my brothers takes notice when I lean into him, but I'm glad Drew stands his ground and doesn't falter. Growing up around the four of them made it impossible to have an openly serious relationship. The Bishop boys somehow found a way to scare everyone away for the most part. Luckily, I've got myself a real man who couldn't give two shits about their dirty looks and empty threats.

"Benita, it was supposed to be a surprise that I was coming to the wedding, but you know how good the Brooks keep secrets." I turn and eye Mom and then look over at Aunt Charlotte and Aunt Patsy. They all shrug.

"A secret?" Benita laughs, brushing her long black hair to the side. "I knew as soon as you told Aunt Rose."

Dad comes downstairs, and Mom makes him a big bowl of gumbo and plops the potato salad right inside the bowl. He eats in silence as everyone chats about the wedding, the new Family Dollar Store being built in town, and who's pregnant. That's 'bout as good as it gets living in West Texas.

I try to find a time to formally introduce Drew to my father. It's so hard to get a word in edgewise because everyone is talking over each other. Sometimes Drew wonders why I talk so loud, but it's because I'm so used to fighting to be heard.

"Dad," I say, leaning toward him, trying not to be too loud. He looks up from his bowl.

"This is Drew, my boyfriend."

Drew turns and looks at my father. "Hi, sir. It's nice to meet you."

"Well, at least he has manners," Dad says and I give him a scolding look. "It's nice to meet you, son."

I give a hard nod. "That's better."

Once the sun completely sets, I start yawning. We all place our bowls by the sink while Aunt Patsy and Aunt Charlotte wash the dishes. Benita comes over to me and pulls me into a big hug as my aunts ask Drew questions about California.

"Your boyfriend is so fucking hot! I just, I can't even," she says.

I pull away and look her in the eyes and can't help a girly squeal from coming out. "I know, right."

"I'm pretty sure my mom is undressing him with her eyes," Benita says.

"Isn't everyone?" I laugh.

"I missed you, Court." She pulls me into a big hug.

"Missed you too."

Drew walks up, and he's smiling. "Apparently, you're not the only one who has cop fantasies."

Benita and I burst into laughter, and we say our goodbyes to everyone. Soon the house is empty other than my brothers and parents. Mom and Dad are in the living room, and I walk in and give them hugs goodnight. Drew tells everyone goodnight as well.

"Spare room," Dad says as we walk up the stairs and I shake my head.

"Told you," I say toward Drew, checking out his cute little butt.

We walk into my room and Drew lets out a deep breath. "You're right. Your dad is intense."

"He'll grow on you," I say, walking to him. "Now, where were we?"

"Mm," Drew moans into my hair, pinching the skin of my neck between his teeth. "You were showing me to my room, ma'am," he tries to say in a Southern accent but fails miserably.

I sigh. "Yes, to *your* room. Because if you stay in here, you'll get murdered. There are too many places to hide a body."

I grab his hand and open the door to the room that's right across the hallway from mine. It's got a big wooden bed with a quilt my great grandmother made and even has its own bathroom. I turn on the lights in the room and give him the grand tour. He pulls me into his arms, and I don't want to let go.

"I'm going to take a shower and go to bed, I think," Drew says. "I wish you were coming with me."

He looks so sexy right now, with his hair pulled back into a ponytail. I think about it for a few seconds, imagining his hard body against mine and realize that I can't. "Too risky."

"I understand. I'll be thinking about you the whole time," Drew dips his head down and kisses me.

"Goodnight." I wrap my arms around his neck. "Thank you so much for coming with me."

"I want it to be our new tradition. I like everyone."

"Really?" I can't stop smiling.

"*Really.*" Drew pulls me in for one last kiss before I walk out and the only person I can think about when I close my eyes is him.

I hear the water come on in the other bathroom and decide to wash the travel stank off too. As soon as I'm out of the shower, I lie in bed and fall asleep with a smile on my face.

The commotion at four in the morning wakes me before the sun does, though I should be used to it. Ranching is early work that must be done every day, rain or shine. I toss and turn until the sun blares through my windows. Worst night's sleep ever, and I truly believe it's because Drew wasn't beside me.

I walk downstairs in my pajamas, and Drew's already awake drinking coffee with my mom and brothers. They didn't stay because they all built houses on different parts of the property, but they're here every single morning to drink coffee before starting their daily tasks. I'm surprised they're all smiling, and I realize Drew is telling them stories about different prostitutes and drug dealers he arrested. I'm pretty sure right now they're all in love with him, which makes me happy.

"Court, I'm trading you in for Drew," John says, and even hard-ass Evan laughs.

"Replaced!" Alex sips a cup of coffee.

"You'll always be my little sis." Jackson comes to me and rubs my hair until it's frizzy on top. "The only one I can annoy."

"Mom!" I yell.

"Leave her alone," she scolds them, but I can tell she's impressed with Drew by the way she nods her head at me and glances over at him.

"Real subtle, Mom," I say, grabbing Drew's coffee from his hand and drinking it.

"You're rude." Jackson jerks the hot coffee from my hand and gives it back to Drew.

"Want to move to California?" Drew jokes. "I need you there when she steals my dinner, too."

"All of you—" I point at them, "—are annoying."

I make my own cup of coffee and try to wake up. No matter where I travel to, no one makes coffee as strong as my mother. I swear it'll make anyone grow hair on their chest, but I drink it down quick.

"What are you kids doin' today?" Mom asks, but I hadn't really thought about it.

"Thinking about taking a side-by-side and driving around the property and showing Drew around."

"Better not let her drive." John laughs.

"I got stuck *once*, and none of you will let me live it down. Did any of you help me? No, I winched that shit—" As soon as the word comes out of my mouth, my mother gives me a pointed look. "Sorry, winched that thang by myself. The only reason any of you knew was because I was covered in mud."

"That's true," Alex says. "And because it wouldn't start again after you parked it."

"Oh, shut up." I playfully roll my eyes at him.

"Keys to the side-by-sides are hanging by the back door. Bring a walkie, just in case," Mom says.

I stand up and Drew follows me upstairs. He walks into my room and closes the door. "I missed you last night."

"Sleeping without you next to me is torture." I remove my shirt, and his eyes go wide. When I take off my pajama pants and he sees I'm wearing a thong, his mouth falls open. I pull out a pair of blue jeans, a t-shirt, and a hoodie, and then grab a pair of mud boots from my closet. Even after all these years, they're exactly where I left them.

"You're going to need some boots," I tell him as I sit on the edge of the bed.

"Should I be scared? You're getting all country on me."

"Before we leave this weekend, you'll be drinking the hooch, dipping, and saying 'y'all'." I burst out laughing. "Sorry, I couldn't keep a straight face with that one."

I grab his hand, lead him downstairs and go into the mud room and grab him a pair of extra rubber boots.

"What size do you wear? An eleven?"

"Yeah, and you know what they say about men who have big feet?"

"They wear big boots?" I smile and hand him a pair, and they fit perfectly. I grab a key from the hook by the back door and breathe deeply when we step on to the back porch. The smell of fresh air and the rolling hills is what I live for. It's easy to miss all this in California.

"Wow," I hear Drew whisper, and I interlock my fingers with his.

"This is home." I remember being a teenager and sitting on the back porch and would stare out as far as I could see. I'd get lost in my thoughts so many times that it was ridiculous. We stand there for a few more minutes as the morning chill rolls in, then I lead him over to the building that has all the utility vehicles.

We walk inside, and he looks like a kid in a candy store.

"Four-wheelers, side-by-sides, and of course, a Jeep."

I look down at the key and see which one I have, then we hop in, and I crank it.

"Do you want to drive?" I look over at him.

"Hell yeah!" He doesn't hesitate to jump out and switch with me.

I laugh, giving him directions as we pull out of the building. We head out on a trail, and I tell him to turn off to another one and give him so many directions, I know he has no idea where we are. Being home and seeing how beautiful everything is makes me realize how much I took this place for granted.

"You'll go down that hill and make a right as soon as you hit the bottom," I yell over the sound of the motor.

Drew sees me stealing glances at him, and he places his hand on my thigh. Having him here with me doesn't seem real. Having him meet my family and love them seems like a dream. My heart races at the thought of how much he means to me, and it's slivers of moments like this that I never want to forget.

He turns down a gravel road, and we travel up the path to a large barn where my father stores extra hay in the winter.

"Pull inside," I tell him and he does. Turning off the side-by-side, he turns and looks at me.

"So, this is a hay barn? I love the smell of it." He leans in and kisses me. "I love the smell of you."

I tap my finger against his lip and hop out and hold out my hand for him to join me. We climb a ladder in the barn, and I sit on the edge of a bale of hay. My heart is racing as he walks over to me and lays me down.

"I wanted alone time with you," I whisper into his mouth. "I couldn't take it any longer." His breath is hot against my skin, and I wrap my arms around his neck, pulling him down until his body hovers over mine.

"I need you so fucking bad," he says between kisses as his

hand trails up my stomach, and he pinches my nipple. My body instantly responds, and I don't know how much longer I can wait to have him. I unbutton and unzip my pants and push them down to my knees. Drew groans and I can see how hard he is when he stands to unbutton his pants.

"I need to have you," he says and hooks his fingers on the edge of my panties and pulls them until they pop. *Oh my God*, Drew Fisher is a panty ripper. He places them in his pocket with an evil grin on his face. Pleasure and pain shoot through me, and I want him *now*.

"Don't be stingy, Deputy," I say, giving him a smirk, holding myself up on my elbows as he stands and admires my body. I stand in front of him, my eyes never leaving his and remove my shirt and bra. His breathing increases as I bend down and take off my boots and jeans. I'm standing naked in front of him and watch as he removes his clothes too.

"Court," he says, taking a step forward and whispering against my mouth, "I've never felt this way about anyone before."

"I haven't either," I respond truthfully.

I close my eyes and allow my mouth to take control as my hands run up his chest. Drew lays me down on the hay and the overwhelming need to have him takes control. I sit up and grab his hands and pull him to me, not wanting our lips to ever part again. Not rushing, he slowly guides himself in me, and I gasp as our ends meet. Staring down at me, we exchange a million silent I need, I want, and I love yous. I take all of him, the rhythm of our bodies moving together in perfect sync. Being with him like this, on such an intimate level, doesn't ever feel like enough. No matter how much I have of him, I need more.

My body swirls with emotions, and I lose myself in his

lips and touch as we make love. I give him a little smirk before I flip over and straddle him. His thumbs press into my hips as he guides me, not wanting to rush this. I take his length slowly, wanting to memorize how good he feels with the sound of his hushed moans in my ear as I lean down to kiss him. Falling down on top of him, we pour so much into our kisses that I don't know how much longer I'll last. As soon as his thumb circles my clit, I lose it. My eyes flutter closed, and I ride the wave, which is so intense I can't keep quiet. Moans release from my lips as I continue to rock back and forth until he tenses and relaxes. I fall on top of his chest, and he holds me and kisses my hair as our hearts return to a steady pace.

"I love you so much, Deputy."

"I love you too, Court. More than I ever thought possible."

We return to the house with guilt written all over our faces and bodies. I try to pretend like I didn't have the most mind-blowing sex of my life, but the pinkness on my cheeks and the hay in my hair are a dead giveaway. Knowing that I'm not a good liar, I make sure we take the super long way back, but as soon as I catch a glimpse of my swollen lips and disheveled hair in the mirror, I know it's a lost cause.

"You have sex face on," Drew says.

"And you look guilty as sin."

"What you meant to say was *sexy*." Drew laughs.

"Yeah, that too." I give him a wink.

Somehow, no one mentions the hay in my hair or my swollen lips, which is a miracle considering how nosy my brothers are. I hurry and grab the keys to the Jeep in the garage and Drew and I head off to town to grab lunch at a little burger joint.

"Do they have salads?"

"No, sir. This is Texas. Only meat and potatoes. Also, this is a cheat *weekend*," I remind him.

As we park, he turns and looks at me, and I can tell there's something he wants to say. He grabs my hand and sweetly kisses my knuckles. "I can't imagine you not being in my life. You make me so fucking happy."

My heart does somersaults, and every time he says something like that, I feel like I'm dreaming. "I'm not going anywhere, Deputy. Not unless you want me to."

"Never," he says, and we get out and walk in.

CHAPTER TWENTY-TWO

DREW

COURTNEY DRIVES me around until it gets dark, then we eat quickly, and sneak upstairs without really talking to anyone. We stand in the hallway, and I kiss her goodnight, wishing we could sleep in the same bed. At home, though we switch rooms when it's time to wash the sheets, there hasn't been a night that we haven't slept together. Even after my shift, I make sure to crawl into whichever bed she's in for the night. Holding her and having her body pressed against mine is something I look forward to every day.

The next morning, we get dressed, and we drive to a winery in Christoval. I can't stop staring at Courtney and how beautiful she looks in that slinky dress that hangs off her shoulders. I'm happy she decided to drive the Jeep so we could be alone, but each time she shifts, I catch a glimpse of her bare thigh.

"You're a naughty boy," she says, giving me a side-glance, but not taking her eyes off the road.

"If you only knew what I was thinking right now."

"I have an idea." She smiles.

We pull up to the winery and I kind of laugh because while it's cute and quaint, it's nothing like Napa Valley. But then again, that's why I like it. There's a big stone cathedral and tons of people are standing outside under a white tent. I catch glimpses of the lanterns hanging from the roof and the tables and chairs with silk covers.

Courtney walks up, and everyone, who didn't know she would be here, is so excited to see her. She never takes her hand from mine and pulls me closer. I love the way she looks at me when she introduces me as her boyfriend. Actually, I love the way she looks at me any time; it's the way she's always looked at me. Her mother takes a picture of us and promises she'll send copies. As she goes to take another one, I bend down and kiss Courtney on the lips. Rose is so happy we're together. It's written all over her face. She makes me already feel like a part of the family.

The ceremony starts, and the ordained minister steps forward wearing leather boots and a black velvet cowboy hat. As I look around the room, I realize that's the Texas tuxedo, and Courtney didn't give me the memo. I'll have to mention it to her later; she'll probably laugh at me.

I listen to the words they say, and I can see the love the two of them have for each other. Benita looks at Aaron like he's her world and when I glance over at Courtney, I see she looks at me the same way. I swallow hard, brushing my thumb against hers as we hold hands.

As soon as the couple begin to exchange their vows, Courtney starts crying tears of joy. "Weddings get me every time," she says and squeezes my hand.

Benita and Aaron kiss and Courtney leans her head against my shoulder. Once the ceremony is over, the happy couple gets together to take family photos and Courtney and I head outside to the tent where the wine is flowing like water. The band begins playing, and Courtney leans into me as she sips.

"Want to dance?" She lifts an eyebrow.

"At this hoedown?"

Courtney hurries and swallows the wine that's in her mouth, then bursts out laughing. "You're so cute, but it's not a hoedown until the sun sets."

"Oh, gotcha." I lean over and steal a kiss.

The fiddles and guitars fill in, and I've never really danced to country music.

"Come on; I'll teach you how to two-step." Courtney grabs my hand and leads me to the middle of the dance floor that happens to be completely empty.

I look around the room and see people sitting at tables, staring at us. "We're the only ones out here."

"Sometimes you have to dance like no one's watching." She places one of my hands on her lower back and interlocks her fingers with my other. "Now you'll take two quick steps forward, one slow step back, and you just do that over and over. Hear the beat of the music?"

I nod, pulling her close to my body and following her instruction. She whispers the steps to me.

"You're doing good!" She smiles proudly.

"It's because I have the best teacher." I grab her hand, spin her around then land back in step.

"Okay, now you're just showing off." She laughs.

We may be the only ones on the dance floor, but at this moment, it feels like we're the only two people in the room. As the song ends, people start clapping and whistling for us. Courtney grabs my hand, and we bow for our audience.

When the bride and groom enter, everyone stands and

claps for them. They look so happy together. Courtney and I give our congratulations to Benita and Aaron, but they are pulled away by family soon after.

"It's okay, we'll catch up later," Courtney hollers across the room to Benita.

We drink and dance more until the appetizers are served, then we stand around and eat bacon-wrapped and fried everything. Once the sun begins to set, the more everyone drinks.

"I'm going to grab another glass of wine. Want one?" Courtney asks, giving me a quick kiss on the lips.

I hold up my glass that's half full and shake my head with a smile. "If I didn't know better, I'd say you were trying to get me drunk."

"I don't have to get you drunk to get what I want." She licks her lips, and I nod in agreement because she's damn right about that.

She gives me a heated look and stands. I can't keep my eyes off her as she walks across the room. Before she makes it to the wine bar, a man stops her. She turns and smiles, looks him in the eyes, then they exchange a hug. But he holds her a little too close and a little too tight. Laughing, she pats him on the chest, and he leans in and whispers something in her ear. She rolls her eyes playfully, and he grabs her hand. Courtney shakes her head and pulls her hand back, but I'm curious as to what she said back to him. I hope she was a smartass, and by his reaction, I think she was.

Jackson and John walk up to the table, and I can't tell them apart until they start talking, *I think*.

"Hey there," Jackson says, or maybe it's John.

I'm starting to get used to the way they over-pronounce their R's.

He notices I'm not taking my eyes off Courtney who's still talking to that guy a little too close.

Jackson chugs his wine. "Oh, that there is one of Courtney's ex-boyfriends. Bastard. If we weren't at a family event, I'd kick his ass for doing what he did to her." Jackson looks over at John like he wants some sort of approval.

I stand up, ready to join him.

"Hold up, Tonto, she ain't got eyes for nobody but you. That loser right there would have never made it with my sister. He cries like a pussy and can't take a punch. So, let's just chill." I know for a fact it's John speaking now because he's the peacekeeper of the two.

Seeing her close to someone else uncovers emotions I hadn't felt before. It's jealousy in the rawest form, but I've never seen someone look at her that way since we've been together, especially someone she has a past with. Sure, guys stare at her often, but it was the closeness and the way he allowed his hand to linger that bothers me.

Jackson and John continue talking about work that has to be done in the morning when their Dad walks up. Jackson tilts his head, and John takes the cue, and within seconds they walk away.

"So," Scott takes a sip of whiskey, and I don't question where he got it because they are only serving wine. "My daughter..."

I look over at Courtney who's still chatting away with the man who's undressing her with his eyes.

"Yes, sir," I say, turning my head toward him.

"There were times I wished my little girl would come back from California and stay home. She gave up her trust fund until I decide otherwise because California makes her happy. Now that I see her with you, I realize it's not California that makes her happy; it's *you*. So, here's your warning, son; don't make me regret accepting this relationship of yours. She's hardheaded, but she loves hard, so treat her right."

He holds out his rough and strong hand, and I take it in mine. There's an unspoken agreement being made, and I willingly accept. When he releases my hand, I have no doubt he could break every bone in my body. His face is worn and rough like leather from working in the sun, but he has soft, caring blue eyes, like the rest of the Bishops. I have nothing but respect for him as he stands in front of me, drinking whiskey like water. Courtney walks up, and she eyes her dad then looks to me before giving him a big hug. He eyes me over her shoulder, and his words are clear—hurt my daughter and you'll regret it. Then just like that, he walks away.

"Did he threaten to murder you?" she asks, her breath smelling like grapes and strawberries.

"In so many words." I wrap my arm around her waist. "So, who was that?" I nod my head over to where they were standing.

"Who?" she asks, nonchalantly.

"The guy who was eye fucking you for the last ten minutes."

"Oh, you saw that. That's Toby."

"Wait, that was Toby? Your ex?" My jaw clenches because I know he'd broken her heart into little pieces. I'd heard the sadness in her voice many times when she'd talked about him.

"He was holding you a little too tight." I finish my wine.

"Oh, my gosh. Deputy is jealous." She's enjoying this way too much.

"I don't like sharing what's mine."

"Just know he's an ex because he couldn't keep his dick in his pants. I don't really like sharing what's mine either, Deputy."

"What's he doing here?" I'm trying to put the pieces together.

She laughs. "He's a family friend. We started dating a long time ago in high school. He moved to California to be with me and cheated like the sorry-ass loser he is. My brothers hated him and hog-tied him a few times to teach him a damn lesson. He made me cry a little too much back then and continued to do so over the years. Looking back at it, I know why they hated him."

"He never deserved you." I don't want to imagine her with anyone else and I know it's been years since their nasty breakup, but just knowing he hurt her makes me want to kick his little punk ass.

She wraps her arms around my neck just as a slow song starts playing. "The only person I want to bring home tonight is you. You know that, right? I think it's cute you're jealous. Kinda gives you a glimpse of what I put up with all those years."

"I don't know how you did it." I place my palm on her cheek and kiss her.

"I wasn't giving up on you, Drew. I would've waited forever."

I pull her into my arms and hope she can feel how much I love her.

COURTNEY

Weddings make me happy. I love watching when two people who are head over heels for each other make it official. And I love that Drew's here with me. Honestly, he's become such an integral part of my life that it would feel awkward without him.

We dance and drink ourselves silly with wine. After the cake is cut, Benita throws the bouquet out to all the single ladies, and I happen to catch it. I squeal, and my mom waves and points at Drew and I try to ignore her because she's being loud and embarrassing. We're not rushing things, but she wants grandkids now, and my brothers aren't ready for family life yet. Hell, all of them are single except for Jackson, which is surprising that he could find someone who puts up with his constant jokes.

As I'm walking over to Drew, his eyebrows are raised, and he's smiling. Evan walks past me and steals the bouquet out of my hand. "Always the bridesmaid, never the bride," he teases.

"You need it more than me anyway," I yell back to him and family around us starts laughing.

I don't even try to run after the bouquet of flowers because I'm magnetized toward Drew and the way he's looking at me at this moment. In the corner of my eye, I catch a glimpse of Evan taking pictures with Benita as he caught it. When Drew wraps his arms around me, and I wrap mine around his waist, I don't care about anything else because as long as we're together, nothing else in the world matters. I think it's always been like that, even before when we were just best friends.

"You'd make a beautiful bride," he whispers in my ear.

"Maybe one day." I wink and grab his hand.

"Your husband will be the luckiest man in the world." Drew's looking at me like I'm the most beautiful woman in the room, and it makes my heart swell. I swallow hard, never hearing him say anything like this before. I never imagined we'd be here, falling so hard for one another, with no end in sight. I wished it, I wanted it, but now that it's happening, it feels unreal. If this is a dream, I never want to wake.

My Aunt Charlotte passes out bubbles to everyone, and we get ready to send Benita and her husband off. We line up outside, and as soon as they walk out, Drew glances over at me and pulls me to the back of the crowd. Once we're away from everyone, he pulls me into his arms and kisses me so hard that he steals my breath away. "I love you. More than you'll ever know. I'm sorry, but I had to tell you right now." His thumb traces my bottom lip before he dips down and kisses me again. No one around us is paying attention because their eyes are focused on Benita, and for once I'm thankful for that.

"I love you too, Drew. I love you so much. Don't ever be sorry. I'm yours, babe. Whisk me away whenever you want."

Bubbles float around us from the way the wind is blowing, and I never want to forget this moment. Once the pickup drives off and the Bud Light cans start clanking against the pavement, the crowd begins to trickle away though the party's still going.

Alex can see we're in no shape to drive and offers to take us home.

"Alex, you're my favorite brother; you know that, right?"

He laughs. "Yeah, sis. It's mainly because I'm not a huge asshole. I know the truth."

I hiccup. "Good."

Alex pulls up to the house and I open the door and Drew holds tightly around my waist as I partially lose my balance. We tell Alex thanks and say our goodbyes because we have to be at the airport at six in the morning. I wrap my arm around Drew as we walk inside. When he looks over at me and smiles, my world feels as if it tilts on its axis.

The lights in the house are off except for the one at the top of the stairs, and I turn around and put my finger over my mouth to shh him, so my parents won't wake. "Walk lightly." With his hand in mine, I drag him up the stairs. I hold back laughter as he looks at the photos on the wall and whispers comments about how I looked as a kid.

"Deputy," I playfully warn. "I'm going to have Viola pull out the family photo album when we get home if you don't stop."

We make it up the stairs and stand outside of our doors. "I don't want to sleep without you tonight," he says.

"It's a death wish," I warn

"You're worth dying for." He gives me a wink.

I stand on my tiptoes and give him a sweet kiss. "Goodnight, Deputy. Early flight in the morning."

"Fine," he tries pouting, but it doesn't work.

I go into my room and toss and turn for an hour before I decide I have to go to him. If I know my parents, they waited up for us to return home and waited to hear two doors click closed. Slipping off all my clothes, I put a robe over my naked body and crack my door open. The only noise I hear is the hard pounding in my chest; otherwise, it's eerily silent. Peeking my head out, I look down toward the opposite end of the hallway toward my parents' room, and from under their door, I can see the TV flicker, which is normal. Sucking in a deep breath, I tiptoe across the worn boards, praying they don't squeak and give me away. I quickly open Drew's door and lock it closed. Breathing hard, I stand with my back pressed firmly against the cool door.

His eyes flutter open, and the shit-eating grin plastered across his face tells me he knew I'd come to him.

"I've been waiting for you, sweetheart," he says. The low grumble of his voice does crazy things to my body. The moonlight splashes across the floor and acts as a spotlight when I remove my robe. It drops to the floor in a pile, and I take a step forward. Drew licks his lips and gets up and moves to me. His warm hands roam my body, while his mouth memorizes every inch, kissing and sucking my skin. My teeth sink down on my lower lip as I hold back a moan, trying to be as quiet as possible. His warm mouth drags across my neck and bites down on my shoulder, causing spikes of pain and pleasure to soar through me. Allowing my hands to take control, I run my fingers through his long hair and force his mouth to mine.

"I was hoping you'd come to me," he says.

"I couldn't stand it another minute. I'm addicted and had to get my fix." I smile against his lips.

"Drugs are bad for you." He smirks.

"It's never felt so good to be so bad."

I wrap my arms around his neck and my legs around his waist. His hands slide under my bare ass, holding me in place against the door as I try to devour his mouth.

"I need you right now," I demand, feeling him hard through his jogging pants. I lean my head against the door as he slips his pants down. He slides slowly inside me, and I let out a sigh as I take him all in. His kisses muffle my moans as I move up and down him. Wanting more, he carries me over to the bed.

"Don't go easy on me, Deputy. I want it hard and rough."

He growls against my mouth and does exactly what I say. I try to stay quiet, covering my mouth with his as he takes me hard. I might break in two by how rough he's being, but I want it this way. Tomorrow on the plane I want to know exactly where he's been. Fucking like animals in my parents' house shouldn't turn me on so much, but it does. He takes my nipple in his mouth and flicks his tongue hard before he flips me over and fucks me from behind.

I grab a fist full of the quilt as Drew squeezes my ass with his hands, so our bodies connecting don't make noise. I look over my shoulder at him and see his lips are tucked in his mouth because he's trying to hold back his moans too.

"Fuck," I whisper, and he grabs my hips and pumps me harder than he ever has before.

"You're so wet, Court." He pulls out of me and replaces his dick with his tongue. I bury my face in the bed, losing myself in the sexual euphoria he's created. His touch sets my whole body on fire and when his tongue swirls around my clit, the orgasm screams out, begging to release.

"Don't come yet," he demands as my body tenses. I press against his face, and I try to hold back, but he's buried so deep in my pussy that my body isn't listening to my commands. While I'm teetering on edge, he pulls away, and I pout because I was so close to spilling over it almost hurts. I try to catch my breath as he crawls over to me and lays beside me on the bed.

"You need to be teased every once in a while, you greedy little thing," Drew says, shooting me a smirk.

"I'll get you back," I say.

"Mm. I'm looking forward to it."

I roll on my side and trail my hand down his chest,

stomach until I've got him in my hand. Leaning over further I kiss him as I slowly stroke his hard cock and he hums against my mouth. Not able to wait any longer, he moves until he's hovering above me, both of his strong arms on either side of my head. I can't help but admire his body he's worked so hard for, and it's almost hard to believe he's mine. The tip of him teases my entrance, and I beg him with my pleading eyes to give me what I want. Instead of immediately taking me, Drew searches my face until a smile covers his.

"What?" I ask, wishing I could read his mind.

"You're just…so fucking beautiful. I love you."

"I love you," I whisper as he pushes deep inside me. I feel like I'm losing my grip on reality because of the intense sensation that follows.

"I love you more," he whispers, nibbling on the lobe of my ear.

"I loved you first," I pull him closer to me and he lets out a low chuckle.

His words, his kisses, and the way he looks at me will never get old. Drew takes me hard and slow, and our eyes never leave one another's.

As he picks up the pace, the bed begins to squeak, and I place my hands on his chest to stop, and his eyes go wide. We stay still, making sure we don't hear any footsteps.

"I think we're okay. But let's move to the floor," I say, knowing it's going to be cold and hard, but I don't care.

We throw the quilt on the floor under the window, and our bodies are lit solely by the moonlight. Goosebumps cover my body as his hands trail up my stomach and over my breast. I let out a whimper, and he roughly grabs my thighs and pulls me to him as he plunges to my end.

"Say it again," I whisper. "I can never hear it enough." It

doesn't take long for the orgasm to rebuild and I'm walking a fine line as he slams into me.

I don't even have to explain myself before he speaks.

"I love you so fucking much, Courtney Bishop. I love you. *Fuck.* I love you," he breathlessly says as the orgasm streams through my body. Scratching my nails hard down his back, I close my eyes, hips arched, and allow myself to get lost with him. He holds me tight and doesn't stop fucking me until he unravels from the outside in.

"Court." His breathing increases and his head rolls back on his shoulders, and I watch his mouth fall open as he allows the intensity of it all to overtake him.

"I can never have enough of you," I whisper.

His eyes slowly open and he sucks in air. *"Never."*

We're both hopelessly addicted to one another, and I'm happy there's no cure.

Hovering above me, he kisses me sweet and slow, and our emotions swirl together. We stay on the hardwood floor, and lie in each other's arms until our breathing returns to normal.

"That's the first time I've ever had sex in my parents' house," I admit.

"Really? I'm glad I could be the man who made you break the rules after twenty-six years." He kisses my nose.

"You're a bad influence, Fisher," I say, cleaning up really quick and putting my robe back on.

"I'm pretty sure you started it this time."

I give him an evil smile. "Maybe I did. But you surely finished it."

"I always do, don't I?" He pulls me into his arms and holds me before I leave because as much as I want to crawl into bed with him, it would just be a fight in the morning. I want my parents and brothers to love Drew as much as I do.

"I can't wait to get home." I squeeze him a little tighter.

He looks down and meets my eyes. "So then you can scream my name as loud as you want?"

I smile. "So, I can have my morning sex before starting my day."

He runs his fingers through my hair and kisses my forehead. "Goodnight, Court. If you stand here any longer, I'm not letting you leave. I'll hold you as a hostage."

I let out a huff, not wanting to go. "Night. One day we'll be able to sleep in the same bed at my parents' house."

His eyes meet mine, and he knows exactly what I'm referring to and doesn't deny it, which makes me so damn happy. "One day we will."

CHAPTER TWENTY-THREE

DREW

SIX MONTHS LATER

THE LAST SIX months with Courtney have been amazing. For the first time in my life, I'm truly happy in a relationship. What we have is real and meaningful, and I understand love in its purest form when I'm with her. Opening my heart and fully allowing her in changed my life and I don't ever want to go back. Being with family during the holidays had a whole new meaning with her around, and I got to kiss my girl on New Year's. I'm in too deep, and there's no going back now.

The workweek has only just begun, and it's always hard going back when we've spent several uninterrupted days together. It doesn't matter what we do when we're together, my time with her is never enough. We're together so much that Viola and Travis have openly started calling us Team Drewtney, because apparently, we're a super couple now. Court eats it up.

Before I head to work, I make a quick protein shake for the road. On the fridge, Courtney left a note on the dry erase board saying she loves me. I quickly grab the marker and write it back. It's become one of our little traditions—leaving notes and seeing how long it takes the other to find them.

On the way to work, I realize how much my life has changed since last year. Courtney is my girlfriend, and Logan is no longer my partner. While I'm happy he was promoted to the position he's always wanted—detective—it's just not the same patrolling without him. He's level-headed, and I knew he had my back on the streets. My new partner, Tyler, isn't so bad, and I try to give him credit, but he's a rookie and has little experience. But I've taken him under my wing just as Logan did for me. Maybe one day I'll be promoted to detective, and my brother in blue and I will be partners once again.

As I pull up to the station, I take a final look at my uniform and make sure everything is tucked properly because the chief has been giving some of us shit for coming to work sloppy. If I ever want to become a detective like Logan, I have to stay top notch. As I walk inside the station, I get a text message.

Courtney: Have a good shift. Stay safe. I love you.

Drew: I miss you already and love you more.

Courtney: Can you call in sick?

Drew: No can do, sweetheart. I'll be home before you know it.

Courtney: Better be!

Most of the night is uneventful as we patrol our area. We do a few routine traffic stops, but for the most part, the hours slowly drift by. Time stretches on; we have dinner and go back to patrolling our area. I'm grateful for nothing dangerous but nights like this make my eyes bulge.

Courtney: Ditch your partner and come home for a quickie.

Drew: Court, don't even tease me.

Courtney: I only need five minutes.

Drew: Damn woman, I wish I could.

I glance over at Tyler, and he's reading a book of state laws. I laugh and as soon as I do a car comes speeding past us and is inches from taking off our side mirror. He's going way too fast, and I know I can't let this one slide.

"Did you see that?" Tyler perks up. "He almost took out that car, too."

"Fuck," I say under my breath and pop the car into drive while Tyler turns on the siren and lights. I give the car so much power we're right behind the vehicle, but it doesn't pull over. Tyler calmly calls dispatch for backup and gives our position as we trail behind the car that's swerving all over the road. The car turns hard and slams into a parked car going full speed. Smoke bellows from under the hood of the totaled car. Tyler calls for emergency assistance. "We have a code ten-fifty. Send rescue."

I get out of the car to check the situation and get ready to draw my weapon, but the man stumbles out of the car with a gun in his hand that's pointed directly at me.

Always be prepared. I learned that in the academy and they drilled it into us. As I stand weaponless with the barrel of a forty-five pointed at me, I know that I wasn't. I should've pulled my gun sooner. I expected someone to be hurt or maybe even texting and driving, but I'm faced with a tweaker who doesn't notice the large gash on his arm and head that's gushing blood.

"Tell your partner to stay in the fucking car," he demands with a scratchy voice, not taking the gun off me.

I swallow hard, not wanting to move my body even to speak. I stay calm, but I'm watching everything I love flash before my eyes—Courtney. Her name is on my lips, and my heart aches knowing this could be the end.

"Tell him!" he screams at me.

I hold out my hands to him, hoping he'll see that I'm not going to hurt him. I yell over my shoulder, "Stay in the car, Tyler!" From my peripheral, I catch a glimpse of Tyler's ghostly face, but he does as I say. It's risky as fuck, but I don't need any sudden movements.

My heart races and my adrenaline rushes. I watch the man, trying to find a chink in his armor, but he's looking at me like I'm the enemy, and I'm sure to him if I'm wearing this uniform I am. I try to find the right moment to pull my weapon and take the shot, but it doesn't come.

"Drop to your knees, pig." He stumbles forward, waving the gun around and I don't hesitate. Coming closer, I'm able to look into his coal-like eyes, and I can't see anything behind him. The man is an empty shell of a human and that scares me more than the gun. All I can think of is how next year my name could be on that list of the fallen officers and Logan will have to stand up there and give a speech of my character. I don't want my life to end by the hands of a tweaker who has no control over himself right now.

"I know what you want to do. You want to lock me up in prison and watch me rot, just like my father," he hisses, tucking stringy grease-filled hair behind his ear.

"No," I say, calmly. "Let's talk about this."

"No! No more talking!" He yells, pointing the gun more violently at me.

At this moment, the only thing that saves me is Courtney. The thought of her warmth takes me away from the fear that's blanketing my body. I just wish I could tell her one last time how much I love her and will always love her. I want her to know that she's changed my life and no matter what happens to me, that will never change. Any minute backup will arrive, and it'll take all of two seconds for him to pull the trigger. The odds of living through a shot at that proximity is little to none. Just as I predicted, I hear the faint sounds of sirens in the distance and try to drown it out.

I'm not done living. I don't want my life to be cut short.

"You should run," I say, giving him his out, but he doesn't take the bait. Instead, he moves closer and gives me a wicked smile and drops to his knees in front of me. His breath smells of decay and cigarettes, and his clothes are filthy. He's losing a significant amount of blood and should be rushed to the hospital immediately, but he's completely unaware. Drugs do that to people. They can take control of people's minds and turn them into puppets. I've seen it way too much on the streets, but I've never been this close to someone so far gone.

Seconds pass, and we're eye to eye. "You won't ever catch me," he growls, then places the gun against my temple. I close my eyes and hear the sound of the car door, and I know Tyler has his gun drawn. My eyes bolt open. This could be life or death, and I wish he would've just fucking listened to me.

"I told you to tell him to stay in the car." The man's dirty fingers grab my cheeks hard, but he doesn't remove the gun. "Fucking pigs are all the same."

The gun feels like poison burning against my skin as he pushes it harder into my temple. Tyler is already loaded, and if he can get a clear enough shot, he wouldn't hesitate, but the positioning we're in makes it impossible and too risky.

The man has the smile of a devil when he slowly begins to pull the trigger. I close my eyes tight knowing this is the end, feeling so much regret for the things I never did, that it overtakes me. I hear the click, and the bullet doesn't come, but I won't be relieved until this is over and I'm walking away.

"Put the weapon down!" Tyler yells, and the man laughs.

As the sirens come, he pulls the trigger again. *Click.*

"You're not changing the world. And you'll never take me," he says, removing the gun from my head and placing it in his mouth.

"No, please," I beg, right before he pulls the trigger and the shot goes off.

I sit there on my knees—frozen in time and covered in blood. My ears ring from the gunfire, and I try to comprehend what happened. Blood, dark black blood is everywhere. It's on my arms, my face, and pouring into a puddle around the body. I can't move because I feel like my knees are glued to the pavement and I'm unable to get away from the nightmare that I'm currently living. I wait to wake up, but I don't, and the relief from the horror never comes.

Strong hands are on my shoulders, and it's Tyler, forcing

me to stand, but my surroundings all seem black and white. The man's body is a lifeless lump on the ground, and I can't stop thinking about how this could've ended differently. It could've easily been me lying there. After a moment, EMS, officers, and firemen are on the scene, and they're securing the area with yellow tape, which is common with a fatality.

"Drew," I hear but don't respond.

"Drew." I turn and see Logan carrying a blanket for me, and he's being followed by a paramedic to quarantine me. I can't get the blood off me fast enough. Logan waits as they strip me of my clothes and wipe my arms and face with a disinfectant.

He gives me a big hug once they walk away. "It could've been you. I'm so glad it wasn't."

I let out a deep breath, and it's hard for me to process everything that's happened in the last ten minutes. Logan asks me a few questions, and I answer like a robot. My body camera is confiscated, and Tyler is surrounded by people asking questions.

"You should use some vacation days and take a few days off," Logan tells me matter-of-factly. "You need to take that time away. Try to purge it from your thoughts, though you'll never be able to forget it." He stares off into the distance, and I wonder if, at that moment, he's thinking about all the people he's lost in his life. "If you need to talk, I'm here and I understand."

I nod and give Logan another hard hug. The chief comes over and walks me to an undercover vehicle and drives me back to the station.

"You're in shock. It's normal when something tragic happens. It's not your fault, Fisher. Don't blame yourself," he says.

"Sir, I'd like to use some of my vacation days, if possible. I need some time to process."

He looks over at me, the hardness on his face never wavering, and gives me a nod.

As I look him over, I realize how much he reminds me of Courtney's father. Then I think of Court, and I feel like I'm drowning and almost gasp for air. The thoughts of her hearing something bad happened to me knocks my breath away. Thankfully, the chief approves my vacation request, and I'll have the next ten days off. The news of what happened spreads like wildfire, and by the time we make it back to the station, everyone knows. Many people offer to listen if I want to talk, but I opt for dealing with it myself— for now. I need to sort out my thoughts and let it sink it before I can talk about anything. My head seems like a jumbled mess right now. It's like I'm trying to force square pegs into circle-shaped holes. I try to push away the thoughts and focus on home to Courtney.

Before I head out, I take a shower at the station and scrub so hard my skin feels raw. I wish I could scrub the memory of it happening away. I grab my stuff from my locker and sit in the truck in complete silence before starting it. Watching someone take their life, knowing it could've easily been mine, puts how dangerous this job is into perspective. When I arrive home, hours earlier than expected, I'll make sure to hold Courtney extra tight because losing her forever almost became my reality.

CHAPTER TWENTY-FOUR

COURTNEY

I'VE NEVER FELT SO scared in my entire life.

Drew's work incident made my worst fears come alive. For the past six months, and even before then, I'd always worried about him on the job. It's a natural feeling that no matter how many times he'd reassure me, it'd never fully put me at ease.

The moment he walked in from his shift early and I saw his face and his glassy eyes; I knew something bad had happened. Drew looked pale, distraught, emotionless. I'd never seen him so defeated before and it scared the crap out of me to see him like that.

Hearing the chief gave him a week off made me happy to know I'd have him home safe with me. Travis and Viola have been just as worried ever since they heard, and I know they're relieved for him to have time off.

It's been two days since the incident, and I'm still not getting much out of him. He's said he doesn't want to talk about it, but I think talking will help him with the coping process.

"Drew," I say, walking into the living room with a sandwich. "I made you some lunch."

"I'm not hungry," he replies firmly. "But thanks."

"You need to eat. You haven't eaten in two days," I remind him. "Please."

I sit down next to him, but his eyes don't avert from the TV. "Will you look at me?"

He blinks, then shifts his eyes to mine.

"Talk to me."

"I want to, Court, but I just can't get the right words out."

I suck my lips into my mouth and slowly nod. I understand he's experienced something tragic and that he blames himself, but I just wish he'd talk to me about it, so he doesn't hold it in and let it burn him from the inside.

"We can talk about anything," I tell him. "Or go do anything."

He shrugs and looks back to the TV. After a silent minute, I set the plate down on the coffee table and walk out. Needing to talk to someone, I text Viola.

Courtney: He won't talk to me, Lola. He's in bad shape. I don't know what to do.

Viola: Just be there for him. He's probably still in shock and it's haunting him. I wish I had an exact answer for you, but Drew is tough. He'll process and get through this.

Courtney: I hope you're right. I hate seeing him like this. He looks soulless.

Viola: Maybe you two need to get away for a few days. Get on a plane and fly somewhere.

Courtney: That'd be nice. Maybe a change of scenery will help. I want to give him his space and time he needs to cope but I also don't want him to sit around overthinking it for the next week.

Viola: You could go to Vegas and get hitched ;) Then get to making me some nieces and nephews!

Courtney: OMG! You're relentless!

Viola: Haha! Seriously. Go. Take his mind off what happened and maybe he'll come around and be ready to talk.

Courtney: It's worth a shot. I just need to find the right time to mention it.

Viola: I'm sure taking your clothes off would help distract him.

Courtney: Get real, Lola. I'm not going to seduce him when he's feeling like this. Although from the stories you've told me about rage sex, perhaps it's worth the risk.

Viola: SO WORTH IT :)

I set my phone down on the kitchen counter and dig around the fridge although I'm not feeling hungry myself anymore. I grab a bottle of Snapple before closing the fridge door, and as soon I try twisting off the cap, it slips from my fingers and falls to the ground.

"Shit," I mutter, as the glass breaks and spills everywhere. I bend down to start cleaning it up when I cut my finger on a piece of glass. "Ouch! Fuck." I suck the blood off my fingertip and as soon as I stand up, Drew catches me from behind.

"Are you okay?" His hands are on my shoulders, and it's the first time he's touched me in two days. It feels nice having him close to me again.

"I cut my finger. I just need a Band-Aid."

"I'll grab one for you," he says, walking away. I thank him and smile.

Once he cleans up my finger and wraps the Band-Aid around, he grabs a towel and starts cleaning up. "Do you want me to help?"

"No, I've got it."

I stand and watch as he carefully grabs the pieces of glass and tosses them out. Once he finishes wiping the floor, he stands in front of me and takes my hand. He brings it to his mouth, and I watch as he kisses my finger gently. My heart flutters as I feel his lips press against my skin. Even after all this time, he still affects me in ways I don't think I'll ever be able to ignore.

"Thanks for taking care of me," I say.

"I'll always take care of you, sweetheart. Even if it's just a little cut." His smile makes my eyes swell. He's been so isolated the past two days; it feels like this is the first time I've really heard him speak.

I wrap a hand around his neck and pull him down to my

lips. He wraps his arms around me and holds me tight. "I'm so sorry I've been distant."

I lean back and look in his eyes. "Don't be sorry. You have nothing to be sorry for. I've just been worried about you."

"I know." He kisses the top of my forehead. "I don't want you to worry. I'll be okay."

I wish I believed him, but I believe he'll try to be. Drew's strong and he has a big heart. I wasn't even there, and the whole thing shook me to my core.

"Wanna get away?" I ask abruptly.

He blinks.

"Let's get out of here. You can't just sit here for the next week." I hope I'm not sounding crazy, but I don't want to lose him either.

"Okay," he says, taking me by surprise. "Let's do it. Where do you want to go?"

I smile and bite my lower lip. He stares at me, waiting.

"Vegas?"

"You trying to get me drunk and take advantage of me?" He flashes a sly smirk, and it makes me giddy to see him joking around.

"Um, always!" I laugh. "Viola practically had to stop me from climbing you like a tree for three years, so I will always take advantage."

"Good to know. I'll be sure to wear my lucky underwear."

CHAPTER TWENTY-FIVE

DREW

No one can properly prepare you for what it's like to watch another human being take their own life. Especially when you thought it'd be your life they were going to take away. It's all I've thought about, and yet, I feel numb inside.

I know Courtney's worried about me. Viola and Travis, too. I don't know what to say to them because I can't make sense of it in my own damn head. One minute the gun was pointing at me and the next it was in his mouth, blowing his brains out. His lifeless body lay next to me as I brace myself for the worst. I don't know what he was thinking, what his thought process was, why he had a gun in the first place, and why he took his own life instead of mine.

The unknown is what's driving me insane. The unanswered questions. The fear of it happening again. The way I felt the minute I realized he was armed and dangerous. I'd never felt my heart beat that fast or hard before. I was a trained police officer with five years of experience. I excelled at the academy and felt ready for anything.

I was wrong.

Nothing prepares you for what it feels like when you think you're about to die. Suddenly, everything looks so much clearer and the things you thought that mattered, you now realize were small compared to the bigger picture.

The images fly through my mind, and as much as I try to push them away, they resurface and remind me of it all. Everything happened so fast, but when it replays in my mind, it's in slow motion. It's fucking torture.

I think about Tyler and how I'm responsible for him and how I would've felt had something happened to him. I think about Logan and how he's the lead on the investigation and what kinds of information he'll find on the guy. Even if he does find out details, I'm not sure it'll ever be enough to feel closure or take away the images that are now burned into my brain.

"Drew?" Courtney grabs my attention back. God, she looks so beautiful. She always is, but I'm noticing everything about her now. The way she drags her top teeth along her bottom lip, the way she scrunches her nose anytime she disagrees with something, and the way she always touches her ear when she's nervous. She has the cutest quirks, and I love her so fucking much.

"Yes," I say.

"Yes?" She arches her brow.

"Let's go to Vegas!" I tell her.

I love seeing her face light up. The way she looks up at me brings warmth back into my soul. I'd do anything to keep that look on her face.

"Are you really sure?"

I tilt her chin and press my lips to hers. "I would go anywhere in the world with you, Court."

She smiles, and I pull her into my chest, loving the way

her arms secure around my waist. I was so close to losing this, and I don't want to dwell on the what ifs when the person I love most is here right in front of me.

But I could do without the images in my head. For now, though, I'll keep pushing them out until they're no longer running through my mind on repeat. A mini-vacation is exactly what we need right now.

The flight is just over an hour long, and we're landing in Vegas before I know it. Courtney is so excited and looks so happy that it's contagious. I don't let what's happened ruin our time together because if I do, I might self-destruct.

We Uber to the Four Seasons with the sun blazing and the streets busy. It's almost noon, and we're both starving, but I can't wait to get her up to the room.

"This hotel is so gorgeous," she says as we ride the elevator. A guy in a fitted uniform brings our luggage up on a cart, so we don't even have to tote them around. I've heard great things about this hotel and wanted to take Courtney some place nice for our getaway.

"What do you want to do first?" I ask as I take her hand and lead her off the elevator. We're on the fifteenth floor, and already I can tell the view is going to be amazing.

"Truthfully, it all feels a little overwhelming. There's so much to do, and I don't even know where to start."

"How about we start with some food?" I smile as we get to our room.

"Yes, definitely some food."

We walk in, and Courtney's eyes go wide, taking it all in. Everything is clean and put together perfectly. The large bay windows overlook the city, and I can only imagine how stunning it'll look at night.

"Holy crap," Courtney mutters. "I definitely think this place'll do."

I pull her back into my chest and cup her face as I kiss her deeply. Being here with her is just what I needed.

A knock at the door interrupts us, and I step away to let the bellboy in with our luggage. Once he sets them down, I hand him a tip, and he's out in less than two minutes.

"I'm going to change, and then we can go find someplace to eat," Courtney tells me. She presses a quick kiss on my mouth and then grabs her suitcase.

I lie on the bed and take it all in. I'd never been to Vegas before, and I couldn't think of a better person to experience it with.

Dozing off, I'm brought back to the scene from two days ago, except this time he doesn't put the gun in his mouth. He puts it in mine. I feel the anxiety creep inside and before the trigger clicks, Courtney is shaking me awake.

"Drew, wake up, baby." Her voice is music to my ears as I realize I'd fallen asleep. She's towering over me; concern etched all over her face. "You were rustling in your sleep. Are you okay?"

I rub my hands over my face and blink. "Yeah, fine. Just a dream."

I don't tell her what about because I don't want to worry her or ruin our time here.

"I'm ready. Should we go?" she asks, smiling down at me.

Looking at her, a smile forms on my face. "You look beautiful." I grab her hand and press a soft kiss on her knuckles. "Too beautiful. I'm going to have to fight anyone who looks at you now."

She chuckles, wrinkling her nose at me. "Don't worry,

Deputy. I'll make sure they all know you're the only one I have eyes for."

"Good. I'd hate to have to punch someone out." I smirk.

We grab lunch and walk the strip hand in hand. It feels nice being with her and I'm so glad she suggested we come here.

"There's so much to do! I don't know what to do first," she says as we look around. It's a little overwhelming. "Are you afraid of heights?"

I laugh. "No."

She smiles.

"You look like you're up to something."

"I've always wanted to try zip-lining," she confesses. "I saw it when I was looking up ideas for us to do here."

"I think I've seen it," I say, contemplating. She looks up at me with hopeful eyes and I know I can't deny her. "Let's do it."

She smiles wide as we make our way to Fremont Street. Every minute with her eases my mind and takes me further and further away from that night.

"I can't believe you're making me do this," I tease as they strap us in.

"You'll love it!" She's smiling so wide, I can't even pretend to be upset.

We opt for the eleven-foot upper zoom line versus the seven-foot where you fly across the line on your stomach like superman. It feels a lot higher than I was anticipating, but there's no greater time now than to live in the present.

"Are you ready?" I shout, gripping her hand. "No going back once they push us over!"

She smiles with a giddy laugh. "Ready!"

It's the most thrilling experience of my life, and I can't stop smiling as we zip-line down Fremont under the video screen. It provides an amazing view of the strip and the five blocks we zip down go too fast.

"That was incredible," she says as we catch our breaths.

"It was."

"So, I looked on one of those romantic-things-to-do-in-Vegas sites, as cheesy as it sounds, but I totally want to visit the Love Locket, visit a fortune teller, and maybe a couple's massage?" The excited look in her eyes makes me so damn happy to be here with her.

"Let's do it all." I bring my lips to hers and playfully nibble on her bottom lip. "I've heard they have a place where you can get your picture taken to look like you eloped. We should do that and send it to Viola and Travis."

She laughs and nods her head, agreeing. "Totally! They will freak!"

We do as many things as possible before we stop for dinner around ten p.m. We hit up a buffet and take pictures of the number of plates we load up. She posts them to Instagram, knowing Viola will be religiously following her.

"Let's take a selfie by the fountains in front of the Bellagio and post it since we're close by." She's so cute when she gets all excited.

We stumble back to the hotel room sometime after three a.m. and before the sun rises. We ended up taking fake wedding pictures and less than two minutes after posting them, Viola calls Courtney.

"Are you fucking kidding me?" I hear Viola scream. "You eloped in Vegas?"

Courtney is dying with laughter, loving the way she's getting her worked up. "You said you wanted nieces and nephews," she reminds her with a laugh.

"I swear to God, you two!"

"Relax, Lola! It's not real!"

"I'm going to kill you both!"

We both crack up laughing before hanging up and end up at the hotel bar. Once we sit down, we find a show to see the next night and purchase some tickets online. We make a plan to gamble beforehand and whatever else we can find. But I'm so hopelessly in love with her, I can barely keep my hands off her, and the only thing I want to do right now is get her into bed and fuck her wild.

I rub my nose along her neck and pull her lobe in between my teeth. "If I wasn't tipsy, I'd carry your ass back to our room and fuck you against the window," I growl.

She blushes and bites her lip. "Just because you can't carry me, doesn't mean you can't still fuck me against the window."

I groan. "You're so fucking filthy."

She narrows her eyes and looks past me, but I can't tell what she's looking at.

"You okay, babe?"

She blinks and refocuses her attention on me. "Uh, yeah. Just thought I saw someone, but I'm pretty sure it's the alcohol."

She sucks down the rest of her drink. I grab the bartender's attention to pay the tab. Once I sign for it, I grab for the keycard.

"Didn't I set it down here?" I ask, looking to see if I dropped it on the floor.

"I can't remember, but I have the other card in my clutch."

"Perfect," I slur. Perhaps I shouldn't have had that last whiskey and Coke, but that's not going to stop me from making love to my girl. "Let's go."

Soon we're stumbling back to our room, and before I can rip her dress off, she's passed out on the bed. I'm soon to follow her.

∿

The sun blazes in through the windows and my head is in a hazy cloud as I blink my eyes open. I haven't slept that hard in months. One minute I was taking off my shoes and the next I'm waking up.

I roll over to pull Courtney into my chest, but she's already moving down under the covers, crawling in between my legs and wrapping her hand around my cock.

"Mm...sweetheart," I growl. "Looks like you're making up for last night."

She slowly and torturously slides her tongue up my shaft before pulling it into her mouth. She works the tip as she wraps her hand back around me and strokes up and down simultaneously, moaning as she devours me. Fuck! I don't know what's gotten into her, but I'm fucking loving it.

"Jesus, sweetheart," I growl as I grip the sheet. She's buried under the blanket, and the fact that she's enjoying herself so much works me up even more. "Fuck, that feels so good."

I'm desperate to touch her and just as I'm about to fist

her hair, she deep throats my cock and curse words start spewing out of my mouth.

My body tenses, and I know I'm not going to last much longer. Her mouth feels so goddamn good. She pushes her mouth down deeper, and that's all it takes before I release inside her perfect mouth.

"Holy fuck," I whisper, trying to catch my breath. I can feel her cleaning me up and I just want to kiss the hell out of her for that morning wake-up call.

"Come up here, beautiful," I say, reaching for her.

She begins crawling up my body, and I can't wait to flip her over and fuck her till lunch. Her blonde hair peeks out from the covers, and I fist a handful in my hand, bringing her closer.

"That was a good way to—"

She lifts her head, and when her eyes meet mine, I nearly choke.

"What the fuck?" I gasp, inching away.

"A good way to what?" She licks her lips.

"Get the fuck off me, *Mia*!"

WHAT'S NEXT

Checkmate: This is Effortless
Drew & Courtney, #2

Courtney Bishop is as sugary sweet as her famous blueberry muffins.
Southern belle at heart, Cali girl by choice.
She barged into my life and easily became my best friend.

All was great as roommates and just friends, but then I fell for the girl who could chop firewood, deliver baby calves, and bail hay without breaking a sweat.
She's the perfect mixture of sugar and spice, and I *love* her.

Being more than friends and trying to build our future isn't as easy as it sounds.
Moving forward and creating memories is all I want for us, but when the past continues to come back and haunt me, I'm not so sure she'll stay for the ride.

Loving her is easy, but losing her will break me. Burning passion combined with an undeniable chemistry constantly pushes and pulls us together. In the end, I'll prove we're worth the fight, even when the game is far from over.

Checkmate, sweetheart.

ABOUT THE AUTHOR

Brooke Cumberland and Lyra Parish are a duo of romance authors who teamed up under the *USA Today* pseudonym, Kennedy Fox. They share a love of Hallmark movies & overpriced coffee. When they aren't bonding over romantic comedies, they like to brainstorm new book ideas. One day, they decided to collaborate under a pseudonym and have some fun creating new characters that'll make you blush and your heart melt. If you enjoy romance stories with sexy, tattooed alpha males and smart, quirky, independent women, then a Kennedy Fox book is for you! They're looking forward to bringing you many more stories to fall in love with!

CONNECT WITH US

Find us on our website:
kennedyfoxbooks.com

Subscribe to our newsletter:
Kennedyfoxbooks.com/newsletter

Join our reader group:
Facebook.com/groups/kennedyfoxbooks

facebook.com/kennedyfoxbooks

twitter.com/kennedyfoxbooks

instagram.com/kennedyfoxbooks

amazon.com/author/kennedyfoxbooks

goodreads.com/kennedyfox

bookbub.com/authors/kennedy-fox

BOOKS BY KENNEDY FOX

CHECKMATE DUET SERIES

TRAVIS & VIOLA DUET
Checkmate: This is War
Checkmate: This is Love

DREW & COURTNEY DUET
Checkmate: This is Reckless
Checkmate: This is Effortless

LOGAN & KAYLA DUET
Checkmate: This is Dangerous
Checkmate: This is Beautiful

BISHOP BROTHERS SERIES
Taming Him
Needing Him
Chasing Him
Keeping Him

BEDTIME READS SERIES
Falling for the Bad Boy
Falling for the Playboy
Falling for the Cowboy

ROOMMATE DUET SERIES

HUNTER & LENNON DUET
Baby Mine
Baby Yours

MASON & SOPHIE DUET
Truly Mine
Truly Yours

LIAM & MADELYN DUET
Always Mine
Always Yours

CIRCLE B RANCH SERIES
Roping the Cowboy
Hitching the Cowboy
Catching the Cowboy
Wrangling the Cowboy

EX-CON DUET SERIES

NOAH & KATIE DUET
Pushing You Away
Holding You Close

TYLER & GEMMA DUET
Keeping You Away
Needing You Close

Manufactured by Amazon.ca
Bolton, ON

18201426R00173